SHADOWS OF SOUNDS

SHADOWS OF SOUNDS

ALEX GRAY

First published in Great Britain in 2005 by
Allison & Busby Limited
Bon Marché Centre
241-251 Ferndale Road
London SW9 8BJ

http://www.allisonandbusby.com

'Sounds and Silences' from *Collected Poems* by Norman MacCaig
published by Chatto and Windus.
Used by kind permission of Birlinn Ltd

A catalogue record for this book is available from
the British Library.

10 9 8 7 6 5 4 3 2 1

ISBN 0 7490 8378 6
ISBN 0 7490 8393 X (Trade paperback)

Printed and bound in Wales by
Creative Print and Design, Ebbw Vale

Alex Gray was born and educated in Glasgow. She has worked as a folk singer, a visiting officer for the Department of Social Security and an English teacher. She has been awarded the Scottish Association of Writers' Constable and Pitlochry trophies for her crime writing. Married with a son and daughter, she now writes full time.

This novel is dedicated to John and Suzanne with love.

~ Even the quietest of nights
          are never silent: hear
          their shadows of sounds.

From 'Sounds and Silences'
      by Norman MacCaig

The man at the back of the Upper Circle sat gnawing his finger-nails and concentrating on the unbroken shadow cast by the proscenium.

Nothing could go wrong, surely. He'd thought of everything. All the details had been double-checked. The musicians who were only coming on for the second half knew exactly when to be on stage. It had been made quite clear during the rehearsal that there would be no sloping off to the bar until after the performance. The Orchestra Manager had driven home that point.

So why the hell hadn't the lights in the Concert Hall been dimmed? The programme was already ten minutes late in starting. He bit a flake of skin from his index finger. It was hard and waxy between his teeth. With an effort of will the man wrenched his gaze from the wings to the musicians on stage, as if trying to make sense of the delay.

On the platform the members of the Orchestra were looking bored. They had already tuned their instruments and were only waiting for the Leader to come on to start the evening's proceedings. Had this been a rehearsal, he knew from experience that the Sunday papers would be spread across their music stands. However, protocol dictated that they assumed an air of gravity towards the actual performance. As his eyes travelled over the players, he saw that the brass section weren't even attempting to hide their feelings. Typical, he thought.

One French horn player was slouched back in his seat whilst the trumpets at desks three and four were deliberately outdoing one another with exaggerated yawns. They totally ignored the dark looks being fired at them by the Second Fiddle.

Only the Chorus sat silently up in the Choir Stalls, music folders open on their laps, ready to begin. From their vantage point above them, the man imagined the members of the Chorus looking down at the paying customers who'd be examining their watches and frowning towards the wings from where the Leader should have emerged. He looked at his own watch. It was almost a quarter to eight.

A hum of talk out in the auditorium became a ripple as the Orchestra Manager slipped onto the platform and bent to whisper to the Second Violin, a lady in black lace. She paused for a moment as if to reflect on his message, merely giving a quiet nod in reply.

A swift smile passed across her face as she performed her duty as Leader of the Orchestra, standing up and bowing to the audience. The brass section sat up just as Victor Poliakowski, the Russian conductor, came striding on to the platform.

The man sank back into his seat, took out a large handkerchief and wiped the perspiration that had gathered on his brow. "Thank God," he whispered to himself.

The house lights dimmed at last then, as the conductor raised his baton, the first drum roll began.

Chapter One

It was business as usual backstage in Glasgow Royal Concert Hall. Now that the wings were cleared of the musicians, there was an obligatory pause in proceedings before the Leader would make his appearance. Tonight, however, that pause seemed unusually prolonged.

"Old George is keeping them waiting again," remarked the Stage Manager to the lanky youth beside him. From his cubicle in the wings he could see the Orchestra on his television monitor; a glance to the left would alert him to any performers arriving from their dressing rooms backstage. The remark might have been intended for the retreating figure of Brendan Phillips, the Orchestra Manager, who was responsible for escorting the Principals to and from their dressing rooms. He gave no sign of having heard the Stage Manager's words, however, as he walked briskly around the corner and out of sight.

"Not wanting to come out to play tonight?" joked the boy who was staring at the empty area behind them.

"Oh, he'll be here all right. Brendan will chase him up, don't you worry," the Stage Manager replied confidently, knowing that Brendan Phillips had disappeared off in the direction of the Artistes' corridor to fetch George Millar. The boy gave a sudden grin and sloped off after Phillips.

"Making you run around after them tonight, eh?" The boy's question made the Orchestra Manager break his stride for just a moment. Colin, the newest recruit amongst the Orchestra's drivers and shifters, was ever eager to fraternise with the Names as he called them. Phillips had tolerated the lad's star-struck behaviour but it was becoming a bit of a nuisance. All the other shifters were downstairs in dressing room 1, where they could drink tea and smoke to their heart's content, no doubt listening to the football on the radio. He pretended to ignore the boy who had latched on to him, continuing along the corridor to the four rooms named after Scottish Lochs that were reserved for guest artistes and management.

Brendan Phillips stopped outside Morar, the second-best dressing room that, tonight, was occupied by the Leader of the Orchestra. Their guest conductor, Victor Poliakowski, would be pacing up and down next door in Lomond, the suite kept for the biggest name.

Phillips was agitated. Normally he would have closed the door stage left after the final musician had trooped out of the wings. Then it was only a short stride to the dressing rooms to alert the Leader. But tonight everything seemed to have gone wrong. He'd spent time dashing back and forth behind the scenes. First it had been a spare reed for a flautist who was temping, then a new set of music for the harpist. She had been sitting stage right making frantic gestures at him until he'd translated her sign language into a plea to fill her empty music stand. So he had been later than usual, forced as he was to go all the way round from the Stage Manager's cubicle to alert the Leader.

Colin, hovering behind him, was an irritant that Phillips could quite do without, yet the Orchestra Manager's desire to maintain an air of composure overcame his annoyance.

Phillips knocked politely, his knuckles light on the blonde wood of the door. There was no response. The Orchestra Manager gave a rat-a-tat that was intended to sound peremptory.

"Maybe he's in the loo," suggested Colin who was still hovering at Phillips's shoulder.

Brendan Phillips didn't deign to answer but twin creases between his brows revealed a growing anxiety. It was his head that would roll if there were a glitch in the proceedings.

The Orchestra Manager turned the handle and stepped into the dressing room.

At first the room appeared to be empty. Only the violin nestling in its open case gave any sign of the musician's presence. Brendan scanned the room before taking a further step inside.

Then he saw him.

Even though he was lying face down, the Orchestra Manager knew it was George Millar, Leader of The City of Glasgow Orchestra.

Brendan was aware of a gagging noise behind him but he couldn't move. Nor could he take his eyes off the body. Half of

George's balding skull shone from the overhead light in the bathroom. The rest was a blackened mass.

Blood from a head wound had dripped onto the blue bathroom tiles creating a dark stain that had spread all the way down, reddening the man's grizzled beard. Brendan could see the tip of his wing collar sticking up like a bright scarlet flag.

In those first moments all the Orchestra Manager could do was stand and stare at the outrage before him. His mind tried to deceive his eyes. Perhaps he'd slipped? Brendan attempted to visualise George's black shoes sliding on a wet patch.

He began feverishly scanning the bathroom floor for surface water. The tiles gleamed back at him, dry and polished but for that red halo emanating from George's head. He found himself blinking hard as if to dispel the vision of the body spreadeagled upon the floor. Even as his mind sought for a decent explanation, his eyes couldn't ignore the obvious.

No slip on the shiny tiles had accounted for George's sudden demise. Beside the violinist's outstretched fingers lay a metal hammer. Brendan recognised it at once. It was a percussion hammer, small, but not insignificant.

"My God, I don't like the look of him." The voice behind him broke into Brendan's stupor, making him turn around. Colin had disappeared. It was Stan, their chief driver who stood there, marvelling at the body on the tiles.

"He's not…dead…is he?" The doubt in Stan's voice sank to a whisper as he caught the Orchestra Manager's gaze.

For an instant Brendan felt himself becoming unreasonably possessive about George Millar's mortal remains, resenting the additional presence of the driver. A sudden irritation pushed his qualms aside, that and a need to make things happen. He straightened his shoulders, placing himself between Stan and the body.

"We'll have to get Security. I'll use the phone next door. We'll need an ambulance," he hesitated for a second before adding, "and the police."

Stan turned to go but Brendan Phillips caught his arm, "Not a word, not from any of you," rasped Phillips. "Not until the police get here."

The Orchestra Manager walked out with Stan who was still trying to peer into the room behind them. Several feet from the doorway Colin had slumped to the floor, his back against the wall. The boy's face was the colour of putty.

"Take him downstairs and make him some tea. Just keep out of sight until I send for you. All right?"

The two men glanced at one another uncertainly. Then Stan stretched out a hand to Colin.

"Come on lad, let's be having you," he said, heaving the shifter to his feet. "Nice cup of tea to make you feel better."

Looking at the boy's grey complexion, Brendan Phillips doubted whether Colin would be able to keep anything down.

The immediate thing to do was to alert Security. Phillips looked up and down the red-carpeted corridor before taking out his copy of the master key and locking the door to Morar. Poliakowski, the conductor, was safely ensconced in Lomond for the time being; thankfully the dressing room on the other side was empty. Phillips slipped inside, picked up the phone and dialled the code for Security.

"Neville?" Brendan visualised the Security man at the stage door as he spoke. He heard himself speaking in a voice belonging to some other person, someone in control, not the same man whose hands were shaking as they gripped the telephone. He couldn't believe that his own words sounded so clipped and emotionless as he explained the situation.

He walked back, unlocking Morar in a daze, still trying to convince himself that he really had seen that body on the tiled floor. Telling Neville about it should have made it real, yet somehow he still wanted to believe that George would be standing there waiting for him, violin and bow in his carefully manicured hands. It would all be a mistake. There would be no corpse on the floor. But when he turned towards the entrance to the bathroom it was still there. Brendan closed his eyes seeking some kind of help. Nothing came into his mind. No childhood prayers from Sunday School. Not even a line from any of his favourite Requiems. All he could think of were the words, "Take this cup from me." When he opened his eyes again the sight of George's body filled him with shame.

Come on, Brendan Phillips, he muttered to himself, think on your feet. That was what the City Fathers were paying him to do, after all, he realised, although the job description had made no mention of bloodied corpses behind the scenes. There were no codes or procedures for this. He couldn't simply stride onto the platform announcing, "Ladies and gentlemen, tonight's concert has been cancelled due to the unforeseen death of the Leader of the Orchestra". But he'd have to make a decision quickly.

Locking the door to Morar for the second time that night, Brendan Phillips felt prickles of sweat break out on his forehead as he agonised over whether he ought to carry on with the concert.

Even as he approached the stage he still wasn't sure if it was the proper thing to do. He hovered in the wings for a moment, aware of curious glances from members of the Percussion section.

He'd have to use the Second Fiddle. That woman, Karen, was ambitious. She'd be only too pleased to take over. And when the police arrived they would clear up whatever had happened back here, wouldn't they?

Chapter Two

Detective Chief Inspector Lorimer pressed the mute control on the TV remote as his mobile rang out. His eyes watched the silent antics of figures on his screen as he listened to a voice that demanded his full attention.

"Okay. I'll be there," Lorimer spoke into the phone. "About twenty minutes."

He flicked the red button and turned his attention to the television once more. A man and woman were having a heated argument. He could see her lipstick-red mouth wide open. The man was slapping the table between them noiselessly. Lorimer switched them off. He knew how it would end. They'd come over all sweet and sorry later on just as they always did. That's why this soap opera had such a huge following, he thought. With its happy endings it was so unlike real life. He couldn't have explained why he'd started to watch it after Maggie had left. She'd have been appalled at how hooked he'd become.

Anyway, this wasn't getting him nearer the start of a new case. And, from what he'd just heard, there certainly weren't going to be any happy endings. There were squads of men being called out from every Division in Glasgow to cope with this one. There would be a whacking great overtime bill by the time all the punters had been screened. Not to mention the musicians. And they'd had a bloody great Chorus on stage too, just to compound the logistical nightmare. Lorimer shook his head. Sometimes it wasn't so bad being a mere Detective Chief Inspector. At least he didn't have to worry about budgeting all of the time.

Lorimer shrugged himself into the jacket that had been hanging on the handle of the lounge door. The remains of a Chinese takeaway lay on the coffee table beside a half empty bottle of Irn Bru. He'd tidy them away later, he assured his absent wife, along with the week's supply of newspapers strewn across the floor. For a moment Lorimer stared into space, seeing the room as it had been only two months before. It had never really been tidy what with Maggie's piles of jotters to mark and both of them leaving books in various corners but now it was simply neglected. Then, at least, the place had been vacuumed and dusted, he supposed or whatever she'd done to make it comfortable. But the difference was really more than mere housework, if he was honest with himself, much, much more.

With a grimace at the sight of it, Lorimer switched off the light and headed for the front door.

"Chief Inspector Lorimer."

The Security man at the stage door looked keenly at Lorimer's warrant card then into the face of the tall man who stood just inside the doorway.

"Mr Phillips, the Orchestra Manager, is waiting for you upstairs, sir," he said. "Trish will show you the way." Neville, the Security man beckoned forward a comfortable looking middle-aged woman. Lorimer recognised her steward's tartan uniform.

"Aye, it's up here, Chief Inspector," Trish started to smile at him, but pursed her lips almost immediately as if she realised that the circumstances demanded some gravity of demeanour. Lorimer followed the woman up a steep staircase and through two sets of heavy swing doors. As they walked along a brightly lit corridor Trish cleared her throat.

"It's terrible, isn't it? The poor wee man." She risked a glance into Lorimer's face but he didn't offer any comment in reply. The woman gave a sigh, whether about the passing of George Millar or Lorimer's reluctance to engage in conversation, he didn't know. They reached the end of the corridor, pushed through another two sets of swing doors and entered an open area that had a low ceiling and no windows. Lorimer saw with some relief that it was already full of uniformed policemen. Some were behind hastily erected trestle tables and taking statements from the musicians who were still in evening dress. A couple of officers from his own Division looked up as he came in, acknowledging his presence with a nod.

"They've set up their stuff in here," said Trish. "It's where the Chorus and musicians usually assemble just before they go on stage. Mr Phillips should be around somewhere. Oh, there he is," she told him, just as a figure in dark tails approached them.

Lorimer's first impression of Brendan Phillips was of a slight, rather dapper man whose smooth, boyish face belied his age. He was probably in his late thirties, Lorimer reckoned. Not much younger than himself.

"Chief Inspector, thank goodness you're here," Brendan Phillips seemed on the point of reaching out to take Lorimer by the hand, but after one look at the policeman's face, the Orchestra Manager's hand fell to his side. Trish, Lorimer noticed, had vanished discreetly.

"The Doctor said you would want to go straight to the dressing room. Where the body is," Phillips added in deliberately hushed tones. Lorimer followed the man out of the claustrophobic room. Round a corner, they emerged onto the entrance to the stage.

The auditorium was brightly lit and there were full spots still directed onto the stage itself. Both, mercifully, were empty. Lorimer followed the Orchestra Manager across the front of the stage, skirting the music stands and the conductor's podium. Several instruments were lying in their cases on the pale, varnished floor. Lorimer had to squeeze past a large harp as Phillips took him towards the stair leading to the other stage exit. He noted a booth with a board full of controls and a close circuit television that showed the empty stage. His policeman's eyes also took in the CCTV cameras angled at regular intervals from the ceiling.

"Who found the body?" Lorimer asked.

When Phillips turned back to answer, Lorimer noticed that he didn't meet his eyes.

"I did," he replied. "It's my responsibility to ensure that all the performers are on stage in time. It's customary to fetch the Leader and the Principals personally from their dressing rooms. It's part of my job," he added with a sigh that seemed to come from his well-polished shoes.

The Orchestra Manager walked on as he spoke. Round a corner they came to another, smaller assembly area.

The regulation incident tape had been fastened across an opening to the left. Phillips stopped and gestured towards an open door leading to a corridor on their right. It was parallel, Lorimer noticed, to another corridor that disappeared into darkness, its ceiling lowered by massive metal tubing. Rows of open fiddle cases lined a shelf on one side.

"These are the Artistes' dressing rooms. The first one, Lomond, is for our conductor. Morar is where..." he broke off uncertainly.

"Where you found the body," Lorimer finished for him. "And then you called Security, I take it?"

"Yes," the man looked thoroughly miserable now, no doubt recalling the event that would give him nightmares for weeks. Lorimer nodded briefly and headed for the second room along the corridor that had been reserved for the late Leader of Glasgow Concert Orchestra.

"Well, hello there, stranger," a blonde head turned to look up at him as Lorimer stepped carefully into the room.

"Ah, Rosie," Lorimer grinned back at the pixie face below him. Doctor Rosie Fergusson, Lorimer's favourite pathologist, was on her knees beside the body, her diminutive frame wrapped inside a clean white boiler suit.

"I'll just wait out here, shall I?" Phillips called out, hovering in the doorway.

Lorimer frowned but before he could speak, Rosie answered for him, "That's fine. Just keep the masses away from here. We don't want to contaminate this area any further. Okay?"

"Yes," Phillips seemed uncertain if he should stay around but clearly didn't relish the prospect of being in such close proximity to whatever they were planning to do with George Millar's corpse.

Lorimer turned back to the Orchestra Manager. This time he laid a consoling hand on the man's shoulder. "Look. You've had a pretty tough time tonight. Why don't you stay down in Security meantime? I'll catch up with you when we're finished in here."

Brendan Phillips gave a grateful nod. The man looked simply defeated, thought Lorimer. A dead body might be all in a day's work for Rosie, and to a lesser extent for a DCI but, Lorimer reminded himself, it was surely outwith the experience of the average Orchestra Manager.

"Well. What have we here?" Lorimer joined the pathologist at the entrance to the tiled bathroom. The preliminary examination had taken place, he supposed. George Millar's body still lay face down, but Rosie would have taken the body temperature as a first measure.

"Time of death?" he queried.

"How did I know you were going to ask me that? You're so predictable, Lorimer," Rosie teased. "Not that long ago, actually. The body was still warm when I got here, but rigor was coming on so I'd narrow it down to say he died two to three hours ago." She looked at her watch. "That's about half an hour, or less maybe, before the concert was due to start. This room's pretty well heated but I don't think that complicates the timing too much."

"Good. So any CCTV footage from about seven o' clock onwards should show us who was around this particular dressing room," Lorimer mused.

The fact that so many people had been in the Concert Hall made this case a potential shambles. But, really, these security devices should eliminate practically all of them.

Lorimer didn't anticipate a lot of bother with this one. Once they'd seen the footage, they'd be home and dry, surely?

Sitting in the tiny space that passed for the Security department, Lorimer scanned the tapes that had purported to show all movement in and around the whole of the Concert Hall since midday. His initial optimism about finding evidence on the tape footage was rapidly being extinguished.

"That's when we change the tapes," Neville explained to him, "There's maybe a two minute delay between taking the last ones out and putting fresh ones in. That's all."

Lorimer frowned. The screen that should have shown the area around the Artistes' dressing rooms had been blanked out from just after seven o'clock.

"And didn't you do something about it when you saw that?" Lorimer demanded of the man.

Neville shrugged. "Our usual technician's off sick tonight. There's just me and I didn't know there'd been a murder, did I? Anyway, the outside cameras are probably more of a concern at that time of night."

"Oh? Why?"

Neville looked uneasy. "Don't get me wrong. It's not me who makes decisions about that sort of thing," he paused. "It's all the beggars we get around here; *Big Issue* sellers and druggies with their wee plastic cups. It's company policy to keep an eye on them."

"So what did you think when you saw that one of your monitors was suddenly blank?" Lorimer wanted to know.

"I was puzzled. But then His Nibs phoned down and told me to dial 999. That was when I realised there must have been something fishy about that screen."

Lorimer gritted his teeth, so much for an easy solution. Whoever had immobilised the CCTV camera upstairs had planned things pretty carefully. At least he knew now that this was no random killing. Premeditated murder would be on the charge sheet in the event of an arrest.

"Okay. Thanks. We'll need the original tapes to take away tonight. I'll have them copied and returned to you whenever it's possible," Lorimer told him. Privately he doubted if they'd ever be returned. They'd be kept as evidence in the case until after a trial, if it ever came to that. He picked up a programme from Neville's desk, flicking through it till he came to the list of performers. This might come in handy, he mused, taking note of some of the names.

Trudging back up the stairs, Lorimer felt suddenly weary. The thought of all those people who'd been backstage tonight filled him with despair. God alone knew who had passed back and forth along the corridor of the four Principals' dressing rooms in the half hour before the concert began. The paying public had already been herded out into the suites of rooms opposite the auditorium. They would leave names, addresses and show proof of identity before being allowed to leave the Concert Hall. Even the Hall's stewards had been hastily drafted in to help the police officers perform this massive job.

It was time to join the troops who were busy taking details from each and every one of the members of the Orchestra,

Chorus and various backstage crew.

The claustrophobia hit him almost as soon as he entered the windowless area with its low ceiling. There seemed to be no space to move amongst the masses of bodies crammed into the room. Even the tables set up by the uniformed officers had disappeared against a wall of musicians in evening dress. A quick glance showed him the various styles adopted by the female members of the Orchestra ranging from plain trousers and blouses to full-skirted gowns. All the men wore black tails.

A buzz of noise filled the room. Evidently a murder in their midst hadn't quelled the odd artistic temperament, judging by some of the louder voices raised in protest at their incarceration in this confined space.

As Lorimer approached the nearest table to speak to WPC Irvine, one of his own officers, the woman opposite looked up at him. She was probably middle-aged, judging by the steel grey hair. Her face, still smooth and youthful looking, had a strong bone structure dominated by the long, determined line of her jaw.

"And who may you be?" she asked in tones that instantly reminded Lorimer of a loud-voiced neighbour in his street who was forever complaining about dog fouling and children playing football near her garden. Mrs Ellis was the self-appointed neighbourhood watch who kept tabs on everybody's coming and going. She had even resorted to ringing his front door bell, demanding Police Action until Maggie had sent her packing with a flea in her ear. Lorimer swallowed his instant dislike of the woman in front of him dressed all in black lace, reminding himself that the Mrs Ellises of this world had their uses.

"Detective Chief Inspector Lorimer, ma'am," WPC Irvine replied for him. "And this is Karen Quentin-Jones." The look on his officer's face showed that she clearly expected the mention of Lorimer's rank to change the woman's tune. Lorimer glanced back at the programme in his hand. Karen Quentin-Jones was the Second Violin.

She must be the one who had taken over when Phillips had decided that the show must go on, Lorimer thought.

"Well, Chief Inspector, just how long do you intend keeping us cooped up here like a lot of cattle?" The woman's sarcasm made WPC Irvine flinch. People who knew Lorimer just didn't speak to him like that in her experience. So she was surprised when Lorimer smiled.

"Would you come with me please? Constable Irvine, may I have this lady's notes. I'll be through in the room marked "Ness". All right?"

Wordlessly, the musician rose from the chair, brushing out the layers of her skirt and followed Lorimer to the door leading to the other end of the Artistes' corridor.

The tape was fastened across the narrow space but Lorimer untied it, indicating that the woman should pass through with him. For a second she hesitated. It was clear she knew what had taken place along here and didn't relish the prospect of such close proximity to violent death.

"If you would just take a seat in here, I'll be right with you," Lorimer told her, holding open the door of the empty dressing room. He closed it behind her and turned to look up in the corner by the corridor door.

The CCTV camera was covered with a dark piece of cloth. Lorimer stood on tiptoe to examine it more closely. It looked for all the world like a black duster. A few strides would take him back into Morar. He stopped at the doorway, hearing familiar voices and realised that Rosie now had the company of the Scene of Crime Officers.

"Sorry. Stay out of here will you! Oh, it's you, Lorimer," Rosie looked up as he came into the room.

"Can I borrow someone for a minute?"

Jim Freely, one of the SOCOs, followed him into the corridor.

"There," Lorimer pointed to the cloth covering the camera. "Can you have it photographed before you take it down, d'you think?"

"Sure," Jim gave Lorimer a quizzical look. "Someone's gone to a bit of trouble to keep themselves off the screens, eh? Can't be one of the performers, then. They're only too keen to be on the telly," he joked, walking back to Morar.

Lorimer stood looking up at the cloth then back at the shape of the corridor. The doorways of each dressing room were deeply recessed in from the wall. He took a step towards the entrance of Ness but did not open the door. Instead, he stood back in the shadow of the doorway and lifted his hand towards the camera. It was several feet away. Whoever had immobilised it must have used something to attach the cloth. Something like a walking stick, perhaps? Lorimer made a mental note to scan the tape again as soon as he could. Meantime Mrs Quentin-Jones was waiting for his attention.

He gave a quick knock and entered the dressing room.

It was like George Millar's room, only not quite so grand. Karen Quentin-Jones had placed herself in the middle of a small settee, her voluminous skirts spread out around her. There was another chair in the corner.

"Sorry to keep you waiting," he began, fetching the chair and setting it down at an angle beside her. "Now. I gather you were acting as Leader of the Orchestra tonight. Is that correct?"

The woman bent her head imperiously, steady grey eyes looking straight at him. "Quite correct."

"As Second Fiddle, you'd go on stage with the other members of the Orchestra. Which side did you come on?"

"Violins came on from stage right," she answered.

Lorimer made a mental sketch in his head. "That's by the Stage Manager's cubicle, yes?"

"Correct."

"And what time did you all leave your dressing rooms?"

"Seven-fifteen. We always have a call at seven-twenty, but usually we're ready to go on before then."

Lorimer remembered the few occasions when he and Maggie had attended orchestral concerts. The members of the Orchestra usually came onto stage in dribs and drabs, adjusting music stands, playing snatches of music until the Second Fiddle gave them their note to tune up.

"So everybody was on stage by what time?"

"Oh, definitely seven-twenty-five. I remember looking at my watch and thinking it would all be over in two hours and twenty minutes. Quarter to ten," she added as if Lorimer was too slow to work that out for himself.

He ignored the sarcasm and continued, "Was anybody late arriving on stage?"

Karen's eyes widened, the reasoning behind that question clearly not lost on her.

"No," she answered immediately. Then she seemed to hesitate for a moment before continuing, "But not everybody was needed for the first half. Some of the brass section and two in percussion would still have been backstage then."

Lorimer was interested in her faltering tone. Her mind was obviously moving on to the consideration of who might have killed George Millar. She didn't want it to be one of her own colleagues, he could tell.

"Did it bother you that you had to take the part of Leader at such short notice?"

Karen made a face. "I didn't have time to be bothered. Anyway, it's not the first time it's happened."

"Oh?" Lorimer raised his eyebrows, inferring that she should elaborate on her statement.

"There was an incident earlier in the season when George was suddenly very sick just before the start of a concert. It turned out to be bad oysters," she wrinkled her nose in distaste. Was she insinuating that the Leader had consumed oysters to boost his sexuality or was she simply the squeamish type? Looking at her, Lorimer was prepared to bet that she had a cast iron constitution.

"What can you tell me about Mr Millar?"

"What do you want to know?" she answered back, almost rudely.

Remembering Mrs Ellis in his street, Lorimer bit back a hasty retort. He knew he'd be given plenty of facts and figures information from the Orchestra Manager who was responsible for the Orchestra personnel but he sensed this woman could provide a different side to the standard "everybody liked him, he had no enemies" routine that invariably met his questions after a sudden, unexplained death.

"I want to know what you thought of George Millar. What manner of man was he?" Lorimer asked quietly.

For the first time Karen Quentin-Jones lost her imperious look and became thoughtful. Perhaps she was finally experiencing some real remorse for the man who had been her colleague, Lorimer thought. Her next words took him by surprise, however.

"He was a total shit," she said calmly, leaning back and crossing her legs in a rustle of petticoats under the black lace.

"In what way?" Lorimer asked, trying to conceal his astonishment at her remark.

"In his relationships. In the way he treated people."

"Care to expand on that for me?" Lorimer asked wryly. "Tell some tales out of school?" The question was blatantly suggesting that the woman before him would relish a good gossip. It was rather out of order under the present circumstances and they both knew it but to his relief he saw the hint of a smile play about the violinist's mouth.

"I really shouldn't be telling you this," she began, "but George was a very naughty boy. Kept all his lovers in a fair old turmoil, he did, playing them off against one another."

"His lovers? Ladies in the Orchestra, do you mean?" Lorimer asked, suddenly wondering if the woman numbered herself among George Millar's lovers.

"God, no!" She gave a harsh little laugh. "George was as bent as his fiddle, darling!"

Lorimer stared at her. The screwed-up face describing the oysters had been an indication of her disapproval of the late Leader's sexual appetite. The way Karen had mentioned his lovers suggested that it had been a rather voracious appetite at that. And were these signs of distaste more to do with a homophobic attitude on her part?

Lorimer thought again of the fearsome Mrs Ellis. He was sure she'd be first in the queue to protest against the gay community if she believed it was trying to encroach on her precious suburban street.

"Did he live with anybody in particular?" Lorimer decided to ask as a way of moving the dialogue forward.

"His wife," answered Karen, her face studying his reaction in amusement. Lorimer didn't return her smile. He was well enough acquainted with homosexual relationships to know that nothing was straightforward. Often a married couple found, sometimes very belatedly, that their sexual orientation was not as they had imagined on the day of their nuptials. It was surprising how so many couples stayed together despite that. Surprising, too, the tolerance shown towards the aberrant one in the marriage.

"Who were George Millar's lovers?" he asked, the question deliberately blunt.

Karen pulled a small evening bag onto her lap. "Mind if I smoke?"

Lorimer did mind, but it was his policy to let any smoker indulge their habit if it relaxed them into telling him what he wanted to know. He simply nodded his head and waited as she fished out a pack of Rothman's and lit up her cigarette with a tiny silver lighter shaped like a harp. He watched as she inhaled deeply then blew the smoke over one shoulder.

"I didn't know who they all were, naturally, only the ones in the Orchestra. I'm sure he had lots of other friends, though."

Was she playing with him, wondered Lorimer, or was she stalling for time, wondering whether she should tell him the whole truth and nothing but the truth?

His blue stare seemed to unnerve the woman, however, as she flicked ash from her cigarette and gave a small sigh.

"Currently he was messing around with Simon and Carl. Simon is our number three horn and Carl plays second viola. We call him the Great Dane. He's six foot six. A big, blond boy," she added with a leer.

Lorimer made a mental note to seek out the two men for interview before the night was out. He didn't relish the thought of prying into their affairs with George but it would have to be done. Karen, on the other hand, seemed to take pleasure in dishing the dirt on George. Lorimer thought he knew why.

"Did you enjoy being in charge tonight?" he asked.

"Naturally," she smiled. "It was a good programme."

Lorimer looked at the order of pieces played in the first half.

"Ah. You'd have played the solo during the Albinoni Adagio, then?" he murmured.

The woman's eyebrows shot up. "Good gracious. A policeman who isn't a complete Philistine. Wonders will never cease."

Lorimer didn't rise to the bait. It was pure luck that he happened to have a recording of this piece of music. His classical discs rubbed shoulders with everything from Pink Floyd to REM.

"Can you think of anything unusual that happened tonight before the concert?" he asked, changing tack again.

"What sort of things?" the woman countered, screwing up her eyes as she exhaled smoke into the air.

"A change to the normal routine. A crisis of some kind."

The woman gave a snort. "There's always a crisis of some kind. Concerts rarely run to plan. Sometimes we have to deputise at the last minute. Other times it's silly things like someone forgetting to pack their evening shoes."

"And tonight?" Lorimer persisted. Why did he get the feeling she was still stalling him?

"Oh Brenda was flapping about like a wet hen. Chloe, the harpist, had no music on her stand. Brenda had to run round to the library box to fetch her some."

"Brenda?" Lorimer queried, but even as the word came out he guessed what Karen Quentin-Jones would reply.

"Brendan Phillips, our very own nanny. Orchestra Manager is his official designation," she added.

Lorimer flinched. Was the man who had made the discovery of George Millar's murder also gay, or was the Second Violin simply unable to talk of her colleagues without making some sarcastic remark? He was beginning to wonder about this woman.

"And that was all? There was nothing else?"

"Not that I noticed," she replied, avoiding his eyes and flicking an invisible speck from her lacy dress. "Is that all? May I go home now?" she drawled as if the interview had begun to bore her.

Lorimer glanced at the notes WPC Irvine had made. Karen Quentin-Jones had given an address in a part of the city that boasted some fine, detached properties, the sort of old houses that required a lot of money to maintain.

Lorimer studied Karen Quentin-Jones briefly, taking in the well-cut hair and jewels at her throat. This lady didn't look short of a bob or two so her reason for working with an orchestra was hardly likely to be financial. It must be love of music, he mused, though she hadn't struck him as the dedicated, artistic type. Perhaps it was different once you were on stage.

Lorimer looked again at her home address. She wouldn't be too hard to find again if he needed her.

"Yes," he answered shortly. "Be sure to sign out with Security at the stage door."

They rose together, the violinist's black skirts shivering against the carpet. Lorimer held open the door then followed her to the end of the corridor where he again untied the striped tape.

"Thank you," Karen Quentin-Jones gave him a small nod and headed for the stairs that would take her back to the musicians' dressing rooms. Lorimer watched her go. There was something in her manner that had disturbed him. Either she had told him too much or else there was something she knew that she was keeping entirely to herself.

The music room was flooded with light when Karen Quentin-Jones stepped towards her French windows. She could see the outline of the beech trees, their bark silvered from the light of the moon. A smile hovered around her mouth. What a perfect night this could have been! She'd played her socks off. Even that great bear of a Russian had tapped his baton against the podium. Laying her violin case on an ornate table by the window, Karen undid the clips that kept it fastened then opened it slowly and for a moment she simply gazed at the instrument. Then, like a woman afraid to awake her sleeping lover, she stroked the chest-nut-coloured wood with one finger.

Giving a sigh, her eyes turned from the violin nestled within its case and she looked again at the darkness outside. She could have had such a triumph but her performance had been brutally over-shadowed. Even in death George Millar had outplayed her. Or had he?

Karen's smile straightened out and her eyes narrowed into a frown. This would mean some changes all round. She would be asked to fill George's shoes, she thought suddenly then shuddered at the image. And it would affect other people too, she thought, her lip curling in contempt.

A sudden impulse made her dart across the room. Her fingers dialled the digits she needed and she listened as the number rang out. At the sound of his voice she paused.

"Well," she said at last, "you won't have to worry about your darling boy any more, will you?"

Chapter Three

The blue lights of Buchanan Street lent an eerie glow to the hill that sloped down from the steps of the Concert Hall all the way down to Saint Enoch's Square. Oblivious to the drama above them, a crowd of football supporters crossed the pedestrian area on their way from Queen Street Station. Their team had beaten Hibs and the post-match jollies that had begun in the inter city shuttle were continuing in raucous celebration.

Flynn sat on the steps outside the Concert Hall cowering into his parka. They were far enough away to leave him in peace. Sometimes he'd take the risk of touting for loose change from the football crowds. They were unpredictable in their response. Flynn knew he could be the butt of abuse from the more belligerent of the fans; sometimes, though, a handful of coins would be spilled into his empty plastic cup. It didn't even depend on whether they'd won or not. Tonight Flynn didn't feel like taking the risk. He watched them in the distance as they disappeared down the stairs of the Underground, wondering if they had ignored the overtures of the *Big Issue* seller outside.

Flynn turned to look longingly at the main doors. They were late coming out tonight. Must have been a good show, with lots of encores keeping the punters in their seats, he told himself hopefully.

Maybe they'd be in a generous mood and he'd have enough dosh to score later on? One of Seaton's mates had been around earlier, tempting him with talk of some good gear. It wasn't too cold tonight and he'd rather spend the next few hours getting smashed than cowering into the dubious comfort of a narrow bed in the hostel.

His eyes searched the glass panels that flanked the beech wood doors. He could make out dim shapes of people moving. That was good. They'd be opening the doors any minute now. Flynn stood up, his body aching from sitting on the stone steps. Suddenly he stiffened. One of the shapes beyond the door was only too familiar; its chequered cap and dark suit showing the presence of the Busies. Flynn put one foot onto the lower step then hesitated. It could be anything, really. Maybe he'd wait and see what was up when the punters streamed out.

The doors swung open to reveal two officers and a lady in steward's uniform. Flynn shrank into the shadows, still watching, still uncertain of his next move. But it was too late. Even as he tried to camouflage himself against the grey walls he saw a man in a raincoat come between the officers and look his way. The man's beckoning finger was impossible to ignore and so Flynn moved grudgingly into the light.

"Been here long, lad?" Raincoat asked him.

Flynn shrugged. Something was up. Two uniforms and now a plain clothes cop. He cast a wary eye towards the detective. It wasn't anyone he recognised.

"Is that a yes or a no?" the question held a note of steel. This one meant business. To mess him around might be more bother than it was worth. All the same, they pissed him off, did the Busies.

"It's a don't know. As in I don't know 'cos I don't have a watch," Flynn replied.

The man grabbed his arm suddenly making Flynn wince.

"Look, pal, I haven't got time for wisecracks. You can answer my questions here or I can send you down to the station. It's up to you."

Flynn's arm was released but Raincoat's face told him that this was serious. His eyes flicked past the detective to the foyer where he could see people beginning to make their way towards the entrance.

"Aye. Well Ah've bin here since they all went in, y'know. Like before the show began." Flynn looked desperately at the punters leaving the Concert Hall. This cop was getting in the way of his bread and butter, not to mention the bit of Afghan he'd been fantasising about all evening.

He sensed rather than saw a change in he cop's attitude.

"That right, eh? Well, well. Maybe you and me should take a wee daunder inside and talk about just how you spent your evening, son?"

Shit! Someone had seen Seaton's mate talking with him earlier on. The wee bastard must've got bust. Flynn made to do a runner but that vice-like grip was on his arm again and he found himself being led into the bright lights of the Concert Hall. Curious eyes turned their way as the cop led the dishevelled youth across the foyer and into the interior of the Hall itself.

Flynn had long been desperate to see beyond the doors of his patch but it wouldn't do to let the Busy notice his eyes roaming around like an over-eager schoolboy. He tried at first to act as if he couldn't give a toss what it looked like, concentrating his attention on the pattern of the carpet as he followed the cop, wondering what the hell he'd got himself into this time.

It was no use. Flynn's eyes were drawn towards the walls as naturally as a moth to the light. He gazed at the huge pictures as he passed them. What the heck was that one? He wondered, marvelling at a painting of some woman with a giant sticking plaster under her mouth. Flynn sniggered to himself. Maybe it was a symbolic way of keeping folk quiet. He knew all about that, didn't he? They passed a large, brightly coloured picture next and then he slowed down, recognising the familiar style in the frame beyond. It was a Howson. The belligerent eyes of the fighter made Flynn take a step sideways, but he still gazed. This picture was great but the one of the big drums was his favourite. You could near enough hear the music of an Orange Walk, flutes, an' all. He'd seen other Howsons in the Gallery of Modern Art. It didn't cost anything to look at stuff in Glasgow and Flynn liked to look.

"In here," the Raincoat was ushering him around into a sort of corridor with a Bar at one end where Flynn saw crowds of folk queuing up against the wall. Were they getting their money back or something?

"Right, you, over here," Raincoat directed Flynn to a corner in the Bar area where there were little round tables and plastic chairs arranged in groups as if people had been sitting having a drink sometime earlier. Flynn suddenly felt like a drink himself.

"Any chancy a cuppa tea?" he asked with a nervous lick of his lips.

"Aye, why not. Milk and sugar?" Now that he'd got him in here, Raincoat had obviously decided to be his pal. Flynn wasn't sure if he preferred this to the previous hard-faced version.

"Aye," he replied, watching Raincoat's every move as the man spoke to a wee lassie behind the counter.

It was only a couple of steps away and Flynn thought about doing a runner. But by the time he'd considered it, Raincoat was back, sitting opposite and looking at him with some interest. Was this about Seaton, after all? Flynn glanced at the lines of people edging towards a table where there were uniformed Busies taking down notes. No, he decided, this wasn't about him and Allan Seaton. This was something a lot bigger.

"Use this pitch often, son?" the Busy enquired, passing a teacup over to Flynn.

"Aye. An' they lot in here know me as well so you can jist ask them if you like," Flynn answered. He took a slurp of the hot tea, one eye on Raincoat.

"I will," he said, then seemed to lose interest in Flynn, letting his gaze wander over the folk lined up beyond the tea bar. Flynn followed his gaze. Raincoat knew what was up, all right, but what had it to do with him?

"Has the band cancelled, then? Is that it?" Flynn asked, drawing Raincoat's eyes back to his own.

"Something a bit more serious than that," Raincoat answered. "Someone got hurt tonight," he paused for effect, staring at Flynn as if trying to see how he'd react to this titbit of information. "We're here to find out how it happened."

Flynn shivered, despite the heat from the cup clutched in both his hands. There was a tone of menace in the Busy's voice that he didn't like at all.

The detective took out a notebook and pen from his coat pocket.

"Right. Let's make a start. Name."

Flynn sighed. How often he'd been through this rigmarole. The mischief-maker in him wanted to say "Mickey Mouse" or something daft. Down the Nick it could raise a laugh but here it would just sound stupid.

"Flynn. Joseph Alexander Flynn. No fixed abode," he delivered the words in a monotone.

"Okay, Joseph Alexander,"

"Flynn. Just Flynn. All right?"

Raincoat looked up, surprised by the vehemence in the lad's voice. "Sure. I'm Detective Sergeant Wilson. Sergeant to you."

Flynn regarded the man warily. Was he trying to wind him up or butter him up?

The dregs of Flynn's second cup of tea were cold by the time Wilson had finished with him. He'd asked him the same questions more than once. Who'd passed by the steps that evening? Had he seen anyone emerge from the Buchanan Street entrance? It was obvious to Flynn that they were on the lookout for a villain. Someone who'd had a go at one of the performers, he guessed; maybe it had been a famous bloke. That was what all the fuss was about. If his guess were correct, then he'd be one of the first to see it shouted from the news stands in the morning.

Brendan Phillips was still downstairs. Lorimer hoped he was in a fit state to be questioned but he'd have to wait his turn. Somewhere in this labyrinth the Chief Executive of Glasgow Concert Orchestra was fending off the Press. It was part of Phillips's job but his boss had relieved him of that under the circumstances.

Slowly the detective walked back towards Morar. The black duster had been removed from the CCTV camera in the corridor, he noticed.

"Hello again," he put his head around the door tentatively. The SOCOs were hard at work gathering fibres from various parts of the room. George Millar's remains had disappeared into a dark zipped body bag. Already the dressing room had assumed an air of quiet industry. It was as if violent death itself had been swept away by the officers' zeal. Jim and Rosie turned at the sound of his voice.

"Anything on that black cloth?"

"Something sticky this way comes," Rosie quipped, holding up the duster in its plastic envelope. "We'll know for certain once it's back in the lab but it looks like the stuff you get from double-sided sticky tape."

"Thanks," Lorimer replied briefly, marvelling as always at the pathologist's capacity for levity in the face of brutality. It wasn't that she was inured to it; it was merely her way of dealing with the daily business of death in all its horrid forms.

The faint sound of music coming through the wall from the next room reminded Lorimer that Victor Poliakowski was still in Lomond. It had been judged that the conductor could stay there safely until he'd been interviewed. Then, and only then, would he be free to return to his hotel for the night.

"I'll leave you to it," Lorimer said. "Call me in the morning, will you, Rosie?"

"Sure will," she gave a small wave of her hand before turning back to discuss some technical detail with Jim.

Lorimer stood outside in the corridor. The door to Lomond was closed but he could make out the sound of a piano playing within. As he pushed open the door, he recognised the Rachmaninov concerto at once, its runs descending in a tinkling waterfall of sound. Lorimer expected the sound to falter into silence but it continued even when he walked from the dressing area into the reception room where he saw Victor Poliakowski seated behind the grand piano.

Lorimer quickly realised that the Russian wasn't ignoring him but he seemed so totally absorbed in his rendition of the concerto that he simply could not see anyone in the room despite the mirrored wall in front of him. Lorimer raised his eyebrows. Some witness this one was going to make!

As he listened, he tried to put himself into the position of the conductor on the podium, his back to the audience, his eyes on the performers.

"What is it you want?" Poliakowski's voice broke into Lorimer's reverie. The music had stopped abruptly and the Russian was rising from his position behind the grand piano.

"Chief Inspector Lorimer, sir," Lorimer was beside him in two strides, his hand outstretched. Poliakowski shook it, a brisk up and down then gestured for Lorimer to sit on one of the easy chairs that were placed around the sitting room. It was, Lorimer mused, a very civilised way to begin a discussion about murder.

"I'm very sorry that you've been so inconvenienced tonight,

sir, but under the circumstances..." Lorimer shrugged and smiled to let the man know that he wasn't sorry at all and that he was merely being polite. He was a policeman doing his job. Poliakowski was a man who had been stopped halfway through his own evening's work. Being a famous conductor didn't come into it, for Lorimer.

"So. They tell me the First Violin is killed. Here, in the room that is next to mine. And you wish to know if I had a hand in it, eh?"

Lorimer sat up. Was he joking? The Russian's bearded face was inclined towards him, the eyes beneath the bristling brows devoid of any sign of humour.

"I'd certainly wish to know that. If you did," added Lorimer, his eyes meeting those of the Russian. For some seconds they stared at each other in uncomfortable silence. Poliakowski looked away first then sank back into the armchair. It gave a leathery creak that failed to mask his theatrical sigh. Lorimer still searched the man's face with his blue gaze.

"No. Chief Inspector. I cannot give you such a simple solution to your search for a murderer. I did not even know of the matter until the interval."

Lorimer listened intently to the man's every word, delivered in near perfect English. There were overtones of an American accent and only a trace of the sort of voices he'd come to associate with John Le Carré's characters. But then he wasn't big on Eastern Europeans of any sort. What he heard told him that this was a clever and sophisticated man. It remained to be seen if he was also a suspect.

"As you say, sir, your room is next to where Mr Millar met his death. I must ask you exactly what your movements were prior to the start of the concert."

The big Russian shrugged again, "My movements," he said slowly as if savouring the words. "My movements were not very much. I was in this room sitting down or standing up. There was no moving outside or a visit to the man next door." He smiled but the smile was simply a perfunctory straightening of his lips.

"You didn't realise that your call was later than usual?"

Lorimer asked.

"No. I take no notice of such things. I do not wear a watch. I do not watch the clock. When it is time to perform, I will be ready. That is all."

"During the time before Mr Phillips came to escort you to the stage, did you hear any noise coming from next door?"

"No. I noticed no noise. Here I have switched on the television where I see the Orchestra. I play a few notes on the piano, perhaps? Really I do not remember what I do in that time," Poliakowski sounded rather irritated by the question.

No cries of anguish coming at you from the other side of that wall, then? Lorimer thought to himself. He listened intently. There were no noises at all from outside Lomond. It was perfectly feasible that the conductor was speaking the truth, that he really had been unaware of a murder taking place so close to this room.

"How well did you know Mr Millar?" Lorimer shifted tack deliberately.

Poliakowski raised his eyebrows, "How well? Ah, but not at all, is really the answer to that. I did not know this man until today. I meet him and I listen to his music. That is all. In fact I could hardly describe him to you." The Russian sounded both sorry and thoughtful as he spoke, looking down at his hands and turning them as if examining his nails for any flaws. Lorimer noticed, though, that his command of English was slipping just a little. A sign of strain would be reasonable to expect under the circumstances. And yet he struck Lorimer as a man with some reserves of strength; he was a big man, not just in his enormous physique. He would withstand interrogation more than most, Lorimer reckoned.

"You are not familiar with the members of the Orchestra, then?"

"Ah, but you are wrong. For me this is the first time to play with them here in Glasgow but I have met one or two of the musicians on my travels. The American lady in Percussion; she was in Russia with another Orchestra some years ago."

Lorimer smiled as Poliakowski rolled the R of Russia. He

sounded much more like his memory of one of Le Carré's Cold War spies now. But the Russian was continuing.

"And a fellow countryman. I forget his name. He is second desk horn. We play together when he is much younger."

"When was the last time you saw Mr Millar alive?"

Poliakowsi stared at Lorimer for a moment, thrown by the question's change of direction. Then he shook his head slowly. "I do not know. I remember he was with the Orchestra at the end of our rehearsal but I do not remember seeing him again." The Russian frowned as if he was trying hard to think.

"And after the rehearsal what did you do?"

"I came here. There was some food brought in to me. Brendan, the good fellow, he sees that I am happy to be on my own with no interruptions until the concert begins. It is my way," he explained to Lorimer.

It could be true. The man might have been quite oblivious to the scene next door. And it was interesting to know that the Russian preferred to keep himself alone in his room during the hour or so between the rehearsal and the concert. Who else would know that?

Lorimer asked him.

"Hm. A difficult question, Chief Inspector. I do not have an answer to that. Perhaps the people I already worked with? Perhaps any person who hears me speaking to Mr Brendan Phillips? Maybe you should ask of him that question, yes?"

"Yes," Lorimer agreed, his mind already working towards that objective.

"Were you planning to leave Scotland immediately after the concert, sir?"

Poliakowsi smiled. "Ah, but no. I will take a little holiday for some days. I do not return to Russia for quite some time. This is my first concert in what will be a short series with this orchestra."

"And where may we find you meantime?" Lorimer asked.

"The Island of Skye. From tomorrow I will be with Lady Claire MacDonald and her husband."

Lorimer was impressed in spite of himself. He had taken Poliakowski for a city type who'd have been booked in to

Number One Devonshire Gardens. But he preferred the delights of Skye, did he? Kinloch Lodge would provide the man with the pleasures of the flesh but the island itself, as Lorimer knew well, would grant him the real soul restoring treatment.

There was something else he had meant to ask the Russian but it had slipped his present thoughts. Lorimer tried to remember what it was, admitting to himself that tiredness was catching up with him. Maybe he'd sleep better tonight.

"I shan't keep you any longer, sir. If you would please let Security know when you are leaving then you may go back to your hotel now." As Lorimer stood up, Poliakowski heaved himself out of the leather armchair and offered his hand. As Lorimer grasped it, he could feel the clamminess on the man's palms. He'd certainly concealed his nervousness well, if that was what had made his hands so moist.

Out in the corridor once more, Lorimer leaned against the wall opposite Morar. His thoughts about the killer were beginning to crystallise. Not only had he foreseen the necessity of disabling that CCTV camera, had he also known that the technician would be off sick? If he was one of the musicians then he might well have known that Poliakowski liked to be left alone in his room. This had the hallmarks of a crime that was prepared well in advance just like an act of terrorism. The thought made Lorimer feel cold.

Yet it could narrow things down, too. How many people would be aware of Poliakowski's preferences?

Most of all, why would anybody want to murder George Millar in the first place?

That was a question he'd like to ask Dr Solomon Brightman, if only he could. Solly's expertise as a criminal profiler had been useful in the past; however he couldn't see the psychologist being involved in this case. Serial killings were more his forte. And this was surely just a one-off murder.

Chapter Four

Lorimer could hear the sound of the telephone ringing upstairs as he opened the front door. His long legs took the stairs two at a time.

"Lorimer," he breathed heavily into the mouthpiece.

"It's me," a voice replied. Her voice sounded as if she were in the next room not the other side of the Atlantic.

He let himself sink down to the carpet, his spine coming to rest against the wall.

"Well, hallo, you," he replied softly. "How're you doing?"

Fine," Maggie gave a short laugh. "God, that's what all the kids say when you ask them the same question. Isn't it maddening? Anyway, I am fine. Just about to make tracks for bed. Thought you might get this as a message in the morning. I didn't mean to disturb you." Her words came out in a rush and Lorimer detected a slight tremor in her voice.

"Have you been trying to reach me tonight?"

"Several times. I thought you were going to be at home," she spoke in a voice that tried not to sound accusing.

"Got called out."

"Oh?" The question offered Lorimer a chance to tell her all about it. Suddenly Lorimer felt desperately tired. All he wanted was to curl up in bed with Maggie beside him and give her some of the story about tonight's case. That was what he used to do. His wife would snuggle in and he'd tell her the less grisly details. Sometimes she'd fall asleep again before he'd finished. Other times she'd make them tea and he'd talk to her until the dawn came up.

"What time is it in Florida?" he asked.

"Just after eleven o'clock. Four in the morning your time."

Lorimer rubbed his hand across his face as if the gesture could dissipate the terrible sleepiness that threatened to overwhelm him.

"We were called out to the Concert Hall. One of the musicians was killed," Lorimer told her, trying hard not to yawn.

"Want to call me back some time tomorrow?" Maggie had

obviously heard his yawn but her voice was sympathetic, not annoyed.

"I will. Promise," Lorimer said.

"Goodnight, love," Maggie whispered.

"'Night," he replied. He listened for an answer then added, "I miss you." He waited for the click but there was nothing. Had she heard these last words?

Putting down the phone on the floor beside him, Lorimer closed his eyes. His body ached for sleep and he knew he should pull himself off the carpet and struggle out of his clothes but something held him there. Maggie's presence was almost tangible. If he held out his hand, would he feel her warm fingers clasping his own?

A sudden gust of wind rattled against the skylight window and broke the spell. Lorimer opened his eyes. The upstairs hall was in darkness. The familiar shapes of the telephone table and waste paper bin were shrouded in shadows. He concentrated hard, trying to bring back the sound of Maggie's voice, but all he could hear was the sound of his own breathing ending in a sigh of resignation. The muscles in his thighs protested as Lorimer stood up and headed for the bathroom.

He switched on the light. The face in the mirror looked back at him, unsmiling. Unkempt dark hair fell over his brow, almost masking the twin frown lines so deeply etched between the blue eyes. The four-in-the-morning shadow made him look like some ageing rock star staring moodily from the mirror. He pulled the light switch cord and plunged the room into darkness, extinguishing the face in an instant.

Lorimer stepped out of his trousers leaving them on the rug beside the bed. Sliding his naked body under the duvet, he groaned at the chill of the sheet. He closed his eyes, wanting to see Maggie again, to hear her voice, preparing himself to lie there awake for hours as usual. With a trembling sigh Lorimer turned on his side, tucking his legs under him.

Seconds later he was asleep.

✳ ✳ ✳

"Whit's up wi' you?" Sadie's voice cut into Lorimer's brain like a bandsaw. He looked at the wee woman behind the canteen counter. Her hair was pulled away from her face making the sharp features that nature had inflicted upon them even more severe. She was standing waiting for him to choose something for his breakfast.

"Just the usual coffee and Danish, thanks," he muttered.

"You look as if you could do with a decent plate o' porridge, so you do. I bet your Maggie would've made it for you if she'd no' been gallivantin' away over there. Where is it she is again?"

"Florida," Lorimer answered, wishing that the woman would keep her voice down. But Sadie was no respecter of persons. Not one of them in the station was above her forthright opinions.

"Florida?" she spoke the word as if he'd said something bad. "What's she wanting to go over there for? Ma Robert went over therr wi' his weans one time, so he did. Came back covered in mosquito bites. It wis that hot they had to stay in the hoose wi' thon air conditioning on. Florida? Ah telt him he should've gone tae Millport. Saved himself a fortune, an' all."

Lorimer grinned in spite of himself as he took the tray back to his office. Sadie might sound like a pain in the neck but she had a heart of gold. Maybe there was something to be said for the blunt approach. And maybe she wasn't too far off the mark, either. Maggie had already told him about the humidity that had hit her like a wall as she'd stepped out of Sarasota airport. Would he ever experience it for himself? They hadn't yet discussed whether Lorimer would take the flight out there or if Maggie would come home for Christmas. There was the problem, too, of Maggie's old mum. She'd hinted about seeing her daughter in Florida. Lorimer would have to take her out with him, if he decided to go there. What would the Yanks make of her? Like Sadie, Maggie's mum was a self-opinionated old so-and-so who expressed herself often in politically incorrect terms. Lorimer loved her.

He was chewing on the last of his Danish pastry when the phone rang.

"Hi there, it's your friendly neighbourhood pathologist. Just thought I'd let you know the latest on your violinist."

"Okay. I'm listening."

"Not a lot to add. A single blow to the skull caused fracture and internal haemorrhaging between the skull and the dura. There were pieces of bone embedded in the brain. The weapon caught him just above his right ear and I've matched the bruising with the diameter of the hammer. No prints on the weapon, though, as 'we thought. Funny it only took one blow. That percussion instrument's only the size of a household hammer. Not such a big weapon, is it?" Rosie asked.

Lorimer heard the note of curiosity in her voice. If she was thinking what he was thinking then his first impressions were probably correct.

"You'd normally expect a whole lot of blows, is that it?"

"Well," she began, "he certainly hit the middle meningeal artery with that first strike, though there wasn't such a lot of blood about. I don't think the killer would have had much to clean off. What d'you think?"

"I'm not sure," Lorimer began slowly. "Either he got lucky with that one strike or he knew exactly how to administer the blow."

"A big man would have been able to bring more force to the weapon," Rosie suggested. "And, from the position of the wound, it seems like the victim had started to turn his head towards whoever came up behind him."

Even as he replied, the image of Victor Poliakowski came into Lorimer's mind.

"I think that we have a very carefully prepared killing on our hands. I don't think George Millar was struck in a moment of blind rage, do you? By the way do you have any results on that black duster?"

"No. Not yet. But I'll fax them through to you as soon as if not sooner. Will that do you?"

"No, but it'll have to, won't it?" Lorimer grumbled. "Was there anything else? Anything under his nails, any fibres worth talking about, or haven't they been processed yet?"

"Nothing on his fingernails. And nope, no results yet on the fibres, of which there are plenty. I'll tell you what, though. We found some powdery substance on his fingertips."

"Uh-huh?"

"No. Not that sort of powder. You lot have narcotics on the brain. It was blue, not white," she replied in a withering tone of voice.

"Interesting. See what your lab. Boys and girls can make of that, eh."

"Will do. Speak to you later."

Lorimer put the phone down. Rosie probably hadn't slept much either but she sounded a whole lot brighter than he felt. Maybe it was fresh air that he needed. There was a pile of reports expected later today from last night's massive exercise. Hundreds of statements had been taken from the members of the Orchestra and Chorus as well as from everybody in the audience. There had been officers drafted in from other divisions to undertake the operation and already their files were being processed on computer.

He'd spent hours talking to Brendan Phillips. The Orchestra Manager would have to supply him with details of the members of the City of Glasgow Orchestra; details that might help him to focus on a reason for George Millar's death.

Lorimer had not visited the violinist's home; that had been a task undertaken by other officers. But he should really make the effort to go out and see Mrs Millar now, he reasoned with himself. If only he didn't feel so exhausted. He reached for the mug of coffee. It was cold but he drained it anyway, knowing he'd need the kick of caffeine.

WPC Irvine scrolled down the list of names on her computer screen. She shook her head in disbelief as the names rolled on and on. How the heck did they get that many people on the stage? It hadn't seemed that big when she'd taken Dad to see Shania Twain for his birthday. Something caught her eye and she slowed down to take a closer look. Funny. The whole list of musicians had been in alphabetical order until that very last name. Maybe he had just newly joined them or something? That Mr Phillips would know. It had been his list that she'd scanned in. Maybe she should mention it?

"Irvine, the Boss wants to see you," Alistair Wilson drummed his fingers lightly over the edge of her desk as he passed by.

WPC Irvine rolled her eyes. "No rest for the wicked," she sighed, wondering what other task Lorimer had in store for her.

Outside the station the rain was beginning to spot the windscreens of the cars in the car park. Lorimer unlocked the door of his ancient Lexus and swung himself into the driver's seat. As always, the feel of leather beneath him gave him a sense of comfort.

He was more at home behind the wheel of his car than in his own armchair at home, Maggie had once told him. And it was probably true.

"Sorry, sir," WPC Irvine flung herself breathlessly into the passenger seat. "It's Huntly Gardens. Number 39."

By the time they'd crossed the city centre, the wipers were flipping back and forth as rain fell steadily. Lorimer needed all his concentration as he negotiated Woodlands Road with cars parked on both sides and pedestrians battling to escape the deluge. The policewoman sat by his side, keeping silent. Chattering to the Boss when he was deep in thought was never a good idea. Up Glasgow Street and over the hill he drove, crossing Byres Road, turning at last into the faded gentility of Huntly Gardens where George Millar had lived.

Lorimer had to park right at the top of the hill. The road was virtually a single lane due to the double parking, Huntly Gardens being one of the few streets off Byres Road that lacked a residents-only zone. As they walked back down, Lorimer found himself looking into the bay windowed rooms of every flat at pavement level. It was a habit of his to gauge what sort of district a person inhabited from the houses of their neighbours. He stared at a variety of window dressings; that hanging wind chime might denote a student flat, those crisply laundered nets probably belonged to a resident out at work and who needed a bit of privacy. There was a grand piano in one bay window with a metronome on top. Music spilled out from behind the fly blown glass window. Lorimer stopped abruptly, checking the address.

"This is it, sir."

As he buzzed the call button opposite "Millar" the music stopped. A crackling sound emanated from the system then a woman's voice asked, "Who is it?"

"Detective Chief Inspector Lorimer, WPC Irvine, Strathclyde Police. We've come to see Mrs Millar."

There was a pause then the same voice said, "Wait a minute."

Beyond the frosted glass panel Lorimer could see a figure hurrying towards him. The door swung open and Mrs Millar stood regarding them seriously.

She was, he supposed, around sixty, though her black jeans and embroidered top gave her a much younger appearance. Her bare feet, thrust into a pair of Birkenstocks, showed purple painted toenails. Lorimer absorbed all this in one glance as he cleared his throat.

"DCI Lorimer. Mrs Millar?"

"Yes," she answered him simply. "Would you like to come on through?"

Lorimer followed George Millar's widow through the hall and into the ground floor flat. She showed them into the front room. Lorimer's first impression was of a high ceiling and lots of ornate plasterwork then his eye fell on the grand piano that sat dominating the bay window. Had that been Mrs Millar playing as he'd passed by? Could you do something as creative as making music the morning after your husband had been murdered?

"Please sit down, Chief Inspector, Constable. Would you like some coffee?" Her tone seemed to indicate that this was merely a social visit. There was no trace of anguish in her voice. Maybe she was still in denial, he told himself.

"Thanks. Coffee would be fine," Lorimer replied, but didn't sit down. Instead he followed Mrs Millar into the kitchen and leaned against the wood panelled wall, watching her as she filled a kettle jug and set about preparing their coffee.

WPC Irvine followed them in and sat by the oak table, glancing up at Lorimer as if trying to gauge what was on his mind.

"I'm sorry about your husband," Lorimer began slowly. "It must have been a dreadful shock." He watched her face as she turned towards him.

"I'm used to shocks, Chief Inspector. Yes, this was dreadful, but it's happened and I can't make it un-happen. Just as I couldn't change the way George was. Don't think me harsh but I've become used to accepting the things I cannot change."

There was an inflection in her tone that made Lorimer realise she was quoting something he'd heard before. For a moment he was at a loss then it came to him. Wasn't it part of a prayer by Saint Francis of Assisi? Or was he mixing that up with something else? Mrs Millar was looking at a corkboard next to the doorway on Lorimer's left. He followed her gaze and saw the small green card. On it was written,

God
Grant me the Serenity to accept
The things I cannot change…
Courage to change the things I can
And Wisdom to know the difference.

She looked back at him, the ghost of a smile hovering apologetically around her lips.

Lorimer didn't know what to say. Even if she was a devout woman that shouldn't stop her from expressing her emotions, should it?

For a moment Lorimer wished he'd asked the officer who'd come here last night for the widow's first reaction. It hadn't seemed necessary. Now he was curious to know how she had responded to the terrible news.

"Thanks," he said as she handed them mugs of coffee. He thought they'd make their way back into the sitting room, but Mrs Millar motioned for him to join his colleague at the kitchen table. She leaned into a chair with a patchwork cushion at her back then raised her mug of coffee.

"To life," she said and smiled in Lorimer's direction.

Her easy familiarity with a complete stranger gave Lorimer some disquiet. For a moment they locked eyes as he raised the mug of coffee to his lips. Lorimer looked away first. There was nothing malevolent about the woman's gaze, just a calm directness. Usually he'd be probing a person's behaviour for undercurrents of emotion, indications that could help in establishing the nature of relationships. But how to get behind that mask of tranquillity, if indeed it was a mask, was a problem.

"I'd like to ask you some questions about your husband," Lorimer began.

"Of course. Whatever I can tell you, Chief Inspector," Mrs Millar's reply was polite, almost but not quite grave. It was as if she were about to discuss someone she'd encountered in the street, not her own husband. Was that telling him something? Lorimer wondered.

"First of all, could you tell me when you last saw Mr Millar?"

"Yes. He was at home yesterday until just after lunch. He left about two o' clock. There was a three o'clock rehearsal call."

"Did he drive into town?"

"No. He took the underground from Hillhead into Buchanan Street. It's the easiest way."

"Was there anything unusual about your husband's demeanour before he left?"

He watched her face as she took another sip of coffee. She was thoughtful, considering her words carefully.

"No. I don't think I noticed anything untoward. He was a fairly cheerful person as a rule. No, he seemed perfectly normal. He was looking forward to the programme, I know that."

Remembering the Albinoni solo, Lorimer wondered if that had been something George Millar would have enjoyed. Something he'd been denied.

"Mrs Millar, can you think who might have wanted your husband dead?"

"My goodness, that's direct enough," she smiled but her eyebrows were raised. "Who might have murderous tendencies towards George?" she mused, looking away from Lorimer and gazing into space.Then she frowned and shook her head. "That's a question that puts me in a difficult position. It makes me have to judge how other people should behave."

Lorimer nodded, silently noting the plural reference. "Let me put it another way, then. Had your husband done anything to provoke anybody?"

"Oh, dear Lord, yes. George was about the most provoking man you could meet."

"I need you to be specific. Who in particular had he provoked?"

She smiled sweetly at him again, "Why me, of course, Chief Inspector. But I'm not the killing type." She glanced across at the policewoman as if to affirm her statement.

"Anybody else?"

"I'm sure he drove many of his fellow musicians mad at times. He was a bit of a perfectionist. And of course he was incorrigibly promiscuous," she added as if it was a mere afterthought.

"Can you give me some details about anyone who may have had a grudge against Mr Millar?"

She shook her head slowly then answered, "No, I don't think I can."

"Do you mean you don't know of anybody or you can't bring yourself to tell me?" he asked.

The woman's head came up and Lorimer saw the first flicker of annoyance disturb that serene expression. He'd rattled her cage at last.

"Chief Inspector, I want to do anything I can to help your investigation. I do not know who killed my husband. Nor do I have the faintest idea who would wish to do something so evil."

"Where were you yesterday evening, Mrs Millar?"

The question took her completely by surprise, Lorimer saw. Her face changed colour as she immediately realised the implication of his words. He could be easy on her, tell her gently that he had to ask such questions, but something made him hold back from the softly, softly approach. This lady had an inner strength of some sort. Well, let her make use of it now. He regarded her as she swallowed the last of her coffee, noting how carefully she set down the mug on the table as if to conceal her trembling fingers. She saw his gaze and hastily drew her hands away out of sight.

"I was here. I spent the evening on my own. I don't think anyone can verify that," she gave a shaky little laugh, "unless somebody upstairs heard me playing the piano."

"We can look into that," he told her sombrely. "Perhaps you

could tell me a bit more about your husband, something about his habits, his personality. It helps to have a picture of the victim when we're conducting a murder inquiry."

Mrs Millar gave a small, involuntary sigh and raised her eyebrows again.

"George was a homosexual, but I suppose you know that by now. He came out a few years ago so it was no secret. He wasn't ashamed of what he was, in fact I think he enjoyed being different." She paused. "You ask about his personality. He was an outgoing man, the sort of person who liked attention. He enjoyed an audience off stage as well as on. But he was totally wrapped up in himself and in his music." She paused. "George wasn't a cruel man, Chief Inspector, I want you to understand that, but he simply didn't think about other people's feelings."

"Even yours?"

"Especially mine," she gave a mirthless laugh.

"So why did you..?"

"Stay with him?" she finished the sentence for him. "Hard to say really, though goodness knows I've asked myself the same question often enough. I suppose it's because he never wanted to leave. He had plenty of lovers but he didn't bring them back here. There would be nights when he didn't come home. And I got used to it after a time. When we were together we got on rather amicably. Does that surprise you?" she asked, seeing the policewoman's bemused expression.

"Well, yes," she admitted.

"George was never bad to me, though he'd been pretty hopeless in bed. Understandable once we knew why. But we got on. We were fond enough of each other not to mind."

"You don't seem terribly upset by the violent death of someone you were fond of," Lorimer remarked at last.

There was silence as Mrs Millar regarded him. She seemed to be searching for a reply then her eyes dropped from his gaze as she said, "Perhaps it hasn't really sunk in yet."

Lorimer drained the last of his coffee. She could have been equally blunt in her response but had chosen to be polite instead.

"Thanks," he said, handing her the empty mug. "I'd be grateful if you did have a word with these neighbours of yours upstairs. Just so they can verify that you were in last night." Lorimer spoke the words more kindly than he had intended, trying to assuage the guilt he felt at his previous accusation. It wasn't, after all, a crime to behave inappropriately at the sudden death of your husband. Still, it would keep him wondering about George Millar's widow for some time to come.

As she closed the door Lorimer lingered on the top step, listening for any hint of anguish from within, even a groan of relief that he'd gone. But there was nothing like that.

Once again he found himself wishing for the familiar sight of the bearded psychologist, his perceptive eyse twinkling behind those horn-rimmed glasses. What would Solomon Brightman make of this woman and her strange reactions? he mused.

By the time they'd reached the street again the melody from the grand piano could be heard once more and Lorimer could have sworn that the newly bereaved Mrs Millar had taken up exactly where she'd left off.

Chapter Five

Simon Corrigan found he was shivering despite the warmth of the room. He'd even had to draw his leg away from the radiator by the table where he'd sat waiting for something to begin. At first it had been a matter of routine, like giving his name and address to the officers the night George had been killed. But now, in this small room in a Police headquarters, Simon sensed that he was in some danger.

Part of him wanted to believe that Scottish police were nice, trustworthy men and women; the polis of his youth who would tell you how to get home if you were lost or give you into trouble for kicking your football into an old lady's garden. But then the polis of his youth had been country constables who'd helped them with their cycling proficiency tests in the playground at Primary School, not the hard-faced lot in the city of Glasgow that you saw on TV shows. He'd heard all sorts of stories about how guys got a kicking down in the cells and no apology afterwards. They knew how to hurt without making a mark for a police doctor to see, he'd heard. Simon shivered again and looked at his watch. How long would they make him wait?

Suddenly he felt angry. He was being detained against his will, wasn't he? The scrape of his chair against the floor alerted the young officer who stood impassively, back to the door.

"Can I help you, sir?" he asked as Simon stood up. His polite, deferential tone made the musician hesitate. "How long will he be? The Inspector, I mean."

"Oh, not long, sir. I'm sorry we've kept you waiting so long. It's always like this, I'm afraid," the constable smiled thinly as if he were taking Simon into his confidence somehow. "Would you like another cup of tea?"

"No. Thanks," Simon replied, sitting down again, his anger evaporating as quickly as it had come. He was wrong. They were simply busy, that was all. His imagination was running away with him. As if they'd be wasting precious time deliberately making him wait; that was the stuff of TV dramas, not real life.

He looked up as the door opened and a blonde woman entered

the room followed by the Detective Sergeant he'd spoken to at the concert hall.

"Inspector Grant, DS Wilson," said the blonde, waving a hand in her colleague's direction as they sat opposite Simon.

"Have you had a cup of tea?" she asked, ignoring the beige plastic cup sitting between them.

"Yes," Simon replied, holding his hands together to stop them from shaking.

"Thanks for agreeing to come in today, Mr Corrigan. As you can appreciate this is a mammoth task we have here, with so many people who were friends or colleagues of Mr Millar," DI Grant began. She smiled at him as if he would understand that a policeman's lot was not a happy one. Simon felt himself relax. It was going to be okay.

"We're really grateful that you could spare us the time. It must be awfully hard to carry on after this," the DI continued.

Simon mumbled a reply and felt his cheeks redden. So, they knew about George and him. He'd suspected as much. That cow, Karen, must have told them. He'd seen her swan off with the tall detective.

"If I could just take down a few details. Sorry about all this. Red tape, but we need it all the same," Jo Grant was all apologies as Simon reeled off his name, date of birth, and current address.

Jo Grant glanced at the man opposite. He was a good-looking lad, with his red-gold hair falling forward over his brow. Green eyes, she'd noticed. Cats' eyes with that measured look as if he were studying her just as she was trying to study him. But wary, too, though he was visibly relaxing now that the preliminary stuff was out of the way. He'd become almost chatty, telling them about his early career and what he hoped to do in the future. Enthusiastic, too, she had liked that. But it was time to slip in the odd reference to a murdered man, to remind them all just why Simon Corrigan, French horn player with the City of Glasgow Orchestra, was sitting opposite two police officers.

"We have to ask everyone who knew Mr Millar about him. It helps us to build up a picture of the victim." Jo saw the man shift in his seat. The word victim always had that effect on the innocent and guilty alike.

"What can you tell us about Mr Millar?" DS Wilson asked.

"What do you want to know?" Simon shrugged. There was silence for answer so he continued. "He was all right, was George. A bit of a scamp, really. Like to spread his favours, if you know what I mean."

"Didn't you mind?" Jo asked, a conspiratorial smile playing about her lips.

"No. Not really. Everyone knew he was an old rogue. Only Carl…" He bit his lip and stopped.

"Carl Bekaert?"

"Aye. Carl, the Great Dane, we all called him. Superb viola player but he took himself too seriously. Had a huge pash for George. Wanted to have him all to himself."

"But Mr Millar was married. Lived with his wife," DS Wilson put in.

"Och, that was different. George would never have moved in with any of us. We were his boys; that was all."

"So there was never a serious relationship between Mr Millar and any of the male members of the Orchestra?" Jo asked.

Simon frowned. "Not like that. I mean there's serious and serious, isn't there? You'd move in with a person if you really were committed, wouldn't you?"

"Tell me about Mr Millar as a musician," Jo said, switching tack.

"Ah, now you're asking something," Simon leaned back in his seat, stretching his long legs out under the table, then leaned forward again. "He was the best, was George. And I'm not just saying this because he's dead. Why he'd never played with some of the big European outfits, I'll never know. He'd been Leader with The City of Glasgow for as long as I can remember. Even saw him perform when I was still at school."

"What was his attitude to the younger players like yourself?"

Simon grinned. "I expect you want to hear if he encouraged us, made some guys his protégés. But it was nothing like that. Sure he hung about with the younger ones, but only in a social sense, like down the pub after rehearsals. He had great stories, you know. We all loved hearing the gossip about people he'd known. I suppose that's how we became friends," he added.

"And how did that friendship deepen?" Wilson asked so politely that Jo Grant had to suppress a grin.

"He asked me to come to bed with him."

"Just like that?" Jo raised her eyebrows.

"Well, we were both a bit pissed. Anyway that's how it all began." Simon smiled down at the table as if recalling some detail from the past and shook his head slightly. "We had some good times. Never thought anyone would have it in for him. Never."

"He was a popular man, then? Within the Orchestra?"

"Not with everyone. Some of the straight women disapproved of him, you know. He could be a right bugger at times, would wind folk up something rotten. But we just laughed. But, yeah, he was liked well enough by most of them. Can't say there was a single soul who'd shown any animosity towards him."

"How did Mr Millar behave on the day of his murder?" Jo asked.

Simon frowned as if trying to recall. "Normal. He was quite normal. There was nothing at all that I noticed that was different from usual. Honestly," he added, deliberately fixing Jo with his green eyes. She recognised it as trick to dominate a dialogue, one she'd seen Lorimer use often enough. But did that mean she believed Corrigan? She stared back at him then lowered her eyes. Let him think he'd the upper hand. Maybe it would make him more careless with his talk. He might have some inkling of how to assert himself, but Jo had been on enough assertiveness training courses to wear out the proverbial T-shirt.

"Did you notice anything unusual at all that afternoon, or evening?"

"Nope. We had a fairly horrible rehearsal, which is par for the course and everything was just as it usually was until George didn't come on stage," Simon bit his lip suddenly and Jo noticed the tightness in his voice.

"I'm sorry," she soothed, "we really do have to ask questions like these."

"It's okay. It's just getting it to sink in, you know? I don't think any of us have really realised that he's not coming back. It's like Karen's just filling in while he's sick, or something."

"I understand. Well, thanks for coming in. If there's anything else we want to ask you or indeed if there's anything you remember that you might think useful, any little thing at all," Jo smiled, "please call us." She stood up and offered the musician her hand. Held in hers for a moment Simon Corrigan's hand felt like a wet fish, bony and sweaty. The musician drew it away suddenly. Mr Cool's cover had been blown and he knew it.

Jo watched him from the upper window, crossing the street and heading off into town, the wind tousling that fine red-gold hair. His shoulders were hunched against the cold but suddenly he straightened up as if he'd caught sight of somebody coming towards him. Jo moved into the corner of the window, straining to see the figure approaching. She noted the laconic walk and the handsome face before the two men met together on the pavement. Their sudden embrace made the Detective Inspector step back instinctively but she continued to watch as the two men clasped one another tightly then broke apart.

When he looked back towards the building he had so recently left, Jo Grant could see that Simon Corrigan's face expressed quite a different mood, now. And, had she been asked, she would have described it as triumphant.

Chapter Six

He was dreaming about Christmas. The tree lights had just been switched on and he could see his Dad's face reflected in the glow from all the different coloured lanterns. He wasn't allowed to touch any of the bulbs but the tree ornaments were a different matter. They were the same ones every year; the wee sailing boat that had long since lost any of its paint, the crimson and gold glass baubles, the box of tiny wooden toys that had come from somewhere in eastern Europe and of course the Fairy with a gauzy kind of skirt that Mum replaced year by year. There was something reassuring about all the familiar objects. Lorimer bent down to pick up the streams of tinsel from the paper bag where they were always kept and then straightened up to meet Mum's eye.

Only it wasn't his mum looking back at him, but Maggie. And he wasn't a wee boy any more; he was aware of being grown up now and Mum and Dad were both gone.

Waking to a feeling of panic, Lorimer lay seeing the people in his dream fade away as he reminded himself of the here and now. Maggie. She was gone too, but not irrevocably, like Mum and Dad. Was that why he'd dreamt it? Was he trying to hold onto her before it was too late?

There was sweat running down his chest and he wiped it away with a corner of the duvet. He'd phone Maggie's mum today. Discuss the trip to Sarasota for Christmas. It was far enough away for him to plan some leave.

Surely this débâcle in the Concert Hall would be done and dusted by then?

The socks in his bottom drawer were the old ones that had worn away in the heels. He'd meant to chuck them out long ago but had never quite got around to it. Now, pulling the washed out pair onto his feet, he was almost grateful for his own lack of domestic organisation. He'd have to do a washing today or else he'd be out of shirts as well. Tonight, he promised himself. He'd do it tonight. What with his earlier resolve to book the Florida trip, Lorimer felt rather pleased with himself. The dream of Dad and the Christmas tree lights flickered and went out as he whistled his way into the bathroom.

Under the hot spray of the shower his whistle was muted to a loud hum. It was only when he had begun to stamp his feet in time to the rhythm that Lorimer realised he was humming the Anvil Chorus.

He was out of the shower and towelling dry his hair in record time. What had happened to the percussionists since their preliminary interviews? That piece was to have been played in the second half. They'd always had two hammers ready. Why had that been? Had he even asked that question? And what had the players who were not needed for the first half of the concert been doing during the time that George Millar was in his dressing room? He'd have his work cut out today to catch up with the transcripts of interviews. Annie Irvine had assured him that the computer files would be updated to make cross-referencing easier. Lorimer growled at his steamy reflection in the bathroom mirror. He'd see if that were true soon enough.

"No breakfast this morning either? That's not good for you, y'know!" Sadie's voice followed Lorimer out of the canteen as he strode along the corridor to his office, trying not to get his fingers too sticky with the icing from his daily Danish.

The file was still incomplete but he'd expected that. There were names and addresses of all the musicians, choral singers and the punters who'd had their evening's entertainment cut short. Or had they? The morning headlines screamed murder at him from the Gazette. There was a grainy picture of Poliakowski that was obviously an old publicity shot judging from the man's slimmer figure. Lorimer was torn between trying to focus on the computer screen and reading the front-page columns.

He gave up and rustled the paper into shape, beginning to read the tabloid version of events in Glasgow Royal Concert Hall. They'd sensationalised it, of course. Poliakowski was their main focus of interest simply because of his high profile in the music world. There had been a short press statement following George's death and a smallish piece had appeared the day following the leader's murder. But now the hacks had got hold of more details and were milking the story for all it was worth. Lorimer had to admit it made pretty bizarre reading.

Poliakowski claimed to have been devastated by George's sudden death and the idea that someone could have got access to his dressing room so easily. There was a veiled suggestion that the killer had perhaps got the wrong victim, that in fact the Russian conductor was the real target and that this was a professional hit. Lorimer reeled at this. It was risible. But then the reporters hadn't got all the facts. They weren't to know about the immobilisation of the CCTV camera outside Morar, were they?

But would that have made such a difference? Lorimer's mind spun rapidly. George Millar had been a fairly short chap, but, like Poliakowski, he'd sported a beard and was thinning on top. The Russian was a huge bear of a man. Surely there could have been no mistaking him if this had been a pro's job? All the other attention to detail ruled that out, didn't it?

The paper went on to discuss the Russian's position on dissident musicians and his own political leanings within his country. There wasn't an awful lot about poor old George, the actual victim. It wouldn't be long, thought Lorimer, before they'd sniffed out the facts of George's homosexuality. Then they'd have a field day. He wondered how Mrs Millar would respond to a crowd of reporters at her door.

Back on the screen, Lorimer could see the names of so many strangers scrolling up past him. The team had done a good job of tabulating the musicians' names and addresses alongside their particular part in the Orchestra, even down to the desk number. Brendan Phillips's hand was in this detail, Lorimer supposed. There had been four percussionists paid for that night's concert, two men and two women. Three were British, one American, Lorimer noted. No Eastern Europeans amongst them. Why had he made that mental remark to himself? Was he becoming paranoid over the Gazette's suppositions? The percussionists' statements all tallied. They'd been together in their dressing room from the time the rest of the Orchestra had trooped on stage to the time they'd been informed of George's death. They'd followed the concert on the TV monitor in the room. Only one of them had been out of the room for more than a few minutes. Cassandra Austen had visited the ladies toilet once during that time. CCTV footage had confirmed her statement. Lorimer was impressed. The team had been hard at work collating what evidence there was and now there could be a proper process of elimination.

The CCTV footage had helped enormously, though not in the way Lorimer had first hoped. The members of the audience who had come into the auditorium had been checked out. Very few had left their seats during the first half of the performance. Most had visited the toilet area by the cloakrooms. One had been seen taking a telephone call on his mobile at the foot of the stairs. He'd been confirmed as a Consultant Surgeon on call. There were no suspicious punters mooching about backstage. To take the audience out of the equation gave Lorimer a huge sense of relief. The members of the Chorus had trooped on stage in a particular pre-ordained order. There was even a peg-board with their names in a seating plan that had been checked against a still from the monitor. That didn't mean there wasn't a killer amongst them, but it did narrow the possible time of death to the twenty minutes before the Chorus had appeared on stage. Prior to that, they'd been clustered on the stairs leading from dressing rooms 5, 6 and 7 for a final briefing from their Chorus master.

Lorimer stopped reading and frowned. Where had the Chorus master gone after that? He scrolled up and down but failed to find the man's name amongst the musicians or members of the Chorus. Odd. After the thoroughness of the rest of the team's efforts this was a glaring omission. He searched back through the list of members of the audience. It wasn't there either. The final check had to show his name amongst all the back room boys, surely? People like Brendan Phillips and other administrators, the drivers and shifters and the permanent Concert Hall staff were all listed in a separate file. But the name was still missing. Lorimer chewed his lip. He didn't even know who he was looking for, simply a name against the designation: Chorus master, City of Glasgow Chorus. When he'd checked the lists again he lifted the phone and dialled Brendan Phillips's number at the Concert

Manager's headquarters.

"Good morning, Chief Inspector. Any news yet?" Brendan Phillips's voice sounded breathless as if he'd been running to pick up the phone.

"Nothing to pass on to you as yet, sir. But I do have a question to ask you. Do you have the full name and address of the Chorus Master?" Lorimer's question was intended to make it seem as if he was querying information he already had rather than fill in an embarrassing blank.

"Could you hold just for a minute?" Lorimer heard the clunk of the handset being placed on Brendan's desk as he waited for the Concert Manager to return.

"Here we are. C. Maurice Drummond, 24 Belmont Street. Afraid I don't know what the C stands for, Chief Inspector. We all know him as Maurice."

Lorimer grinned to himself. This was a piece of pure luck. Phillips would think he needed the man's Christian names. Whatever C stood for it wouldn't make Chief Inspector Lorimer look a right Charlie. He'd follow it up, nonetheless, he thought as he scribbled down the man's telephone number. Someone would have to go and check this one out. He'd enough to do without running around the West End every minute of the day. Lorimer dialled another number and gave instructions for a visit to be made to Mr C. Maurice Drummond.

Funny, though, he mused after he'd spoken to WPC Irvine, how he had slipped through the net like that.

By Rosie's reckoning the murder had taken place before the musicians had gone on stage. The events behind the scenes during that half hour before the scheduled performance were pretty much visible on the CCTV footage. He'd spent hours watching the screen show men in dress shirts milling around their dressing rooms, folk smoking outside at the back door, musicians and members of the Chorus alike wandering through the warren of corridors backstage. And in the minutes before that particular camera had gone blank there was only an empty corridor. The last people seen moving along there had been Brendan Phillips and one of the female stewards. If Lorimer's hunch was right, the camera had been tampered with by someone coming in from the area behind stage left, not someone who had calmly walked down the corridor towards it.

Rosie's latest report had shown the substance on George Millar's fingers to be nothing more sinister than resin from his bow. Lorimer supposed things like that were kept in the man's violin case. The black duster, on the other hand, showed traces of a stronger adhesive than mere double-sided sticky tape. It was an industrial strength adhesive not usually found in the normal outlets like newsagents or supermarkets. Bostik 6092 had only one supplier in Glasgow. It was a place up in the Balmore Industrial estate, according to Rosie. Lorimer grinned to himself. It was tiny details like these that could be followed up and become promising leads in a murder investigation. The murder weapon itself had been wiped clean. Lorimer imagined a figure bending over George Millar's body then placing the percussion instrument where it might easily be seen.

The detective's grin straightened into its customary frown, the twin creases deepening between his eyebrows. Had that been a deliberate ploy on the part of the killer? Had he been trying to draw attention to one of the percussionists? Poliakowski had mentioned working with Cassandra Austen, the American percussionist. She might have known the famous conductor's habit of closeting himself in his dressing room, certainly. But why would she have left such an obvious clue as the murder weapon behind her? No. He could rule that one out on the grounds of simple common sense. But what if one of the men in that section had been having a clandestine affair with George Millar?

Lorimer harked back to Karen Quentin-Jones' statement. She'd told him that George's two current boyfriends had been a French horn player and a viola player. But, according to his wife, the lead violinist had been a promiscuous old boy. Lorimer drummed his fingers on the edge of his desk. The two men had already been invited in for questioning. Perhaps their statements might shed some light on whether George had been playing around with anyone else in the Orchestra. Brendan Phillips had provided a CV for them both, Lorimer remembered, riffling through the papers in front of him. There it was, stapled to DI Grant's report.

Simon Corrigan was a young man from Fife who'd come up through the ranks of local brass bands, going on to study at Glasgow's prestigious Royal Scottish Academy of Music and Drama. He'd been with the Orchestra since graduating, Lorimer read. Carl Bekaert wasn't much older than Corrigan, although his CV showed he'd had experience of other orchestras before coming to Glasgow. Lorimer was puzzled. He'd still to meet them both, it was true, but he couldn't help wondering what on earth these two young musicians had seen in an older man like George Millar.

His thoughts were interrupted by a knock on the door and he looked up to see DI Josephine Grant. Lorimer gave a perfunctory nod. Jo had been one of Superintendent Mitchison's officers and had transferred to their Division not long after the Superintendent's appointment. It was a promotion they all thought had been Lorimer's for the asking. But Jo Grant had been more than simply one of Mitchison's old team, Lorimer reminded himself. He recalled the Superintendent's blonde companion at his previous boss's retiral dinner. She'd scrubbed up well, too, as he remembered. The long running friction between himself and Mitchison could extend to any of his acolytes if Lorimer let it happen, but so far Jo showed no signs of taking sides with either of her superiors. Nor did it seem as if there was any lingering relationship between the Super and Josephine Grant.

"This has just come in on email from Dr. Fergusson," Jo said, handing him a sheet of paper. "Thought you might want me to do something about it," she added as he read its contents. Rosie had underlined one of a list of George's personal effects, things that had been taken away for forensic examination. It was the bow for his violin.

"Strange, don't you think, sir?" Jo Grant was watching his face as Lorimer took in the fact that no fingerprints had been found on the bow.

"Yes," he replied, his mind flicking back to the scene in Morar where George Millar had breathed his last.

"Any ideas, Jo?" he leaned back in his chair, steepling his fingers as he regarded her.

"Well, obviously the killer had touched it and had to wipe it clean of prints," she replied, then made a face, "But why did they touch it in the first place? That's what you're asking isn't it?"

Lorimer nodded. "Yes." His mind was racing with possibilities. "Listen, Jo, can you find out the exact length of that bow for me?"

"The length? It's about that long, isn't it?" she spread her hands, measuring a space in the air.

"Maybe. Tell you what. See if you can do a little experiment for me. You won't get that bow back from Rosie, so find one from Phillips and take it back up to the Concert Hall. You're above average height, aren't you?"

"Five feet nine and a half in my bare feet," she answered, a mystified expression crossing her face. "Why?"

"Let's say for the sake of argument that our killer was your height. See if you could use the victim's bow to fix that black duster onto the CCTV. Hm?" Lorimer waited for her reply.

"Do you think that's how the killer immobilised the camera?"

"Possibly. It had to be done with something long and thin that wouldn't get covered in adhesive. A bow might just have done the trick."

"Wouldn't there be any traces of the black duster on it?" she asked. "I mean the horsehairs are so soft and fuzzy aren't they? There might be something already there for forensics to see."

She was sharp, thought Lorimer. They'd be looking for prints on the varnished wood, but there might well be traces on the mass of hairs strung tautly across the bow.

"Get back to forensics, will you, Jo. It might even give us a vague idea of the killer's height. Or at least eliminate all the wee guys," he said in a tone of mock despair that made the woman smile.

After she'd gone Lorimer sat back and thought about his DI. She'd come straight to him, no messing about. Did she see it as her duty to keep him informed of all the details? If Lorimer had got that email first, he'd have got on to forensics himself, thrashed ideas about with them or else worried away at the facts until they'd produced some kind of solution. Why hadn't Jo done that? Was DI Grant trying to ingratiate herself with him? He knew she wasn't lacking in initiative, he would say as much in her appraisal when the time came. Lorimer shook his head. He had to stop thinking of her as a spy in the camp. She'd come up the ranks on her own merit, even serving as an undercover officer for a spell. Her past association with Mitchison might be nothing at all. Perhaps she'd simply been a colleague he'd asked to accompany him to the dinner. Mitchison wasn't married and never had been, to Lorimer's knowledge. Perhaps he'd been wise enough to see the pitfalls of trying to establish a career and have a stable relationship into the bargain, he told himself, lapsing into a mood of cynicism. He was always immaculately turned out, thought Lorimer, ruefully examining the creases in his own shirtsleeves where he'd forgotten to iron. Maybe constant bachelorhood fostered the kind of discipline that he lacked himself.

Association of ideas took Lorimer back, inevitably, to Maggie. He'd have to get down to the Travel Agent's soon, he told himself. Best phone the old girl, see what she had to say about it.

He dialled her number, a grin on his face as he imagined her response. Maggie's mum was fairly predictable.

"Hello?" a voice answered. She never gave her name and number, something that Lorimer hadn't had to tell her.

"Hello. It's me. Have you a minute to spare or are you rushing off to that hotbed of gossip you call the Senior Citizens' Club?"

"Och, it's yourself, William. What are you doing phoning me in the middle of the day? Are there not enough criminals for you to be chasing in Strathclyde these days?" Mrs Finlay sounded as if she was scolding him but he knew her well enough to tell when she was teasing.

"It's about Christmas," he began. "D'you want me to book a flight for us to go out and stay with Maggie?"

"Oh." Mrs Finlay sounded lost for words, something that didn't happen too often in her son-in-law's experience.

"I'm due leave. I thought we could go out for a fortnight. Ten days, even, if you thought the heat might be too much."

"I don't mind the heat," she answered abruptly. "It's just…"

"I'll pay for us both, of course," Lorimer cut in. "Just call it your Christmas present from me," he added.

"That's very generous of you, Bill. Are you sure?" His mother-in-law's voice had softened and Lorimer knew he'd done the right thing.

"Sure. Leave it with me. I'll see the travel agency later on today and fix it all up."

After he'd rung off, Lorimer felt a frisson of excitement that was tinged with apprehension. He'd be going to see Maggie on her new home ground. Would she make him welcome? Or would her temporary teaching post in Florida be fulfilling enough for her without him? Those were questions he'd just have to leave unanswered until he saw her again.

Chapter Seven

Flynn hesitated before pushing the heavy doors open. The CCTV cameras would be recording his entry, but, hey, they'd record the entry of everybody who came in here, whether it was to go to the booking office or buy stuff down in the wee shop. You could even go for a pee if you felt like it, his mischief-making inner voice told him. Even as the idea coaxed a grin onto his face, Flynn's other voice told him not to be so stupid. They could turf him out as soon as look at him.

The interior of Glasgow Royal Concert Hall looked quite different during the daytime. Flynn passed by the booking desk. He was aware of the woman behind the desk regarding him with interest so he took his time at the nearby stand, leafing through the stacks of flyers for forthcoming events. There were none yet for Celtic Connections, which was one of the few programmes that might have taken his fancy. All the Christmas stuff was there, though, he noticed. There were loads of carol concerts during December, many of them featuring the City of Glasgow Orchestra. They'd been playing the night old George had copped it, he thought to himself. Wouldn't be a very merry Christmas for that lot, he reflected.

He sensed rather than saw the eyes of the woman behind the desk boring into his back so he grabbed a few of the Mozart by Candlelight flyers and stuffed them into his inside pocket. She'd try to make eye contact with him, Flynn knew, so he deliberately turned away and sauntered round the corner towards the coffee bar where he'd been questioned by the Busy.

It was nearly eleven o'clock and the coffee bar already had several folk sitting at tables sipping their cappuccinos. Flynn looked at the legend above the bar and rattled the coins in his pocket.

"Pot o' tea for one, please," he told the boy behind the counter. "And can ye let me have a pot o' hot water as well?"

The boy nodded and turned towards the urn. He'd not given Flynn the once over like that wifie at the booking office. What was it she'd seen? He'd often been told that he looked like the big dreepy one in "Only Fools and Horses". It was true that he had the same long face and woebegone expression. That had been cultivated to catch the sympathy of the punters, of course, but it seemed these days to be Flynn's permanent expression.

"Make a face an' when the wind blows it'll stick like that" his foster Mammy used to tell him. Well the winds of change had blown through his life all right. Maybe his face had stuck like that now, as if there was a deep well of anguish that rose unbidden to be reflected in his eyes. Another glance at the waiter told him it was okay. He was just another punter coming in out of the cold for a cuppa.

Flynn paid for his tea and took it over to the window where the rows of seats were padded and comfortable looking. He'd stay in here for as long as he could without risking curiosity. He looked around at the other people sitting in the coffee area. Some were talking in muted voices as if they didn't want to disturb any rehearsal that might be going on in the auditorium. One guy was engrossed in the morning papers, his empty cup still on the table in front of him. That was a ploy Flynn had used before, especially in bookshops where they let you in to read stuff while you had your café latte or whatever.

He'd raked in a bin to find the papers the morning after the murder. It was all about the Russian guy, really, as if being foreign made him prime suspect. The papers were so uncool about foreigners, thought Flynn. You'd think half of them had never heard of the Race Relations Act the way they'd rumbled on about Poliakowski. It was the same with the footie. Our fans were the greatest. Tartan Army rules ok. The English were scumbags of the worst order, if you believed the sports pages. Flynn had seen running battles in this city between Scots fans of different loyalties, wee boys going mad because there was nothing else for them to get excited about. Then someone would bring out a blade and change the course of someone else's life, or stop it forever.

George Millar, now, he was nothing like the big Russian from his photo in the Gazette. The Busy hadn't mentioned any names that night. He'd wanted to know who Flynn had seen coming and going out of the main doors into Buchanan Street. Flynn could've told him other things, though; things that the papers might pay him for. That was partly why he'd come in here again, to think about it.

Flynn drank the sweet tea slowly, looking around him until his gaze fell on the pile of newspapers by the bar. He hadn't clocked them when he'd ordered his pot of tea but now that he saw them Flynn realised they were there as a courtesy for the customers. Maybe there'd be an update on the murder? Maybe someone else would've spilled the beans on old George before he'd had the brass neck to do it himself? He sauntered across to the bar trying to appear nonchalant, no simple task for Flynn, used as he was to the hostile stare of passers-by. Unease lay about his shoulders like a cloak. Nobody said a word, however, as he lifted that day's Gazette from the counter and took it back to his place by the window. Even as he shifted his glance from left to right there were no accusing eyes staring in his direction.

There was nothing about the murder on the front page and Flynn riffled the pages as he scanned the columns up and down. Yes! There it was, a headline on page four and a wee photo of George with his missus. It was a better one than they'd used before although it was a lot older. George had more hair in this one. Flynn concentrated on the article. It was both a disappointment and a relief. They'd raked up loads of stuff about George's musical life, like where he'd travelled with the City of Glasgow and the other orchestras he'd played with. There were even bits about recordings he'd made with his wife in some chamber orchestra or other ages ago. But there was no mention of George and his boyfriends. Flynn found himself grinning and in that moment he knew he'd not be going along to see DS Wilson. Oh, no, he had better fish to fry.

The hot water jug remained full as Flynn left his seat and headed for the exit. He wasn't cold at all now and a brisk walk up to the Gazette's offices would keep him warm, for sure.

"Jimmy Greer," Flynn said to the woman behind the desk.

"Wait a minute will you, till I see if he's at his desk," the voice that answered his enquiry was as broad Glasgow as his own but as she spoke into the headset her manner was quite different. Flynn had heard it every day of his life on the streets, a voice for the likes of him and a voice for those and such as those.

"Have you an appointment?" she asked him. Flynn was ready for this. He'd prepared his patter on the way over from the concert hall.

"It's to do with George Millar. Tell him his son's here." Flynn waited as she relayed the message. He'd thought about calling himself George's nephew but that wasn't close enough. Even if Jimmy Greer did a quick check, he'd not really be able to tell if Flynn was the real thing or not, would he?

"You've to go on up. Take the lift to the second floor and Jimmy'll meet you there," the receptionist told Flynn.

As the lift doors closed on him, Flynn felt his pulse begin to race. It was a bit of a thrill, this masquerading as old George's son. He'd have to come clean eventually, but what was the worst they could do to him? Throw him out? They'd be too busy to involve the police, Flynn told himself.

All at once the doors opened and Flynn found himself facing a tall man with white hair and a moustache.

"Jimmy Greer?" Flynn stepped forward, cautiously.

"Aye. And who are you, son?" The journalist was looking at him intently and Flynn felt himself wilt under the man's stare.

"Can we talk? I've information about George Millar. Stuff your people don't seem to have a hold of." Flynn's words rushed out as he sensed his imminent departure.

The journalist's eyes narrowed. "Wait here till I get my jacket." Flynn watched Greer disappear beyond a phalanx of grey partitions that separated the news desks. Eventually the man reappeared, fastening his padded jacket as he strode towards Flynn.

"We'll have a wee coffee while we chat, eh?" Greer suggested. Flynn nodded, suddenly feeling unsure of himself as the man pressed the lift button and gave the boy a smile that didn't reach his eyes.

They walked in silence to the coffee bar in the pedestrian precinct, Flynn half a step behind Greer who loped along as if he was deliberately trying to put a distance between the boy and himself.

"Two espressos, doll," Greer demanded, slapping down a pile

of coins on the glass topped counter. The girl didn't even look up as she relayed the order to another server.

The reporter took the two cups over to a table by the window and Flynn quickly slipped into the seat facing into the coffee bar. It wouldn't do to be recognised, especially as they were so close to the concert hall.

"Right, pal, what's all this about?" asked Greer, emptying three long packets of brown sugar into his espresso. "Better not be a waste of my time," he added. The phrase "or else" hung unspoken between them. Flynn gave a weak smile.

"Well, I'm not really George Millar's son," he began.

"Never thought it for a moment," Greer came back, his voice laden with sarcasm.

"But I can tell you about his personal life better'n any son could," Flynn assured him.

"Aye, go on then," Greer answered. He was trying to play it cool but Flynn could see a spark of interest in the man's eyes.

"He wasn't just your regular straight bloke, like? Old George was one of the boys, know what I mean?" Flynn tried to make his remark sound as salacious as he dared just to see which way the reporter would jump.

"And how would a wee scruff like you know that, eh?" Greer was leaning forward, his face so close that Flynn could smell the nicotine on his breath. He made himself sit still though he couldn't help bunching his fists unseen below the table.

"How d'you think?" he leered.

"You're not telling me that a member of the City of Glasgow Orchestra got his kit off with the likes of you?" Greer scoffed. "Now that I just don't buy, pal."

"Naw, naw, no me. Ah'm no' that way inclined anyway," Flynn hastened to assure him. "Ma pitch is up at the concert hall. Ah've done him a few wee favours, like. Put him in touch with some good gear, know what I mean?" Flynn lowered his voice as he spoke.

Jimmy Greer nodded, never taking his eyes off the boy for a minute.

"There's a story in this for you an' all," Flynn hesitated. It wouldn't do to give it all away too soon. It was worth a hell of a lot more than a lousy cup of espresso.

"Aye. Maybe there is and maybe there isnae," Greer spoke softly, an expression of greed flitting across his face.

"Well, what's in it for me? Information's no' cheap, man," Flynn came back at him swiftly, sensing the other man's interest.

"Fifty if it's any good," Greer said immediately.

Flynn hesitated. "Naw, I'm no sure. Ah think it's worth a lot more'n that."

Greer drained his coffee. "Waste of my time then, son," he said and made to stand up.

"No," Flynn protested, his hand raised suddenly as if to prevent the journalist from leaving. "All right then, fifty," he said desperately, cursing Greer inwardly for having the whip hand.

Greer called out to the girl by the coffee machine, "Two more espressos, doll. Oh, and a jammy doughnut," he grinned at Flynn as he turned back. "For you," he added. "Just call it a wee sweetener." He paused. "So. Do you know anything about how George Millar was killed?" Jimmy Greer whispered.

Flynn looked the man straight in the eye. "No I don't. But I know some of the stuff he was involved in."

"Okay, pal. Let's have it."

Flynn took a deep breath and began his story.

Chapter Eight

"Keep out of his way if you know what's good for you," Sadie advised the young policewoman.

WPC Irvine made a face. Lorimer's moods had grown worse since his wife had left him to work in America. The rumour factory was working overtime and it was said that the DCI wasn't sleeping too well. At least he hadn't hit the sauce like some of her colleagues whose marriages had ended in acrimony. The station gossip was ambivalent about Maggie Lorimer, though. Wee Sadie insisted Maggie would be back home "to see to her man" as she put it but other voices cast doubt on that scenario. As for Lorimer himself, well, you could hardly just go up and ask him, could you? Now this case had made more headline news, the kind of news that would make Lorimer blow a gasket. Sadie was right. It would be sensible of the young policewoman to keep her head below the parapet this morning.

As luck would have it, Lorimer had not seen the Gazette that morning. It was only when Superintendent Mitchison came storming into his room that he had any inkling of the matter.

"...and not only is your victim a cocaine user, he's been fingered here," Mitchison slapped the page with his hand, "as a receiver of stolen goods. Musical instruments, to be precise."

Lorimer looked at the man across the desk. He'd noted how George Millar had suddenly become his victim as if the DCI had been personally responsible for the man's demise. The Super was still glaring at him as Lorimer gathered his wits together.

"He's also a homosexual, or did that piece of information not come out in the Press?"

"That's not an offence. Drugs and reset are!" Mitchison's face grew paler with an anger that seemed to be hugely out of proportion to any imagined oversight on Lorimer's part.

"Perhaps if you let me read it?" he suggested, holding out his hand.

"Be quick about it, then, because I want you to nail that hack, Greer, before he has time to write another word!" Mitchison threw the paper onto the files and documents that were already cluttering up Lorimer's desk and stomped out of his office. Lorimer looked towards the door after the Superintendent had gone. It was ajar so he got up and closed it quietly but firmly and returned to his desk.

The paper's headlines stared up at him. "Murder Victim's Shady Dealings" it read. Lorimer scanned the columns, his brain taking in the salient points of the article. George Millar, claimed the journalist, had been a cocaine user known to the drug dealers in Glasgow. Which ones? Lorimer asked himself, his mind running over a list of snouts that might be able to verify this. The article continued with the breathtaking accusation that the late leader of The City of Glasgow Orchestra had been a source of "hot" musical instruments that he had sold to other musicians.

Not only that, the article went on to hint that the violinist funded his cocaine habit from his nefarious profits.

Lorimer sat still. For some reason it was not the bollocking that Mitchison had given him that was uppermost in his mind but the face of Mrs Millar when she read this over her morning corn-flakes. He felt suddenly sorry that she must endure this kind of shame. Then he stopped himself. Had she known about it, after all? Was that why she had been so unemotional about her husband's death? Despite the obvious piety, was she involved in any way?

Lorimer looked back at the paper. Jimmy Greer, whoever he was, was in for a short, sharp shock when it came to withholding information from the police. Lorimer reached for his phone. The sooner he got this particular business over and done with, the sooner he could concentrate on finding George Millar's killer. But before he dialled the number for the Gazette, he recalled Mitchison's white face and his unnatural anger. What had that been all about?

Edith Millar pressed her back against the wall, its cold surface making her shiver. Were they never going to go away? It had been bad enough when the phone calls had started but now, crowding up onto the steps of the flat, trying to peer in at the front window, that was just too much to bear. She thought of the young policewoman who had come to break the news about George.

She'd been solicitous but awkward in the way that some young folk were. The kids from the Mission treated her like that too, as if her advancing years made her somehow slow on the uptake.

She was only sixty-two, for heaven's sake, and coped a dash sight better than most of those kids ever would. Yet the thought of the policewoman made Edith realise that right now she wasn't coping well at all. She wanted somebody to be there, to make the reporters go away. Maybe she should call that man, Chief Inspector Lorimer. There was something about him that had given Edith several unquiet moments but he also had the sort of strength that she could use just now.

If only George was here. He'd have sent them packing. He'd never suffered fools gladly and had always dealt with tiresome people in his own peculiar way. Edith felt the first hot tears prick behind her eyes as she realised George would never be there again. It was only now that she let herself indulge in remembering the few good times they had had all these years ago. George Millar had been quite a catch in those days. Edith had hovered on the fringes of his bohemian set but hadn't known enough to understand George's true sexuality or his need to merely assume the conventions of life. It had been enough for Edith to have been wooed and won. She remembered thinking that marriage would have brought all sorts of rewards, like children. Only there never had been any children for Edith and George Millar. And she'd allowed herself to drift along, remaining in a sterile relationship that had come to be based on sheer habit, her youthful hopes long ago withered in the bud. The Mission had been her refuge since then. There she had found some shelter from the storm and it had provided all the family she'd wanted.

Edith's chin rose as she thought of her late husband. George had made her life a misery when he'd been alive and now he was making things worse, so much worse.

Her mouth firmed into an angry line and the tears were gone as suddenly as they had arisen. She heard the letterbox being rattled again and another voice call out her name. She'd pulled the phone out from the wall but she supposed she'd have to connect it again to call the Police.

Taking a deep breath, Edith Millar marched into the sitting room and drew the heavy curtains across the window, leaving the reporters to gawp at the William Morris pattern instead of peering in to catch a glimpse of the widow of a man who'd been exposed as a criminal.

The telephone was on the floor, its cord splayed across the polished wooden surface. She picked it up and plugged it into the socket. As she dialled the number, Edith Millar looked at her hands. There was no sign of a tremor. She smiled a brief, wintry smile, pleased to be in control of herself once more.

Jimmy Greer was smiling as he picked up the glass of Laphraoig. The sweet taste of success always went down better accompanied by a smooth Malt, he decided. The glass was half way to his mouth when he felt the tug on his jacket sleeve.

"What the…" As he swirled round, the whisky arced in an amber rainbow catching the sunlight. It came to land several inches below his mouth, the smile vanishing in an instant. A tall man was looming over him, his blue eyes staring down into Jimmy's.

"Look what you've done! That was a good whisky, pal!" the journalist's voice came out in a whine as the man's stare began to unnerve him. He'd expected one of them to confront him sooner or later but hadn't thought that it would be DCI Lorimer turning up at his howff. Jimmy knew who the guy was, of course, though they'd never met until now.

"Don't expect me to buy you another one," Lorimer said quietly in a voice that told Greer his sweet moment was suddenly turning sour. There was silence for a long minute as Lorimer towered over the journalist. Greer took out a handkerchief and rubbed ineffectually at the wet whisky stain on his shirt, a ploy to avoid those disturbing eyes more than a need to wipe up a wee bit of spilt Laphraoig. The reporter felt the vinyl seat creak beside him as Lorimer sat at an angle of the banquette. He only turned when the sound of a rolled up Gazette hit the table in front of them.

"Okay. So I got there ahead of youse," Greer shrugged. "Cannae help it if my enthusiasm ran away with me now, can I?"

"There's such a thing as the Police Press office. You know that, so don't try it on, eh?" Lorimer replied in a voice that told Greer he was long since fed up with time wasters. "We can throw the book at you for this one. If we want," Lorimer added. Jimmy Greer looked at him out of the corner of his eye. Was the guy serious? He knew there'd be rapped knuckles but hadn't thought too far ahead. That was what editors were for, after all, wasn't it?

But now, with Lorimer sitting there and no whisky to console him, Jimmy Greer wasn't so sure of himself.

The journalist gave a sigh. "What d'you want?"

"All of it. How you got your story, your sources, names, addresses. And don't miss out a single detail," Lorimer told him.

Greer glanced over his shoulder towards the bar. "Mind if I order another?"

Lorimer gave a shrug. Greer might as well have his tongue loosened. The Detective Chief Inspector certainly wasn't buying and he didn't feel much like drinking either.

"So," Lorimer began, still keeping Jimmy Greer pinned with the stare that had discomfited not a few hard men.

"Who was it?"

Greer pretended not to hear as he signalled the barman for another whisky but one look from Lorimer made him respond.

"A wee nyaff. A bum. Comes to me with his story, right. I do a bit of checking up, that's all. Seems the toe rag's got some real handle on the violinist, so I goes to my editor and, bingo! Front page with my byline. Not bad, eh?" Greer pulled out a packet of Benson & Hedges and lit up a cigarette without offering one to Lorimer. As Greer blew the smoke over their heads, Lorimer saw the man's eyes narrow speculatively. He's wondering just how much of this bravado I'll let him away with, he thought. Part of him wanted to haul the journalist to his feet and shove him into the nearest squad car. Let him stew for a bit in Police Custody. But that could wait. Right now, what Lorimer wanted were facts and a bit of co-operation.

"Name?"

"Said he was George Millar's son. Loada' rubbish of course. Millar never had any weans. Told me his name was Flynn. Hangs about in front of the Royal Concert Hall. That's his regular pitch."

"Is he a *Big Issue* Seller, then?"

"Naw. Just a wee bum. No fixed address."

"So what exactly did he tell you and, more to the point, how did he get his information?"

Greer took another drag on his cigarette, his fingertips stained ochre with nicotine. "Well, that's the thing. His sources, as he put it, weren't up for grabs.He obviously hangs about with some druggies in the town. That much was clear. But I didnae get any names and addresses. Didnae expect to," Greer glanced back at Lorimer but the expression on the policeman's face hadn't changed.

"And?"

"He knew our fiddle-man. Like personally. Must've come across him at the Concert Hall. Anyway, the wee nyaff does his stuff for Millar. Puts him in touch with the coke machine. Ends up being the man's gofer."

Lorimer frowned. There was more to this street bum than met the eye. "How did he know about the reset? I don't believe for a minute that George Millar would have confided in this low life you're describing."

"Naw, you're right there, Chief Inspector. Seems he kinda stumbled across it. I didnae ask for too much detail."

Lorimer left that one. He'd need to find the boy himself and prise these details out of him if he could.

"So, how did you go about verifying this Flynn's story?"

Greer paused in mid-drag, giving Lorimer the impression that he was considering his reply.

"Well, now. That might be incriminating to some other people, know what I mean?"

"Names," Lorimer snapped back at him.

"All right. There were a few of the musicians who'd bought Millar's hot goods. One of them was his boyfriend, that big Danish Guy, Carl. Had a word with him on the Q.T. He was daft enough to admit that George had sold him a suss viola. He was fulla' shit about not being able to afford a top class instrument and how good it was of old George to help him out. Even said George had let him pay by instalments. Anyway, it's all there," Greer flicked his hand towards the Gazette on the table.

"And the others?"

Greer gave a half smile as he spoke. "Aye, there were others, but I only went to see one. A lady. Dead posh, she was. Name of Karen Quentin-Jones." Lorimer's eyebrows lifted in surprise. Greer stared back at him and nodded, adding, "Thought that myself, squire. Why did a rich bitch like that get mixed up in a reset scam?"

"And did you ask her?"

"Ho! Ask her? My God, she gave me the bum's rush and no mistake. Wanted to know who'd sent me. Fair rattled that one's cage and no mistake."

Lorimer watched the journalist as he took a swig of the whisky. There was no apparent tremble to his hand.

"Saw the instrument, though. It was right there in its open case. Couldn't help but notice it as I passed the French windows, could I?" Lorimer suppressed a smile. The journalist was still skating on thin ice as far as the law was concerned, but Lorimer had to admire his persistence in following up a juicy story.

"How much did you pay this Flynn character?"

Greer's hesitation in replying told Lorimer that whatever he said would be a lie.

"Ach, the wee bum touched me for a ton. Said he'd sell the story elsewhere if I didn't cough up. Well, my editor agreed, y'know. Ye have to speculate to accumulate, know what I mean?" Greer's yellowing teeth showed in a smirk below his moustache. Lorimer drew in a deep breath, controlling an urge to wipe the grin off the journalist's face. He supposed the story had been told in confidence and that this Flynn was totally unaware that Greer would be spilling the beans on him. But like rats coming out of a sinking ship, Greer had to scuttle away from any promises made to save his own skin.

"You'll need to go down to make a written statement," Lorimer told the journalist. "Better make it now." Lorimer's tone told the journalist he was telling, not asking. Greer's shoulders twitched in a shrug then he swallowed down the remaining whisky, set it down beside the folded paper and followed Lorimer out of the pub.

"Flynn? Joseph Alexander Flynn?" DS Alistair Wilson's voice was incredulous.

"He didn't give me first names. Why?"

"From your description it must be the same fellow I picked up outside the Concert Hall the night of the murder."

Lorimer gave a snort. "Would you believe it? So where's this Flynn's statement, then?"

Wilson smiled as he indicated a file well to the bottom of the heap of paperwork on Lorimer's desk.

"Interviewed him and gave him a cup of tea. Poor blighter looked frozen. Scared, too, though that's the norm when we come into contact with those boys. They're suspicious of us being suspicious of them. Can't seem to break the vicious circle, more's the pity."

Lorimer knew what Wilson meant. There was little trust between the street people and the Police but sometimes a relationship could be built up and one of them would trade information for a few quid to keep body and soul together.

"Any address or is that a daft question?"

Wilson's raised eyebrows told Lorimer that it was. "Could try to find him around the town, though. He hangs about between the Concert Hall and St Enoch's, usually. I'll go out, if you like, since I've got his ID."

Lorimer nodded, still reading what little information the boy had given his Detective Sergeant. It was coming up to midday and the streets crowded with lunchtime workers might well tempt the beggars into the city centre.

"Okay, do that, but don't ask around for him just yet, I don't want him doing a disappearing act. Just see if he's in the city."

Once Wilson had left, Lorimer stood looking out of his window. Greer's revelations had given him some disquiet. Not only had George Millar been mixed up in various shady dealings, he'd involved Karen Quentin-Jones. He recalled the woman's superior attitude and her obvious dislike of the late leader of the

Orchestra. Why on earth had the woman bought her violin from him? She'd struck Lorimer as a very knowing type. Surely she'd been aware of the Leader's scam?

Well, there was one way to find out.

Chapter Nine

The girl with the long dark hair put down two brimming lattes and sat beside her companion, a young man who was hunched into his leather jacket. He seemed not to notice the coffee for she had to slide it closer to him and nudge his knee to make him sit up. The lights from the mosaic floor in the centre of Princes Square reflected on the glasses, making miniature stars on their sides. She pushed one glass of coffee closer to him.

"C'mon, Chris. You have to have something. It's no good moping like this. That's not going to achieve anything, is it?"

"No, I suppose you're right." The young man smiled. "Still trying to be the amateur psychologist, are you?"

The girl gave a self-deprecating laugh. "Maybe. Sorry. I didn't mean to be so bossy."

"Getting just like your mum, you are," he told her, taking a sip of the latte.

"God, don't say that! I've not been that bad, have I?"

"It's okay. I probably need a bit of geeing up. It's not that easy to cope with, y'know. Who'd have thought that George…"

His voice broke suddenly and he felt for a handkerchief in his pocket but the girl was too quick for him and passed him a tissue from her handbag.

"You'll all miss him, won't you? Especially your own section," the girl whispered. The strings had all looked up to George Millar, she knew. She had even heard her own mother, who was Second Violin, admit what a great Leader he had been. Chris had simply doted on the man.

Around them the buzz of lunchtime shoppers merged with the sound of a piano playing. Strains of Rhapsody in Blue floated over the cafés clustered around the atrium. Nobody paid any attention to the young man blowing his nose or of the anxious glances he was receiving from the girl by his side.

"What'll you do now?" she asked.

"Don't know," he sniffed. "Maybe move back in with Si?"

"Is that wise?"

"Probably not, but we'll have a lot of fun cheering one another up."

The man's sudden grin transformed his face at once making the girl sigh.

"Oh, Chris. Why are all the loveliest boys unavailable?" she whispered, but there was a hint of mischief in her eyes as she spoke.

"I'm always available for you, pal. You know that," he replied, his hand covering hers.

"Aye, for coffee and sympathy," she groaned. "Just as well I don't fancy you, isn't it?"

"Bit of a waste of time that would be," he laughed in reply.

A shadow blocking out the light from the circular floor made Chris Hunter look up but it was just someone pausing to look around. Possibly looking for a seat? Chris twisted round and watched the figure disappearing in the direction of the escalator. Funny, he thought to himself. Just for a moment he thought he'd recognised the man. Don't be daft, he told himself. It's just shadows playing tricks with your imagination. Anyway, wasn't he bound to be jumpy after what had happened?

"That's right," Brendan told her. "He changed his address recently and it was scored off my original list. No problem, Constable. Anything else I can help with, just ring me."

Annie Irvine slotted the name neatly into its correct alphabetical place. Hunter Chris, c/o 135 Ingram Street. Not a permanent residence, she saw. Fairly new to the Orchestra, Brendan Phillips had told her. Funny he'd had two addresses already then, wasn't it? Maybe digs were hard to come by for musicians, she supposed. They weren't all that well off, were they? Still, he'd been interviewed at the concert hall. There wouldn't be much cause to call on him at home, would there? Annie flicked the mouse button and the list of names vanished into its file somewhere in the ether.

Alistair Wilson stepped out into the middle of the pedestrian precinct, looking this way and that. Anybody glancing his way would have seen a well dressed middle-aged man out doing his shopping, the Habitat carrier bag part of his camouflage. A strong sweet scent told him he was nearing the corner where the perfume from soaps and bath ballistics wafted out of Lush. Betty loved stuff like that. And it was her birthday soon. He stopped to look at the beribboned boxes stacked by the door. He could always get them to make her up a big box of stuff, couldn't he? Wilson told himself. But his shopping would have to wait. It certainly wouldn't be today when he was trying to find one particular boy in all these crowds of shoppers and lunchtime diners.

Outside TGI Fridays there was often a wee lassie selling the Issue. She had a special knack of appearing to be on her last legs and Wilson always gave her the obligatory quid. She wasn't there today and still there was no sign of Flynn.

The area outside the Concert Hall had proved fruitless. The *Big Issue* sellers were there all right, but there had been no sign of any beggars who might look like Flynn. He hadn't been daft enough to go back to his usual haunt around there. It was probably a waste of time but he'd make his way down to St Enoch's underground station before calling it a day. Wilson thought ahead to how he might join the queue at the cash point in order to scan the area around St Enoch's Square. The policeman strode past Fraser's shop windows. There was a distinct chill in the air that lent itself to the winter display in the windows of the department store. He paused for a moment to scan the dresses and sparkly accessories strewn artfully behind the glass then set off towards the Underground.

Wilson stopped as he reached the corner. To his right, just protruding from a shop doorway he could see the familiar bundle that told of yet another down and out. Abandoning the crossing, he moved towards the huddled figure.

As he approached the beggar, his eyes widened. It was Flynn. He was sitting with his back against the steps to an upstairs restaurant, polystyrene cup in one hand and a ragged blanket tucked over his legs. Wilson ducked behind a woman weighed down with bags of shopping in both hands. But it was too late. The boy had clocked him.

In one swift movement, Flynn leapt up from the pavement discarding the blanket as he ran, loose change scattering all over the pavement. Wilson broke into a run, dodging between the shoppers, barely pausing to apologise as they were elbowed out of his way.

As the boy headed off along Argyle Street, Wilson was aware of passers-by turning to see what it was all about. It was only a short burst to the next junction and the lights were at red. The boy put on a spurt, turning into Mitchell Street, his boots thudding on the cobbles. Wilson's face broke into a grin. Just around the corner, concealed by the bend in the road, a Police car was waiting. They'd corner him then, for sure. Wilson saw his breath fog out in the frosty air as he thundered after Flynn. The backs of warehouses and the department store leaned over them.

Pedestrians stood back to let them pass as Wilson gave chase, their faces registering alarm.

He felt his feet slipping on the icy stones but he could afford to slow down now that he was certain Flynn would be caught in their trap.

Just as the squad car came into view, Flynn turned round and stared wildly at the Detective Sergeant. The boy hesitated for a moment then looked towards his left. Wilson could read his mind. Flynn was thinking of making a dash into the NCP car park. But how could it offer a hope of escape? They'd get him in there just as easily. Surely he realised that?

Flynn suddenly swerved away towards the car park then, to Wilson's horror, a white van emerged from the shadows of the off-ramp.

Wilson made to dash after him but a squeal of brakes rooted him to the spot.

As Flynn's body made contact with the bonnet, the policeman heard a collective gasp of anguish from the folk standing opposite. It was like seeing a bundle of rags tossed skywards then coming to earth with a sickening thud.

"Oh, my God! The poor laddie!" a woman's voice exclaimed. Wilson put out his hand to stop anybody crowding around the broken figure lying in the road.

"Police. Keep back, please." The words had their intended effect though there was a marked reluctance amongst those who had witnessed the accident to move away. The two uniformed officers further up Mitchell Street had left their car and were heading towards him as Alistair Wilson bent over Flynn's body.

"Ah couldnae help it. He jist came like a bat oot o' Hell!" The driver had slid from his seat and was standing over Wilson, white-faced and shaking. He was a young guy with cropped hair and a silver cross dangling from one ear.

"Aw naw. Whit's he done?" The van driver clutched Wilson's arm. "This is terrible. Ah've only just got this delivery job, no' right used tae the van yet, but it wisnae ma fault."

"No, it wasn't. I saw what happened. The lad didn't see you coming. He just dashed right in front of your van," Wilson assured him.

"Ah wisnae goin' fast or nothin'," the driver's voice cracked.

Wilson nodded. He'd not been going fast, but even so, the van had travelled those few agonising yards towards the running fig-ure. Then there'd been that awful thump as human flesh and bone met 3000 kilos of metal. From experience Wilson knew that would be the memory to stick in the driver's mind.

It wouldn't be the sight of the body on the road but that noise as he'd braked, pulling on the steering wheel as if to rein in a run-away horse.

The man let go of Wilson's sleeve and leaned against the van door for support.

"No, son. Not your fault," Wilson answered him shortly, one half of his mind wondering if in fact the fault lay at his own door.

Flynn's body lay twisted, his arms flung out like a sawdust-filled doll. There didn't seem to be any motion visible from his chest so Wilson lifted one wrist to feel for a pulse. There it was. A flicker, but at least he was still alive.

"Get an ambulance!" he barked as the first officer joined him beside the body.

"He's not...?"

"No. But I don't rate his chances much," muttered Wilson. "Keep this place clear, will you?" he added, indicating the folk hovering in the edge of this tragedy.

Lorimer touched the breast pocket of his jacket. The feel of the tickets tucked away gave him a tingle of pleasure just to know they were there. It had cost him a whack, though. He'd have saved plenty, the wee girl at the travel agency had informed him, if he's booked up sooner. Everyone wanted to go to Florida for Christmas these days, it seemed. Anyway, it was done now and Maggie's mum would be pleased. And what about Maggie herself? Lorimer made a mental note to phone her later on when the time difference linked his bedtime with his wife's evening meal. Would she be glad he'd booked the trip?

Lorimer's thoughts were interrupted by a knock at the door. WPC Irvine hovered in the doorway, one hand on the handle as if she were too afraid to come right on into the lion's den.

"You know that woman you wanted in for questioning, sir? Mrs Quentin-Jones?"

Lorimer looked up. Annie's expression was a dead giveaway that something was wrong.

"Yes?" he drawled out the word slowly, leaning his elbows on the desk and folding his hands beneath his chin.

"Well, she's gone. I mean she's not at her own place and Mr Quentin-Jones doesn't know where she is."

"Why don't you just sit down and give me the whole story, eh?"

The young policewoman closed the door behind her and came to perch on the edge of the chair that faced Lorimer across his desk.

"She was at some late rehearsal in the Concert Hall last night and she didn't come back home, he says. Her husband, Mr Quentin-Jones, is a consultant up at the Southern General and was late getting back from an operation. He didn't realise his wife hadn't come home until this morning. Says he was so tired he just went out like a light. Woke up and she wasn't in the bed beside him. He was going to phone the Police when he got a call from us asking for his wife. Poor man was in some state when we spoke to him. Thought we were going to tell him she'd been in an accident or something." The policewoman's earnest expression made Lorimer wonder. Did Quentin-Jones have any inkling of what his wife had been up to? In fact, did anybody really know?

It was only Greer's dirt-raking that had brought her name into the equation. And Lorimer still wasn't sure if the journalist had got all his facts correct.

"Where is he now?"

"Downstairs, sir. He insisted on coming over. Asked for you personally, sir." WPC Irvine sounded apologetic, as if the consultant had no right to have called on someone of Lorimer's rank.

Lorimer sat and thought for a moment. If Quentin-Jones was as overbearing as his lady wife had been, he wasn't sure that he wanted to deal with him. Maybe she was in the throes of some extra-marital fling. It wasn't his job to find out things like that.

On the other hand, if Karen Quentin-Jones had read an early edition of the Gazette, could she have done a bunk? Lorimer considered this. Maybe she'd risen before her husband had awoken, seen the front page and high-tailed it?

"Okay, tell him I'll be down to see him shortly. Take him into the canteen and let Sadie look after him," Lorimer suggested.

"Aye, right, sir," The WPC was grinning as she left. Sadie Dunlop never stood on ceremony with folks, be they consultants, Chief Inspectors or whoever. Mr Quentin-Jones would just have to sit and take his tea and toast like the rest of them.

Derek Quentin-Jones was pacing up and down in the corridor when Lorimer arrived. He was a man of middle build whose grey hair added to his distinguished appearance. He'd taken the trouble to don a double-breasted pin-striped suit, Lorimer noticed. Was he trying to create a good impression or was that just the normal workaday clothing of a consultant?

"Chief Inspector Lorimer. Mr Quentin-Jones?" Lorimer offered the man his outstretched hand. Quentin-Jones took it at once, gave it a firm shake, looking the policeman straight in the eye. The Second Violin's husband was clearly a worried man if the creases between his eyebrows were anything to go by.

"What's all this about? You called my home to ask me about my wife."

Lorimer indicated the stairs to their right, "We can talk up in my office, sir." The two men were silent on the short flight up to the CID rooms.

"In here," Lorimer ushered the man into his own room, pulling a chair from its position against the wall so that they were facing one another.

"I take it you had some tea or coffee downstairs?"

Quentin-Jones shook his head. "Sorry. It was kind of them but I couldn't take a thing right now."

Lorimer nodded briefly. If Sadie Dunlop had failed to force her canteen hospitality down this bloke's throat, then he was certainly not faking his anxiety.

"I suppose this has something to do with George Millar's death."

"Yes," Lorimer replied. "Have you seen today's Gazette?"

"No. It's not a paper I read. Why? What's going on?"

Lorimer fished a copy out of the waste paper bin and handed it over. The front page carried a photograph of George Millar and Quentin-Jones stared at it for a few moments before opening the page out to read the article alongside.

"I see," he said at length. "That's why he was murdered. Drug-related. But what's that got to do with my wife, Chief Inspector?"

"How long has Mrs Quentin-Jones owned her violin, sir?"

The Consultant's face turned pale as the implication of Lorimer's words sunk in.

"Karen's violin? You mean it was stolen?"

"We do have reason to think so, yes."

"My God," the Consultant leaned forward, burying his head in his hands and groaning. "I had no idea. I'd never have..." the man broke off suddenly.

"Never have what, Mr Quentin-Jones?" Lorimer rapped out.

"Never have bought it for her," the words came out as a whisper.

"You're telling me that you purchased the violin from George Millar?"

Derek Quentin-Jones nodded silently. He looked simply bewildered, Lorimer thought. Was he telling the truth, or was this just a desperate attempt to cover up whatever scandal might attach itself to his wife?

"Karen's fortieth birthday was coming up."

"When was this, sir?"

"Oh, two, no nearly three years ago, I think. George told me he could get hold of something a bit special. He said he'd been contacted by a friend overseas who was retiring and wanted to make the sale."

"And you believed him?"

"Of course. There was no reason not to," Quentin-Jones protested.

"What did you pay him for it?"

Quentin-Jones hesitated but it was the hesitation of a man to whom questions about money are naturally distasteful.

"Sixty-five."

"Sixty-five pounds?" Lorimer frowned.

"Sixty-five thousand, Chief Inspector," Quentin-Jones's smile was almost apologetic. "It was a Vincenzo Panormo. The 1780 edition," he added as if that would explain the matter to the Chief Inspector. Lorimer merely nodded as if he were accustomed to discussing violins that cost more than he earned in a year.

"How did your wife react when you gave it to her?" Lorimer asked. Unbidden, a bitter little thought came into his mind; just how much love could a £65,000 violin buy?

"Well. I don't remember, really. I'm sure she was pleased with it," the Consultant said slowly as if trying his best to recall the moment.

"Do you think your wife may have known where it really came from?"

The Consultant shook his head. "I don't know. That's the honest truth, Chief Inspector. I can't imagine Karen being mixed up in anything underhand. Whether she'd know about the violin's provenance, well, that's another matter," he said. "But I will tell you one thing."

"Yes?"

"She didn't like George Millar. She wouldn't have bought an instrument from him of her own volition. That I do know. So I didn't tell her where I'd bought it."

"And didn't she think that was somewhat strange? Wouldn't

she want to know how you'd managed to procure such a valuable instrument?"

Derek Quentin-Jones sighed. "I suppose in the light of George's death it all seems a bit shady, but at the time all I wanted was for Karen to have a lovely surprise. I thought it best not to mention the connection with George."

"So you lied to her?"

"Yes. I told her I had a patient with an interest in violins. She didn't question me much, now I come to think about it."

Lorimer grimaced. No, Karen Quentin-Jones might not have asked too many questions but Lorimer wondered if the woman would have recognised that particular instrument.

"What I'm most anxious about right now isn't a stolen violin, Chief Inspector, but the whereabouts of my wife!"

"Don't you think the two may be linked?" he asked.

Quentin-Jones frowned back at him, "How's that?"

"Your wife was approached recently by the journalist who wrote that article. I imagine she may not have been too eager to speak to the police about the violin. Incidentally, do you know if she took the instrument when she left?"

"It wasn't in the music room. I looked for any signs that she'd come back from the rehearsal last night. There were none. And I haven't seen her since breakfast yesterday morning. God, that seems so long ago!"

Lorimer leaned back, eyeing the consultant. The man was sitting on the edge of his chair, hands bunched tightly together, the very picture of anxiety. And it was real anxiety, Lorimer guessed, but whether for his missing wife or for his own involvement with George Millar, it was hard to tell.

"I think it might be wise to take a statement from you at this stage, sir," Lorimer told him.

Quentin-Jones's eyebrows shot up in alarm. "Is that really necessary? I mean, I've done nothing wrong, so…"

"It's perfectly routine, sir. Your statement will help us to piece together other information already received."

"Ah," the man relaxed just a fraction, adding, "you mean I'd be helping the police with their enquiries,"

"Just so, sir."

"But Karen…?"

"My officers will do everything in their power to find Mrs Quentin-Jones, sir. Given the nature of our current investigation we cannot yet treat her as a missing person. She may have wished to be elsewhere at present."

Quentin-Jones looked steadily at Lorimer, meeting his blue eyes. What he saw there made him glance down with a small sigh of resignation. "Yes. I think I understand what you're saying, Chief Inspector. And of course I'll do anything in my power to help."

Lorimer lifted the phone and dialled Jo Grant's extension. His DI was just the woman to make the consultant feel calm enough to give a proper statement.

After Quentin-Jones had left in Jo's wake, Lorimer dialled another number.

"Glasgow Royal Concert Hall," the switchboard operator announced.

"DCI Lorimer. Put me through to Brendan Phillips, please."

There was a knock on his door just as Lorimer heard Brendan Phillips's voice answering. The DCI was aware of Annie Irvine hovering in the doorway, her face crumpled into its customary worried look. Lorimer waved his hand in irritation, signalling the policewoman to go away, but much to his annoyance she remained, hand on the door as if in a dither of indecision.

"I'm looking for Karen Quentin-Jones. She was at your rehearsal last night, wasn't she?" Lorimer swung his chair away from the policewoman's gaze.

"Of course. What seems to be the problem?"

"I don't know if there is one yet. Her husband thinks she's disappeared."

There was silence on the other end as the Concert Manager digested this piece of information.

"Sorry. She was here last night, all right. Had to be, seeing she's taken over as Leader. It's in her contract. Do you want me to ask around, Chief Inspector? See if anybody saw her after the rehearsal?"

"Could you? I can rely on your discretion, of course," Lorimer replied.

"Of course," Phillips answered, both men knowing full well that Lorimer was telling, not asking.

Lorimer swung back in his chair. Annie Irvine was still waiting by the door, her impatience barely concealed.

"Okay. What's up?"

The policewoman moved swiftly towards Lorimer's desk and, putting her hands on the edge, sat down in front of him without being asked. Taking a closer look at her, Lorimer realised that she was seriously agitated.

"It's Sergeant Wilson. He's at the Southern General."

"What?" Lorimer was half way out of his seat when the policewoman waved her hands at him.

"No. It's not him. There was an accident. That lad he was after. The one he spoke to at the Royal Concert Hall. He was knocked down. He's in a bad way, seemingly. Can you go down, sir? Sergeant Wilson wanted me to ask you right away."

But Lorimer was already on his feet, pulling his jacket from the coat stand.

"Thanks, Annie." He noticed her white face and suddenly felt guilty. "Don't know how you put up with me sometimes," he added, patting her shoulder as he strode past her.

"Me neither," Annie whispered under her breath, closing Lorimer's door behind her.

Chapter Ten

Being dead was the biggest buzz that Flynn had ever experienced. There was an absence of pain, an absence of any kind of feeling in his body but a real burst of fireworks inside his brain. He'd not expected it to be so white or that the white could be full of such brightness as if someone had switched on a 1000 watt light bulb in his head. The sensation was of floating weightless in a sea of shining clouds. Flynn knew instinctively that this would go on forever. Eternity was here and now, moving slightly forward towards another light even more dazzling than the one he was leaving behind. It smashed against the optic nerves like molten metal and he felt the old sensation of screwing up his eyes against the brightness of the sun.

When he opened them the first thing he saw was another pair of eyes gazing down into his own. They were pale blue like a sky washed clean after a rainstorm and they held a question in them. Flynn was helpless in the blueness, his clouds of light melting under him as he answered the question. Yes, he was alive after all. Yes, he was here, wherever here might be. Flynn let the blueness wash over him like a blanket, surrendering to its strength, then a small sigh escaped him and he drifted into a dreamless sleep.

"There was nothing I could do," Alistair Wilson shook his head in despair as the two men walked slowly down the hospital corridor. "He just took off like a rocket and before I knew it that van was screeching to a halt. It all happened so quickly."

Lorimer gave a sigh and patted Wilson's shoulder. "I know that and the folk that witnessed the accident know that but we still have to convince Mitchison."

"I suppose he's got steam coming out of his ears, then?" Wilson asked.

Lorimer didn't answer for a moment, chewing the ragged end of a fingernail. "He's got a bee in his bonnet about this case. I can't quite figure it out."

"Money, probably. The resources on this one are phenomenal."

Lorimer shook his head. "There's more to it than that. He seems to be on a permanently short fuse. It's as if…" He stopped as a trio of chattering nurses passed them by.

Wilson looked up, noting the thoughtful expression that flitted across his DCI's face. "As if?" he prompted.

"As if he knows something about George Millar. Or Poliakowski. Or Jimmy Greer," Lorimer raised his hands and slapped them against his thighs. "God! I don't know. Maybe it's lack of sleep. Imagination playing tricks on me. But I persistently get the feeling that the Super knows more than he's letting on."

Wilson raised his eyebrows. "Mitchison? No. I don't buy that for a minute. He's too goody-goody. Mr Do-It-By-The-Book. No. You just need a decent night's kip."

The two men turned out of the corridor towards the exit. Grey clouds that had built up all day were now leaden in the night sky. Lorimer zipped up his jacket against the blast of cold air that hit them as they stepped out of the warmth of the Southern General Hospital. It was the kind of wind that his mum had always described as "blowing off snow". Looking at the weight of clouds above them, Lorimer thought she'd have been right. It was still only late October but it wouldn't surprise him to wake up to a white world tomorrow.

The Lexus was parked beneath a street lamp. It had been hours since he'd left it there. Hours that had been passed sitting by the bedside of Joseph Alexander Flynn of no fixed abode, willing him to come back. The boy's head had been swathed in bandages, his eyes two blackened masses. Lorimer had sat next to the figure beneath the sheets watching his stillness. The longer he remained the more compulsive it became to remain, waiting and watching. It was only when Flynn opened his eyes, screwing them up as if in pain that Lorimer knew he had reached him.

For a moment he wondered if that was what fatherhood felt like, that rush of protection for someone more vulnerable than oneself. Then the moment was gone and Lorimer knew it was time for them to make a move.

As he swung out into Govan road, Lorimer thought about Mitchison. Would he really throw the book at Alistair Wilson or would his Detective Sergeant convince him that there had been no dereliction of duty on his part? He remembered George

Phillips, his old Super. Curmudgeonly, loud and sometimes iras-
cible, the Superintendent had nevertheless dealt fairly with each
and every one of his officers.

There would never have been this absurd feeling hanging over
them, a feeling of uncertainty, as if every move made or initiative
taken were somehow going to be judged.

For a time Lorimer had contemplated a move away from main-
stream detective work. There had been a job going at Tulliallan
for a training officer, but he'd never really got around to applying
for it. He'd sent for details, right enough, but that was as far as he'd
taken the matter. For now he was stuck with a boss he couldn't
respect and a job he couldn't abandon.

Chapter Eleven

Solomon Brightman looked out over the skyline of Glasgow as the taxi made its ponderous way through the slushy streets. It was a view he had come to love. He knew this from the first time his heart had lifted on returning from London all these years ago. The train pulling into Central station had crossed the River Clyde and Solomon had seen the cranes, the hotels and the familiar spire of Glasgow University. That was the time Glasgow had truly become home to the man with the black beard and shining eyes whose exotic appearance did not excite remarks more provocative than, "Y'all right, pal?" or "Aye, son, another lousy day, i'n't it?"

Today was a lousy day, right enough, but it had begun with a gasp of pleasure as Solly had thrown open the velvet curtains on to a landscape purified by the overnight snowfall. His windows looked out over the west of the city above Kelvingrove Park and the graceful curving terraces that marched up from Woodlands Road. The morning had brought two new elements to sour his outlook, however; a light drizzle had turned much of the snow into a soupy brown mess and Superintendent Mitchison's ingratiating tones over the telephone had ruffled his senses with an irrational feeling of disquiet.

Now the psychologist was heading into town to the Division where he was to meet Mitchison. Lorimer hadn't been in touch for weeks but Solly knew about the murder at the concert hall. It would be hard not to know from the way the media was stepping up its interest, but Solly had information that came from quite a different source. Rosie Fergusson had kept him up to date about the violinist's death from the start. She'd even suggested that he should be involved in the case, but Solly knew better than to offer his services as criminal profiler until he was asked. Officially. Superintendent Mitchison was one of those vexatious persons the Desiderata on Lorimer's desk urged one to avoid. It was an irony not lost on Solly that the Detective Chief Inspector had opted to ignore the lofty advice that stared him in the face each day.

The cab swung away from the main road, spraying a fan of decomposing slush from its wheels. Solly leaned forward as the vehicle came to a halt, ready to pay the driver. As he stepped out his feet slipped on the uneven surface and he had to grasp the door handle to save himself from falling.

"A'right, pal?" the taxi driver grinned from the safe interior of the cab. "Mind how you go, now, eh?"

Solomon managed a weak smile in reply and steadied himself. As he drove away from the kerb, the driver shook his head and glanced at the bearded man's reflection in the rear view mirror.

Elsewhere in the city the early snowfall was still making its presence felt. The melted snow had created a steady trickle of water running off the Glasgow rooftops now that the winter sun had penetrated the early morning clouds.

It caused extra work for caretakers who were trying to clear the drifts from doorways and stop the drains choking with débris swept down with the sudden heaps of melting snow dislodged from the roofs above.

That morning the staff at Glasgow Royal Concert Hall had to contend with another sort of misfortune than the scandal surrounding the late George Millar. The security guard noticed it first as he tried to flush the toilet downstairs. When nothing happened he listened for the familiar sound of gurgling in the pipes. What he did hear was a low rumbling noise coming from the ceiling. Neville put his hand up as if to ward off the noise then, realising the cause of the rumble, wrenched open the toilet door just in time before the gloss painted ceiling bulged like a naked, overfed stomach. He heard the crash behind him even as he bounded up the steps that led to the ground floor then a gush as water cascaded out of the burst pipes.

Like a tree whose trunk and branches are all that is visible to the passer-by, Glasgow Royal Concert Hall has hidden roots that penetrate deeply into the subterranean spaces. The water that fell from the pipes found its lowest level, as water will inevitably do, obeying the laws of physics. Puddles formed down in the dungeon, covering dark shapes then submerging them completely so that by the time the maintenance crew waded in there was a veritable lake of slimy water. Several bits of detritus bobbed on its surface, illuminated by the flashlights the two men carried.

"We cannae do this ourselves," one of the men remarked in tones of protest. "It's a job fur the Fire Brigade."

"Aye. Looks like it," the other remarked. "Whew! They're welcome to it, 'n' all. That smell'd gie' ye the boak."

"Must've been something rotten in the drains, eh?"

"Well, ah'm no' waitin' tae find oot. 'Ur ye comin'?"

As the two men sloshed their way back from the edge of the water their torches made arcs of light against the dripping walls.

Suddenly one of the men gave out a cry, "Jesus, Hughie! Whit the hell's that?"

His companion stopped and turned, following the torch beam directed towards a corner of the cave-like storeroom they called the dungeon. For a moment his eyes stared, uncomprehending, then the shape fixed beneath the torchlight took on familiar proportions. Despite the darkness he could make out a paler shape that could only be a face. He took a deep breath as his innards churned and his breakfast threatened to escape. Then Hughie McCallum swallowed hard and whispered, "'Sno' the Fire Brigade we're wantin', Rab. It's the polis."

Solly clipped the visitor's identity badge onto his lapel and turned away from the reception desk. Mitchison's office was on the third floor with a view that looked out towards the Kingston Bridge where traffic constantly flowed north and south over the River Clyde. He would wait here until someone came to escort him into the Superintendent's presence.

For once the psychologist was on time for his meeting at Police headquarters. The snowfall may have caused some chaos early on during rush hour but his journey here had been without incident.

"Doctor Brightman?" A young WPC stood at the entrance to a corridor, holding back the door for him to follow her.

"Terrible day. You got here alright, though?" she commented.

"As you see," Solly nodded, unwinding the knitted scarf from his neck. "It's fine now. A trifle slippery underfoot, but that's all," he smiled at the girl, considering the small talk that always centred upon the subject of weather. It might be an idea to throw that into a tutorial with the first years. Could be interesting to make them think about the ways strangers interacted with one another. He could use comparisons from other cultures too, he mused, as they entered the lift. Or he might use the idea of conversations in another way altogether. How did a murderer first approach his victim? By commenting on the weather?

The answer to his hypothetical question remained unanswered as the lift doors opened.

"Superintendent Mitchison asked me to ask you if you'd like some tea or coffee, sir," the WPC told him.

"Ah," Solomon replied, his mind shifting from the tutorial room to the matter of hot drinks. His tongue watered at the memory of strongly brewed tea. Police catering didn't include camomile or peppermint, he was sure.

"A glass of water, perhaps?" he beamed at the girl who raised her eyebrows in surprise. He could almost hear her thoughts as she knocked on the door marked Superintendent M. Mitchison. Cold water? On a day like this?

"Come," a voice commanded.

Solomon stepped inside the beige office. He hadn't been here since that spring morning when Mitchison had requested his help with a case involving what had looked like stranger killings.

It had been Lorimer's case, really, but he'd put in his tuppence worth to good effect. Now he'd been summoned here again and he was curious to know what the Superintendent's request would be this time.

"Do take a seat, Doctor Brightman," Mitchison stood up to greet him, the handshake just the wrong side of perfunctory. "I suppose you know what this is all about. Can't escape it with all the media brouhaha."

"The murder in the Concert Hall?"

"Murders," Mitchison answered shortly, "There's been another one." He glared at the psychologist as if he were somehow to blame. "A body was discovered at the Concert Hall this morning. Lorimer's there now," he added. He continued to look at Solomon, expecting a response, but the man across the desk merely nodded, the ghost of a smile hovering around his lips.

Mitchison leaned forward in his seat, wagging a finger toward Solomon. "It's been a shambles of a case up until now. The press have been out of line and so far there's little in the way of forensic evidence to give us any leads." As the Superintendent spoke, Solomon wondered if there was a veiled criticism of Dr Rosie Fergusson contained in his words, a criticism that Mitchison intended to be communicated through him.

For a moment Solomon felt a heat suffuse his cheeks. His relationship with the pathologist was nobody's business but his own. As he stared back at the Superintendent Solly experienced a sudden revelation. Not only was he acknowledging to himself that he and Rosie were in a relationship but he saw just how ready he was to protect and defend her. The insight made him smile. He decided not to respond, waiting instead for Mitchison to spell out the reason for his invitation to headquarters.

For a second time a cordon was flung around one of Glasgow's focal points. But as yet it was an invisible cordon as there was no telltale scene-of-crime tape.

The Bath Street entrance to the Buchanan Galleries was closed off, much to the annoyance of its manager. It was a real inconvenience to all his shoppers, he protested, but neither he nor they had any knowledge yet of a body floating deep below the city pavements. Nor would they know if the Police Press office kept the news strictly to itself for a while, Lorimer told himself. All that was apparent was the presence of a Strathclyde Fire Brigade truck, its hoses snaking into the emergency exit at West Nile Street and down into the roots of the building.

Lorimer stood for a minute regarding the grey lines disappearing into the darkness. The steps down into the dungeon looked dank and unwholesome as if the triangular shadows in each corner held some poisonous muck. He could see flickering light from the firemen's torches down below, somewhere out of sight. The beams they cast made ghosts dance upon the streaming walls. Lorimer's mouth felt dry as he swallowed. This unnatural fear that had haunted him from childhood seemed to grip him by the throat, rendering his whole body useless for the task ahead.

He gritted his teeth, cursing his weakness then forced one foot in front of the other as he began the descent down into the bowels of the Concert Hall. The soles of his shoes squelched against the sodden carpet, its blood-red colour blackened both by the flood and the many pairs of booted feet that had preceded Lorimer down into the lowest levels of the building.

As always the walls seemed to close in on him, and he had to fight the impulse to raise his hand to ward off their phantom approach. He swallowed once more and continued down each slimy step.

Round a bend in the staircase Lorimer saw with some relief that the dungeon was a fairly wide space though the roof, as he'd expected, was oppressively low.

As the stairs ended, Lorimer felt the water gather round his ankles. It took an effort to move forward, sloshing one foot after the other towards the middle of the plant room. As he ducked to avoid the metal cable trays overhead, the pencil torch he was carrying picked out red lettering on a bank of control panels: DANGER 440 VOLTS. Lorimer felt the sweat trickle down between his shoulder blades. There were electric cables above his head and all along the walls of this room.

One flick of a switch by a careless hand could send them all to eternity.

"Keep back, will ye, sir?" one of the firemen called. Lorimer, peering through the intermittent darkness could see that they were draining a lake of black water. As his eyes adjusted to the gloom, he could make out two white-clad figures bending over what looked like flotsam washed up on the far shore of the pool. On either side of them were drive shafts that led up towards a flat ceiling where a dim rectangle of light illumined the activity below. Measuring the space between the pool and the roof above, Lorimer calculated he was standing almost directly below the stage.

He gazed back at the two white figures. Their ghostly appearance held no terrors for DCI Lorimer who grinned as he recognised the diminutive Doctor Fergusson and Dan, her burly counterpart from Pathology. Looking down at his shoes, Lorimer gave a sigh.

"Another pair for the bin," he muttered.

"Aye, you should've brought your wellies right enough, Chief Inspector," one of the firemen grinned up at him. His face in the torchlight gave the man the look of a demented sprite, his eyes shining under the yellow helmet. "If ye wait another wee while we'll have the place sucked out and ye can get across to your body," he continued. Lorimer raised his eyebrows and smiled in spite of the darkness that was pressing down upon him.

The man's matter-of-fact words brought the situation into a new perspective. They were all just doing their jobs. That realisation often made the filthier business of death a lot easier to handle. Lorimer raised his hand in acknowledgement and stepped back against the wall as the hose threatened to sweep him off his feet.

Over on the far side he could see Dan and Rosie prepare a stretcher to carry out the half-submerged corpse. They moved slowly, their hooded suits making them look like astronauts attempting some grotesque ritual. The sound of water being siphoned away filled the space between them and Lorimer concentrated on the surface water. So long as he focused on the middle of the room he'd be okay. It was an old trick that helped keep the worst of his claustrophobia at bay, like watching the horizon to overcome seasickness.

"That you, Lorimer?" Rosie's voice sounded hollow as she called out in the darkness.

"Yes. D'you want me across there yet?"

There was a pause as Rosie murmured something indistinct to her colleague then, "No. We'll be up there shortly." There was another pause then she added, "No need for you to get your feet any wetter." The usual teasing note was absent from her voice making Lorimer stare through the murk. Whatever grimness lay before the two pathologists had wiped out any sense of levity.

With a feeling of relief, Lorimer turned and started back up the tunnel of stairs that would take him to ground level and into the blessed daylight.

Rosie and Dan had moved the body out of the dungeon and

into the room used by the technicians and shifters where natural light flooded in from a window set high above them.

A light knock on the door made Rosie turn her head, a frown on her face, ever ready to repel boarders. Her brow cleared, however, when she saw Lorimer slip quietly into the room. His gaze immediately fell on the sodden corpse lying on a sheet of tarpaulin. Rosie watched as his expression suddenly altered.

"You know her, then?" she asked wryly for it was clear that the Chief Inspector had recognised the woman whose lifeless body lay centre stage before them. Lorimer nodded slowly, never taking his eyes off the bloated face, its shape distorted by the wire twisted around her neck.

"Karen Quentin-Jones," he said at last.

"But that was..." Rosie broke off, remembering the imperious figure who had swept down the Artistes' corridor. The pathologist gave her head a shake as if to clear the mental picture. But it persisted. Even as she recalled the woman to life, Rosie could not help but remember that other violinist's corpse, a corpse she'd been in the process of examining when she'd caught sight of the figure clad in black lace. The body on the floor was fully dressed, coat buttoned up as if she had been about to step into the winter's night. Only some other hands had stopped her. Hands that had held a wire across her throat, cutting off breath and life.

"I'll have to do a full post-mortem, obviously, but you can see for yourself..." Rosie indicated the wire criss-crossing the neck.

Lorimer bent down, pointing to the ends of the wire. One end was curled into a neat little loop; the other held a small round of white plastic. He knew better than to touch anything. "Any idea what it might be?" he asked.

Rosie made a face. He knew she hated to speculate but he always asked her just the same.

"Guitar string?"

Lorimer looked more closely at the wire. Its silver coils were wound round and round the throat like some obcene African necklace. "Too long for a guitar," he muttered to himself.

"What about a harp, then?" Dan offered, his large hands making circles in the air as he mentally unwound the filament, calculating its length.

"Could be. We'll know soon enough," Rosie replied briskly.

Lorimer stood up again, the tone in her voice telling him it was time to leave the pathologists to their duties and begin his own. With his mouth set in a grim line, Lorimer realised that one of the first of these duties would be to inform Derek Quentin-Jones that his wife was no longer a missing person.

Chapter Twelve

When Maggie Lorimer stretched out her hand to halt the alarm's intrusive bleep, she had no idea that another hand was at that moment unwinding a wire ligature from the neck of Karen Quentin-Jones. Maggie's first thoughts on wakening were to remember the day of the week then calculate what time it was back home. She stretched her feet down to the coolest part of the bed then drew the single sheet up towards her chin, creating a tiny draught of air. The fan whirred quietly on the ceiling above, a noise she'd ceased to notice after all these weeks in Florida. Five more minutes, she told herself, five more minutes before the day need begin. She'd shower in the tiny cubicle adjacent to her bedroom then pad barefoot through to the open plan kitchen/living area, switch on the various machines that would deliver her breakfast while she rummaged in the closet for something suitable to wear. Waking up slowly gave her time to breathe before the rush began and, better still, gave her time to reflect.

Her mouth curved in a wide smile as she remembered last night's telephone conversation with her mum. They were both coming out for Christmas! How Bill had fixed that, she couldn't imagine. Mum had always been adamant that nobody would catch her flying on an aeroplane. But somehow Bill had sweet-talked her into it.

Bill. Maggie breathed a long sigh. They'd be here for two whole weeks. He'd promised. There was leave long overdue and he was taking it, he'd assured his wife. Maggie's right hand drifted unconsciously to the place where her husband would lie. Two weeks. They'd be together, on holiday, for all that time. Okay, Mum was going to be there too, but the nights would be theirs alone. Maggie closed her eyes and conjured up her husband's face, the rough places around his jaw when he'd been too long away from a razor, the mole on his left cheek and the way his eyes crinkled when she made him laugh. She swallowed hard. Dwelling on such things would undermine her resolve. Better to think about practicalities.

There was so much they could all do during the holiday.

Maggie forced her thoughts towards all the sights she wanted to share with the two people she loved best in the world. Some of these were right here in Sarasota. Mum would love the Marie Selby Gardens, especially all those orchids and she'd have to take them to the Ringling Museum, its mock Venetian Palazzo looking out over Long Boat Key. There were other sights they might want to visit; places further afield that she'd been saving up to explore. Maybe they could take a mini-break down to the Keys? Her head buzzed with the possibilities. It would be fun to show off the bits of Sarasota that she knew so well, now. Okay, she'd only been here for eight weeks, Maggie calculated, but already she felt proprietorial about the place. Her place. A few more weeks and they'd be arriving. She longed to show her husband the apartment. Maggie screwed up her eyes tightly. No. What she really wanted was to show him that she could do this thing on her own. It mattered that he saw her in charge of her life.

Maggie listened to the noises of traffic outside her window and that cawing bird she'd yet to identify. Bill might know what it was. How he'd love the birds out here, especially the brown pelicans flying idly over the water. Her mind raced ahead, skimming over the prospects of those precious two weeks. A sudden thought intruded like a cloud blotting out the sun. What would she feel once they'd gone home again? she asked herself. Loneliness? Regret? So far work had been a balm to soothe those self-inflicted sores. In January the new semester would begin. She'd have six more months of being busy at the High School before her exchange was up. Then what? a small voice asked. She pushed the thought away as her hand threw off the crumpled sheet.

Maggie's feet hit the wooden floorboards that were already warm with the morning sun penetrating the slatted blinds. Sitting on the edge of the bed, she hauled the cotton nightshirt over her damp curls. Shower first, she told herself, then coffee, then...? Then the day would materialise into its usual pattern dominated by assertive teenagers and voluble colleagues, a weary voice reminded her. Her five minutes of peace were up. It was time to join the frantic tilt at accumulating credits that passed for education in this part of the world. That really wasn't fair, she scolded herself. Maggie heaved a sigh. Okay, so she had to confess: it was no better or worse than the system back home. At least it was warm here, she smiled ruefully, running fingers through her moist tangle of curls.

As Maggie Lorimer switched on the shower, her naked flesh responded gratefully to the tepid spray sloughing away the sweat of another restless night.

Four thousand miles away, Doctor Rosie Fergusson laid the harp wire on a tray beside Karen's body.

"You can see the ligature marks now, can't you?" she asked, glancing up at Chief Inspector Lorimer who was standing close to the viewing window. Despite the toughened glass they could converse easily through the Mortuary's sound system.

Lorimer looked at the marks left by the twisted wire. The depth of the ligature was quite dramatic. Even after Rosie had removed that last twist, the neck bore a deep cleft as if the wire were still biting into the woman's dead flesh. The wound told its own tale, one of passionate determination to put an end to Karen Quentin-Jones. To stop her breath, to stop any sound she'd ever make again, except that last choking as the wire finally did its work.

"What are these scratch marks near the wound?"

"Fingernails. We might find traces of her own skin under her nails. She'd been trying to get the wire off." Rosie looked down at the body below her. "Didn't help though. She'd have lost consciousness in less than a minute."

"Not enough time to have made any cries for help, then?"

Rosie shook her head. "Hardly a peep. Still," she added in a cheerier tone of voice, "it looks worse than it is."

Lorimer glanced at the swollen, reddened face then looked away again.

"She'll look better after the post-mortem once the blood's drained," Rosie assured him.

"So," he began, "when did she die?"

"When was she last seen alive?" Rosie countered.

"Wednesday night. They had an evening rehearsal. Finished at ten."

"Hm. Can't be precise, but it's possible she died not long after that."

Lorimer nodded. Karen Quentin-Jones should have been on her way home shortly after that. CCTV footage showed no sign of anyone leaving the building later than eleven-fourteen.

The last member of the Orchestra to leave had been Carl. The great Dane, she'd called him, Lorimer remembered. The camera had shown him hurrying away from the stage door, coat collar up against the chill wind, his viola case tucked beneath one arm. And could Karen's missing violin have been inside that case? It would have been easy enough to conceal the instrument under a coat or within a music case. Easy for any of them, come to that.

Most of the musicians had left and walked uphill, towards the car park, their faces scanned only for the briefest of moments and some totally obscured beneath hoods and umbrellas. But there was no mistaking the Dane. He'd scanned that section of film over and over, watching the man's retreating back, asking himself if he was looking at a murderer. A few of them were being invited in again for questioning, Carl Bekaert among them. Lorimer tapped a fingernail against his front teeth, oblivious to the surgical procedure that was taking place in front of him. The big Dane. Could he have fixed that duster across the CCTV lens with his bow? He was certainly tall enough. And he was one of George's lovely boys, darling, a voice reminded him. Lorimer started as if Karen's haughty drawl were coming through the glass.

"No. That's it. Cause of death: strangulation involving a ligature," Rosie's words brought him back suddenly. "No signs of any other trauma. No evidence of sexual assault."

"Any idea yet where the killing took place?"

"We're still working on that one. It'll keep the SOCOs busy for a while. It wasn't done in the plant room, that's for sure. The trap door was only opened when we arrived. The maintenance boys' idea to give us more light on our subject. Did more than that, though didn't it?" she caught his eye and grinned.

"The body was directly under the trap door in a position commensurate with having been dropped through from just that height," Rosie said.

Lorimer nodded. Whoever had killed Karen Quentin-Jones must have had some nerve. Someone had shoved her body through that space in the stage. He tried to visualise the darkened auditorium and the stage set out with music stands for a concert that was certain to be cancelled, now. The vision of the abandoned stage made something flicker in his brain as if someone had struck a match, but whatever it was guttered and died as suddenly as it had appeared. He gave a shudder that had nothing to do with the cadaver lying a few feet away. All at once he needed to be somewhere else, finding out answers to more questions than the ones Rosie was asking.

"Okay," Lorimer raised a hand. "I'm off. Send me a copy of the report whenever you've finished, will you?" He fished in his pockets for the car keys, his thoughts already elsewhere.

Rosie smiled briefly then turned her attention to the body on the slab. The Police would have their paperwork, but first she had to complete the examination as thoroughly and tenderly as she could. It was something the living owed to the dead, Rosie always told herself; especially to those whose ending had been particularly violent.

The rain on his windscreen closed Lorimer off from the outside world as he sat next to the City Mortuary. Karen Quentin-Jones' face came back to him as he'd first seen her. A woman with a fine opinion of herself, he remembered.

Not the least sign of apprehension had shown in that cat-like smile. No, she'd had nothing to fear, of that Lorimer was certain. So why had she been the second victim? Had she known something about George's killer? Perhaps. But her violin was missing too, he remembered. People had been killed for less than a sixty-five grand violin, Lorimer knew.

Lorimer switched on the ignition and instantly the rain was swept away showing the different shades of grey on the city street. He turned the Lexus towards Glasgow Cross, reflecting on the history at the heart of the old town. Here wealthy merchants had amassed their fortunes trading with the Virginia tobacco plantations. Here too, was the site of all the public hangings that had taken place, the Gallowgate. Lorimer gave a thin-lipped smile thinking how apt it was that the city's mortuary and the High Court were situated in this part of Glasgow. Justice was still being meted out in some form, at any rate.His smile creased into a frown as thoughts of the dead woman returned. Had that been somebody's warped idea of justice?

Lorimer hardly noticed the swinging bells and dancing angels being erected on each side of George Square. His mind was taking him on a walk through the depths of the Royal Concert Hall to the stage elevator pit. Every set of lights along Saint Vincent Street changed to red as the big car approached but for once Lorimer didn't curse them. Who had access to that trap door? And what would have happened to Karen's body if the dungeon hadn't been flooded? Lorimer shuddered at the memory of that dark, enclosed space beneath the stage and the twin steel pillars that rose and fell to raise sections of staging.

Had the killer thought that her body would be crushed under the weight of the hydraulics? Or would the mechanism have failed because of the corpse lying in the sunken area below the stage?

It seemed no time at all until he was across town and into the City of Glasgow Orchestra's private car park.

Brendan Phillips was sitting at a desk leafing through a pile of paperwork when Lorimer walked into the room.

"Oh! Oh! It's you!" The Orchestra Manager was half out of his seat, his face turned towards the Chief Inspector.

Lorimer's eyes narrowed. In that split second when he'd been disturbed, Brendan Phillips had visibly jumped from fear. While one part of his brain told Lorimer that it was entirely natural given all the poor man had been through, another part was asking questions.

"You all right?"

"Yes, of course," Phillips began, then, sinking back into his seat. "Well, no. No. I'm not all right. How could I be?" A querulous note entered his voice. Lorimer shrugged. Of course the man wasn't all right. He was a bundle of nerves.

"I came to ask you some more questions," Lorimer told him

gently, taking a seat beside Brendan Phillips' desk.

"There's nothing else I can tell you," Brendan began, his eyes pleading with Lorimer to leave him alone. "I really don't know what's been going on any more than you do."

"Okay. I'm sure that's how it seems. But the normal day-to-day things that might not mean a lot to you could have huge significance when we put them into a different context. You follow?"

Brendan Phillips closed his eyes and drew his fingers back and forth across his brow as if something pained him. Lorimer waited. He recalled Karen Quentin-Jones's derision when she had referred to the Orchestra Manager as "Brenda". The man was certainly living up to her sneer. Lorimer had seen more backbone in a young child. Still, he was in a world where artistic temperaments abounded and sensitive souls were probably the norm.

"Take me through the last rehearsal. Just tell me everything that took place."

Brendan sighed. "It was just a routine rehearsal for the Christmas Classics concert, nothing that was too taxing. There was nothing really very new. It's for the older audience. You know? 'White Christmas', 'Sleigh Ride', 'Lara's theme' from Doctor Zhivago; that sort of stuff."

"And you were using a harpist?"

"Of course," Phillips' eyebrows were raised in surprise. "Christmas. Angel harps. Trumpets. It's all very traditional music."

"And you were using Chloe Redpath again, weren't you?"

"Yes, as a matter of fact. Our usual girl was sick. Having a bad time with her pregnancy, actually."

"So Chloe's been your main harpist all the time since October twenty-second?"

"Not all the time. Just occasionally."

"When we questioned her that night," Lorimer began slowly, "she was adamant that she had never removed any of her music. Yet when she went on stage for the concert it had gone." Somebody had created a series of jobs for Brendan Phillips that night, Lorimer guessed. Unless, of course they had been deliberately manufactured by the Orchestra Manager himself?

"Really?" the Orchestra Manager's eyebrows lifted. "She didn't pass that information on to me," he added querulously.

"Well, events did rather overtake everyone that night," Lorimer answered dryly.

"But, to get back to that other night. The night of Karen's death," he began, ignoring Brendan Phillips's sudden flinch, "nothing out of the ordinary happened at the rehearsal?"

"No. The musicians turned up. They rehearsed. They went home."

Lorimer chewed his lip. That was what it was meant to look like, certainly, but not everybody had gone home. Someone had stayed behind with the First Violin to make sure she would never go home again.

"Who was on duty from the administrative side of the Orchestra that night?"

"I was. They don't need anybody else on a rehearsal night. The sound technicians and the lighting people are all employees of the hall. There's a security man downstairs and some staff in front of house earlier on in the gift shop and at the box office. By the time we're ready to leave it's pretty quiet."

Lorimer was thoughtful. This was information he'd already had from the Concert Hall's security boys. Surely Phillips realised that.

Or was he deliberately trying to take away from the fact that he had been solely responsible for the Orchestra's management that night? Was he experiencing guilt for what had happened?

"So. You were on your own. Did you watch the rehearsal from the wings or were you out front?"

Brendan frowned. "A bit of both. I have to take the register so I'm always in the Hall until everyone's arrived. But I wasn't on my own. Maurice Drummond was there too. It was a Chorus night, you see. Once they'd started the programme and I knew they all had music and everything, I stayed out front with Maurice and listened for a while. It helps to get an idea of the balance of sound," he added.

"Then?"

"Then I'm back in Ness. That's the room I always use here. Everybody knows where to find me. There are people popping in and out all the time."

"I've got a list of everyone who took part in the rehearsal," Lorimer said. "It looks like everyone who was there also took part in the concert that was on the night George Millar died."

"And why should that be significant?"

"Well, think about it. They've hardly got over that night. Surely some of them are still in shock. It wouldn't have come as a surprise to find that certain people had pulled out and had to be replaced at short notice."

"Chief Inspector. Don't forget these are professional musicians we're talking about. They are well able to cope under strain. But, remember this: performing isn't simply a matter of choice for most of them. It's their bread and butter."

The Orchestra Manager had become more assertive, thought Lorimer as he sought to defend his Orchestra. The mother-hen act came naturally to him, he realised wryly. Brendan Phillips was probably just the right sort of bloke to have around an organisation like this.

"You mentioned once before a library box, I think you called it, where spare strings and reeds are kept. I take it you had this at the rehearsal?"

"Oh, yes. It's with the Orchestra every time they play."

"And would you have noticed if there had been anything missing?" Lorimer looked keenly at him. Neither man needed to mention the harp string that had been wound around the neck of Karen Quentin-Jones.

"Yes. But not right away. I make a note of all the items used about once a month. Partly to replace them if we're short, but also to keep tabs on the costs as we reorder," he added.

"And where is this record kept?" Lorimer asked.

Brendan Phillips coloured up at once. Lorimer could see his Adam's apple bobbing up and down in his throat as he swallowed. He broke eye contact with the detective and rustled in among the papers on his desk but it didn't take too much attention on Lorimer's part to see that the paper in question had been on top of the pile.

"So," Lorimer gave him a lopsided smile. "You were there ahead of me, were you?"

Brendan Phillips raised his eyes to the heavens. "What do you expect? I'm not stupid. Of course I wanted to check if there was a missing string."

"And?"

"Yes. There was. There should have been a number 34."

"Can you describe it to me?"

"Yes. It's a fifth octave string, wire, not plastic, and it, it…wasn't there." He looked up tentatively and Lorimer knew what he wanted to ask so he nodded.

"Perhaps you wouldn't mind having a look at the one we have in Pathology?"

The man's shudder was possibly exaggerated but his sense of horror was quite real. There was a pause before he whispered, "I suppose I have to, haven't I?"

Chapter Thirteen

Solomon Brightman had been asked in as an observer to this second interview with Carl Bekaert. Lorimer had scanned Jo's notes accompanying his first statement made shortly after George Millar's death. Reading between the lines, DI Grant had seemed to feel sorry for the Danish viola player. He'd blustered about his friend George, but had stopped short of admitting any closer relationship with the victim. Jo hadn't pressed the point. Why?

"Sit somewhere out of the way," Lorimer had asked him, hoping that the psychologist might be discreet. It was pretty hard to hide such a man, however; his black beard and curling locks drew the eye even in the darkest corner of the room.

Nevertheless he was out of the Dane's line of vision and Lorimer hoped to keep it that way throughout the interview.

Carl Bekaert had stooped as he'd entered the poorly lit room. His eyes flicked back and forth as the Chief Inspector motioned him to sit in the chair on the other side of the desk. Even as the musician folded his long limbs under the table that lay between them Lorimer saw that he kept his eyes fixed to the floor.

From his corner position Solly watched the man's body language give up its secrets.

Carl held his hands together, pressing fingers against knuckles until the tips showed blood red. His head was bowed in a position of utter defeat as if he were waiting for something he felt was inevitable: an accusation, perhaps? Or was he simply afraid to admit his homosexuality? His pale, blond hair was cut close to his ears like a schoolboy's, Solly noticed. In fact the man's whole demeanour was like that of a recalcitrant boy facing his headmaster.

"Carl Bekaert?" Lorimer's tones were entirely neutral but the man's head jerked up as if his name had been screamed out.

"Yes. I am he." He lifted his head and looked at his interrogator for the first time. Lorimer's initial impression was of a human being devoid of any colour; all the life seem to have leached out of his skin and hair making him look like a faded sepia print. Even his eyes had that pale yellow tinge. It was as if the Dane had emerged from years of dwelling in some subterranean chamber. Was he always so anaemic looking or was this the effect of grief? Lorimer continued to study the musician. Carl's hands clutched the sides of the chair making him sit bolt upright. A muscle on his right cheek twitched involuntarily. Lorimer shifted in his chair.

"We asked you in again today, partly to discuss your relationship with George Millar." Noticing Carl pursing his lips in defiance, Lorimer held up a hand. "Don't try to deny it, please. It will only make things worse for you in the long run."

A tide of colour rose over the Dane's clenched jaw, instantly making him appear more human.

"It was known," he faltered, rubbing his finger against his nostrils. "Our relationship. The other members of the Orchestra, they know about George and I."

"Yes," Lorimer agreed, "It was Karen Quentin-Jones who told me about it."

Carl nodded, "So. She tells tales and then she is put away. That is what you want to talk to me about, yes?" The musician leaned to one side, searching in his trouser pocket for his handkerchief. He took it out wiping his nose briefly.

That was interesting, Solly thought to himself. He'd instinctively used a euphemism for death. She is put away. What was he afraid of: death in general or the act of killing? Or had he tried to blot out the horrors surrounding the two murders? Solomon Brightman could understand that reaction. He'd been close enough to cases of murder to know the emotions such events could produce. And was the musician so choked with emotion that he needed to wipe his nose? That hadn't been apparent from his voice. Maybe he just had a cold coming on. Solly's eyes shifted to the Chief Inspector. Lorimer's expression betrayed nothing at all, neither kindliness or harshness. His was the face of the trained professional, open and receptive, welcoming any statement that might help the case. Any change in that expression would work on the person who had to endure his unflinching gaze.

"She told me that you and Simon were both lovers of George

Millar. Is that true?"

Carl sat back in the chair, hands below the level of the desk, avoiding Lorimer's stare. There was a momentary silence as if the Dane was struggling to decide what his answer should be. Then he looked up at Lorimer, a sudden light in his eyes. "Yes. Yes it is true. We love that man. Okay? What's so bad about that, Chief Inspector? Love. It's not a dirty word, no?"

Lorimer raised his eyebrows. "Your relationship with George Millar only concerns me insofar as it concerns his death." He clasped his hands together on the desk. "Tell me, Mr Bekaert, were you still on good terms with George Millar at the time of his death?"

"Good terms! What you mean good terms? We were friends. No, more than friends. I admit it now. Okay? We were lovers!" The Dane's voice rose in a crescendo.

"At the time of his death?" Lorimer persisted.

"I was not there at the time of his death. I tell this to the other officer. She writes it down. Okay?" Carl was leaning forward now, glaring at Lorimer.

"What I mean is, you were still lovers right up until Mr Millar's death?"

Carl sank back once more into the plastic seat, the rage taken out of him by Lorimer's measured tones.

"Of course."

"And Simon Corrigan?"

"That one was never serious. They just fooled about. George laughed at him. That was all."

Lorimer didn't respond. Simon Corrigan's statement backed this up, but only to a point. Had George Millar been quite so dismissive of the horn player?

"I'd like you to describe what happened after the rehearsal for your Christmas concert."

"What happened? Nothing happened. We put our instruments back into their cases, took our coats off their pegs in the dressing room and went home."

"Which dressing room would that be, sir?"

"Number One. We have decent tables in there so we can eat

our food in a more civilised manner."

Listening to the Dane, Solomon realised that his English was becoming better and better the more he grew in confidence. Had the stilted responses been an act, then? Had he been cultivating an imaginary language barrier? That was a ploy that could gain sympathy in confrontational situations. Interesting, the psychologist nodded to himself. And was Lorimer aware of it too? He wondered.

"You left the concert hall at fourteen minutes past eleven. That was over an hour after the rehearsal had finished. Do you mind telling us what you were doing in that time, Mr Bekaert?"

Carl Bekaert's eyes avoided those of Chief Inspector Lorimer. He mumbled something to himself.

"Yes, Mr Bekaert?"

"I was in the men's lavatory."

"For a whole hour? Mind telling us just what you were doing?"

Solomon looked up. Lorimer's voice had an edge to it that the psychologist recognised. He looked from one man to the other. Lorimer's demeanour was as impassive as ever but Solly knew that it was like a snake waiting to strike.

"I had some stuff with me. It took a while, that's all."

"Stuff?" Lorimer was playing the innocent, Solly knew, grinning in his corner as the conversation batted back and forth between them.

"Cocaine," as the word was wrested from the Dane, he clasped his hands behind his neck and gave a sigh concentrating his gaze towards the floor.

"I see. And is there anyone who can verify this?"

Carl Bekaert looked up, clearly shocked. He'd come clean about his relationship with George Millar and had admitted being a cocaine user. What more did this policeman want?

"You think I have others there watching me?"

"Perhaps someone saw you going into the gents? Maybe someone who could testify that you were there for, how long did you say?"

"I don't know," the Dane replied, his face now troubled. "I think other people came and went. I heard voices but I was, well, preoccupied."

"Was it generally known that you were a user?"

The musician shrugged his shoulders. "Who knows? It's not something I discussed with the other players."

"How long were you actually in there?"

Again the Dane gave a shrug, "I don't know. It's hard to tell when...well, when you're...," he sighed as if trying to find the right words, "when you're experiencing something uplifting," he said, meeting Lorimer's eyes to see if the policeman was maybe on his wavelength. But there was no empathy from the blue stare that met his gaze.

"We have something of a difficulty here, Mr Bekaert. You see, unless you can give us proof that you were exactly where you say you were, then we may have to look at the possibility that you were with Karen Quentin-Jones."

From his corner, Solly listened in admiration. Despite the gravity of the situation Lorimer managed to sound as if he were discussing the man's overdraft rather than an alibi for murder.

Carl Bekaert simply stared, slack-jawed, as if the notion of being a murder suspect had never dawned upon him. He looked at Lorimer in disbelief then turned to see who else in the room had heard the detective's words. The duty officer at the door made no movement and the bearded man in he corner merely smiled sadly as if he would like to help but couldn't.

Then, "No. No. You must not think these things. I did not see Karen after the rehearsal was finished. As far as I know she went to the ladies' dressing room and..."

"Did you actually see her go into the ladies' dressing room, then?" Lorimer interrupted.

"No. No. I did not see her at all. What I mean is...she must have gone there. Where else would she go?" Carl Bekaert shook his clasped hands frantically.

"I have to tell you, Mr Bekaert, that you appear to have been the last member of the Orchestra to leave the building that night." Lorimer spoke gently as if breaking the worst possible news to the musician. "We have close circuit camera evidence to back this up."

Carl looked around him, his eyes wide with fear. "You think I put an end to her?" he whispered.

Solly raised his eyebrows. That euphemistic phrase again. Was the man displaying one half of a split personality, one that denied the brutal act of murder, one that feared the violence of its alter ego or simply the consequences of its action? Or was this the behaviour of a man innocent of the ultimate crime? Watching him, Solly pondered these options, wondering how far Lorimer was prepared to take this.

"Did you kill Karen Quentin-Jones?"

"No," the Dane shook his head vehemently. "No. Never. I would never do such a thing!"

"Even although she might have told the police something you wanted to hide?"

"No," the man's protest came out high and strangled. "I tell you everything. About George. About my viola. Now you know I take the cocaine!"

He was less in control of himself now, Solly realised. Lorimer was in complete command of the situation.

"So you won't object to a police surgeon examining you?"

"Why? Why examine me? What do you want to do?"

Lorimer spread his hands in an open gesture. "Simply to take some samples. Then we may be able to eliminate you from our enquiries."

Solomon frowned. Lorimer sounded so plausible, but as far as he knew Rosie had no real DNA samples to work on. What was Lorimer up to?

The policeman's words seemed to have an effect on the musician however, for he slumped back in his chair with a sigh.

"Sure. Go ahead. Then can I go home?"

Lorimer smiled briefly. "Let's hope so."

"Why didn't you charge him?"

"With what? Doing a line in the Gents' toilets? We have no evidence even of that! There's absolutely nothing we can do until we have something concrete. Being the last man out doesn't even help. The security man was still there. The murderer had fixed the CCTV cameras once. Who's to say he couldn't have done it again?"

"You think whoever killed George Millar also killed the woman?"

Yes," Lorimer sounded surprised at the psychologist's question then frowned. "Why? Don't you?"

Solly was silent for a moment, chewing his lower lip. "There are reasons for supposing it might be. The locus is the same. The murder weapon on each occasion was part of a musical instrument. There were many people about so it looks as if he is a risk taker. Not too many of those, I shouldn't imagine."

Lorimer grinned. Solly had his engine up and running. Any minute now, though, he'd throw a spanner into the works.

"But?" Lorimer prompted.

Solly looked up at him. "You see it too?"

"Nope. I could feel it coming though."

"Ah. The But. Yes there is a But, I'm afraid. Someone tried to hide the woman's body. There was no effort to do the same for George Millar."

"And no opportunity, either. Come on, Solly. Don't you think the first murder was carefully planned? Think of the duster over the CCTV camera. It would have been easy for a tall man like him to place it there with the bow. And wouldn't he have known that the Leader would be on his own in Morar?"

"Ah, that's just it. I do believe the first murder was planned out. It's the second one I'm having difficulty with."

"You think he just happened to have a harp string in his pocket? Give us a break."

"No. But he might have lifted it from that library box on impulse."

Lorimer frowned. "What are you getting at?"

"I think," Solly began measuring his words carefully, "that the second killing was a matter of opportunity. Not planned, not thought out at all. She was in the right place at the right time. And hiding the body was a stroke of sheer luck. The trap door on stage provided that."

"It also suggests someone who knew their way about the place, doesn't it? And even you can't seriously suggest that this is the work of a different killer."

"No," Solly admitted, "but it's something I think we ought to consider."

Lorimer shook his head. He didn't want to consider anything of the sort. As far as he was concerned there was one person to profile and one person alone. Okay the modus operandi was different but in his view that wasn't as crucial as the fact that two musicians had met their ends in the same place, Glasgow Royal Concert Hall. And if Carl Bekaert's DNA matched any trace on Karen's body, he'd have him charged with murder.

Chapter Fourteen

Brendan Phillips watched as the conductor took the Orchestra through their paces. Poliakowski was rehearsing the programme as if nothing had happened. Were they all such cold-blooded types? Brendan wondered. He'd always felt a stirring in his soul from listening to Russian musicians. And, watching the conductor, Brendan realised that Poliakowski exuded such passion. Funny how some people changed the minute they walked off a platform. Like Karen, a voice came unbidden into his mind. Brendan shuddered. Concentrate upon the music, he told himself, watching the conductor once more.

The rehearsal was well under way and the musicians caught in the Russian's spell. Poliakowski did not hold a baton but guided the players only with his hands.

Brendan stared at him, fascinated as the conductor's fingers rose and fell rhythmically like a puppeteer commanding the movements of his dolls from invisible strings. They'd been lucky to have the Russian's help at such short notice. Their own resident conductor had been in a car crash and would be out of action for weeks. Poliakowski had agreed to come over to Scotland for the remainder of the year, thus solving Brendan's problem. There were other problems still to be resolved, however.

Simon and Carl were both being questioned by Strathclyde CID and the third fiddle was obviously nervous about taking the Leader's position.

"I don't know, Brendan," the man had told him in all seriousness. "It's a risky business stepping into the shoes of two dead people." The police presence on each of the exits had done little to reassure his musicians. If anything it served merely as a stark reminder of their murdered colleagues. Brendan had urged the Chief Executive to cancel all the remaining concerts for the year but his boss's argument about keeping a sense of normality for the players as well as the public had won the day. The Orchestra Manager had hoped the shambles beneath the stage might go some way to cancelling all their commitments but the backstage crew had assured Brendan that this lower area was okay now.

He'd had a hard time explaining the Executive's decision to Derek Quentin-Jones, though. The man had been beside himself with rage when he'd learned that the Christmas concert would go ahead as scheduled. Listening to his tirade on the telephone, Brendan could only sympathise.

There was a sense of unease throughout the whole Orchestra. It would go away in time, he supposed, but he might not wait around that long. Already the Orchestra Manager was casting his mind to other jobs away from the Glasgow music world. Brendan Phillips wanted a fresh start in a place where he was not constantly reminded of that blood-stained body on the tiles of his dressing room or the coiled harp string that had been stretched around a woman's throat.

Victor Poliakowski strolled into his dressing room. The rehearsal had been awful but he'd kept his temper as he made the players go over and over the same bits of score.

They had further rehearsals before the Christmas show and by then their confidence would have returned. The familiar old tunes would steady their nerves, no doubt. Still, he thought as he towelled his sweating face, there were quite a few who looked as though they'd not slept since the night George Millar had been found dead in his room. Poliakowski gave an involuntary glance towards the wall that separated Lomond from Morar. That policeman asking questions had given him lots to think about. For instance, who had alibis for the time when the lead violin was being killed? It didn't bother the Russian too much that he himself had little in the way of an alibi. For he was Maestro, and nobody questioned his judgement, not even a tall policeman with fire in his eyes.

A knock on the door made Poliakowski turn.

"Your tea, sir," one of the women in tartan uniform came across and laid a tray on the main table by the window. Her eyes did not meet those of the conductor as she performed her task and hurried out. Poliakowski tossed the damp towel over the back of a chair and sat down to enjoy his pot of tea. It was not so bad then, having to stay on awhile in Glasgow if the people became familiar with his little ways. His tea, for instance, was something they brought up automatically when he came off stage. Victor heaved his huge frame onto the leather settee and began to pour out the strong brew. He spooned four sachets of sugar into the teacup and stirred, his mind going over the Orchestra's listless performance and what he would do about it next time. Even the brass section, which could normally be relied upon to liven things, had failed to come up to scratch. The first trumpet's rendering of a horse's neigh at the end of 'Rudolph the Red-Nosed Reindeer' had sounded more like a hyena with a bad cold.

Victor frowned a little. He could have been at home now with Valentina and their grandchildren instead of sitting in this over-heated dressing room sipping black tea.

Christmas was coming, the snows had carpeted Moscow and there were things he'd need to do before the family took its customary holiday to the dacha. Lady Claire MacDonald and her husband had been kindness itself towards the Russian conductor, he mused, letting him bask in the warmth of their country house hotel. And such excellent cuisine! Victor swallowed a mouthful of tea as memories of Lady Claire's table came back to him. It had been some compensation, truly, for his enforced stay here in Scotland. Brendan, the good fellow, had an open ticket for his return via London Heathrow. Surely by the time he'd conducted the Christmas show in a few weeks' time there would be no need to detain him further?

Another knock interrupted the conductor's thoughts and another face appeared in the doorway. Poliakowski scowled at the intruder, then his face cleared as he saw the man's dark beard and twinkling eyes. This was a compatriot, no?

"Mr Poliakowski? May I come in?"

"Sit down," Victor drawled, curious to know the identity behind the London accent. Not a Russian, then, but a Jew, by the look of him.

The stranger held out his hand, then, realising he was still wearing gloves, hastily removed them. He held his hand out once more, a shy smile playing about his lips.

"Solomon Brightman. I'm helping Strathclyde Police with

their investigations."

"Ah. Another policeman," Poliakowski made a dismissive face.

"Oh, no. I am working on the investigation but my role is somewhat separate from that of the police. I'm a psychologist."

Poliakowski's bushy brows rose in renewed interest. "Psychologist," he rolled the word thoughtfully around his mouth as if he could taste it. "You do the profiling of the criminal mind, then? Eh?"

Solly nodded, his smile less shy now, his dark eyes already absorbing the Russian.

"Are you free for the moment, sir?"

"Yes," the Russian answered slowly. "Why do you ask?"

"I thought perhaps you might be my guest for dinner this evening. I'd like to hear your views on the Orchestra and thought we could talk while we eat."

Victor Poliakowski did not reply at once but sat fingering his own beard as if considering the psychologist's invitation.

"Very well. But please allow me to pay for dinner." He gave a sudden grin that transformed his sombre face into that of a caricature villain. "They hold me here on a contract that includes my bed and board," he added, seeing the psychologist's doubtful expression.

An hour later the conductor was sitting across from Solomon Brightman contemplating the menu in Café Rogano. He had remarked on the black and white portrait photographs of celebrities lining the walls and the pithy texts that accompanied them. From where he sat, Solly was aware of Nancy Astor's beaky disapproval looking down upon the diners.

I married beneath me, all women do, her words declared.

Solomon glanced around at the other diners. One or two, like him, were intent on reading these famous quotations from another era.

A bottle of Gerwutzraminer rested in the ice bucket at the side of their table, its contents already well depleted by the conductor. Solly sipped his wine carefully, taking in his companion's mood as Poliakowski chose his dinner.

"Back home my wife already prepares for Christmas with the

baking of cakes and pastries," he said. "She does it every year at this time. This is what I am missing."

"You're with the Orchestra as guest conductor until Christmas, then?"

"That is so. My wife is so used to me being away for work and so we value the times when we can be together," he growled, taking another gulp of the dry wine. "You are married, Doctor Brightman?"

Despite his best intentions, Solly blushed and shook his head.

Lowering the menu, Poliakowski caught his expression and grinned wickedly, "Ah. But you have a lady friend, no doubt. Is she pretty, then?"

Solly tried a smile and nodded. Yes, Rosie Fergusson was pretty, all right. He had a sudden vision of his flat full of the smells of baking and domesticity, Rosie in an apron stirring something that they'd share for Christmas dinner. Is that what she'd like, he wondered, realising for the first time that the pathologist had not mentioned any plans at all for the festive season. Or would the lovely blonde rather dress up and be taken to one of the city's many fine restaurants? Solly made himself a promise to ask. Suddenly it was rather important that he shared Christmas Day with Rosie.

A waiter approached and took their order, Poliakowski asking about several of the dishes with the authority of a practised gourmet.

"Now," began the conductor once the waiter was out of earshot, "you want to know about the City of Glasgow Orchestra, yes?"

"Can you cast you mind back to the performance on October 22nd?"

Poliakowski smiled wryly, "You think I could forget it, then?"

Solly shrugged. "Tell me what you remember about the Orchestra's performance that evening."

"Hm. Damn sight better than today, I assure you, my friend," he remarked. "This is a good orchestra. I tell this already to your Chief Inspector Lorimer. They have style. Panache. And always ready for the good time afterwards," the conductor grinned conspiratorially. "But today," he threw his hands up in a gesture of despair, "the nerves, the mistakes, the lack of life."

"On October 22nd," Solly reminded him gently.

"They play well, you know, the programme is varied, it shows off their virtuosity."

Solly stared into space for a moment. Lorimer had clued him up about this meeting with Poliakowski. Ask him what he saw from the podium, the Chief Inspector had urged. That was what Lorimer had meant to ask that first night, he'd told Solly, but somehow the question had been lost in the conversation.

"You have a unique insight into their playing, do you not?" Solly began. "You face the musicians as they play. You are totally aware of every nuance, every note that trembles in the air?"

Poliakowski smiled. "You should have been a poet, my friend. Such depth of perception."

"It's what a psychologist requires also," Solly told him gravely.

"Yes. I see all these things. I hear every shade within the music. But what of that?"

Solly paused before answering. "Was there any particular player who seemed to be off form? Did any of the musicians make uncharacteristic errors?"

Poliakowski pushed back his chair and crossed one leg over the other, staring at the psychologist.

"You think I can identify a person with a guilty conscience, is that it?"

"Perhaps."

The Russian looked down at his hands, examining the finger-tips carefully. His silence, Solly knew, suggested that he was remembering something that he now saw as significant. But would he reveal this to the stranger sitting opposite?

Poliakowski closed his eyes and leaned back with a sigh. At last he spoke, slowly, as if he were trying to see the City of Glasgow Orchestra in his mind's eye.

"The violinist. She plays like the angels. Now, alas, she is with them for all eternity. The brass section, they are full of spirits. These horns! Ah, such jokers!" The Russian shook his head as if recalling some incident. Then his expression grew sombre. "Yes,

Doctor, I do recall mistakes. So. A trombonist slides too early? A viola is off the beat. What else? I think the harpist shows the nerves. Yes, she trembles when I look her way."

Solly hid a smile. It was not difficult to imagine a nervous player buckling under the Russian's sweeping gaze. The harpist had been in a flap before the performance too, he remembered from Lorimer's notes. But was the DCI looking at this the right way? The psychologist considered his question to Poliakowski. Perhaps he had seen a few musicians off form but would poor playing necessarily have been the response of a killer? Would there not have been some elation in their demeanour, an extra verve to their playing?

Solomon knew he would soon be voicing this point of view to the DCI even although it cast him in the role of Devil's advocate. Again. Still, he'd made a promise to Lorimer so he pushed on with the policeman's idea.

"And the Chorus?"

"Ach, they do what they must do. They look at Maestro and they sing their notes. No mistakes, Doctor. The tenors, well, they could be more forte, you know. It is not unusual for a weakness in that section. But the sopranos, ah, they have the passion!"

"What sort of weakness, exactly?" Solly asked, wondering about the tenors and if any of them had been friendly with the late George Millar.

"Numbers. Always numbers. It is so hard to recruit sufficient for the balance of sound. They are not the professional Chorus, you know?"

Solly shook his head. "No. I didn't know. You mean you use an amateur choir in the concert hall?"

"But of course. There are so few groups of singers who are professionals. Your own Scottish Opera is one, of course. Amateur, you use this word. It means only that the singers themselves are paid nothing. In all other ways they act as professionals, I assure you. And that is why we have these particular rehearsals at night, you see. The singers, they are mostly at work during the daytime."

"You mean the rehearsals for the Christmas Gala concert? I did wonder about that."

"You think it too early for the Christmas songs, eh?" Poliakowski laughed. "Ah, but I am told to take the opportunities to rehearse with the Chorus. When the concert hall is free, you understand.That man, Mr Drummond, he is most insistent that the Orchestra is made available to his singers."

Solly shrugged. He obviously had a lot to learn about the classical music world from the other side of the podium.

His thoughts were interrupted by the waiter bringing their supper and for the next hour Poliakowski refused to give himself up to anything other than the delights of the table. The conductor was an excellent dinner companion, regaling Solly with anecdotes from his travels, many of which centred upon the gourmet high spots of Europe. He had seen all the major capitals of the world, apparently, and talked animatedly of his times in the Far East.

"The Japanese are like us Russians. They take their music seriously. It is a question of nurture, Doctor," he said, raising a glass to his lips. As Solly inclined his head Poliakowski elaborated. "They take a child with genius and they protect him as they would an opening flower. I do not see so much of this here," he added, wiping his mouth with the white linen napkin. The psychologist saw something flare in the Russian's eyes. That was good, he thought, to be passionate about the educational side of music. He could understand more than ever why Poliakowski commanded such respect.

"Did George Millar share your views?" he asked.

"The Leader? How would I know? I scarcely spoke two words to the man." Poliakowski's fingers closed on a piece of tablet and Solly watched as he popped it into his mouth and smiled. "Ah, these sweetmeats. They know how to make them, yes?" The conductor leaned back, his voice deliberately raised to attract a waiter passing them by.

"I'll fetch some more, sir?"

"Ah, good fellow," Poliakowski beamed as the waiter set off again. "You bring me to a splendid restaurant, Doctor. I thank you," Poliakowski lifted his glass in salute and drained the last of his Beaume de Venise.

Solly nodded, wondering just what the City of Glasgow Orchestra's accountant would make of the Russian's bed-and-board expenses.

Solomon glanced towards the main restaurant area as the doorman collected their coats. A melody from the Thirties wafted across the laughing heads seated around the darkened bar, reminding him of the bygone era that was encapsulated in this Art Deco jewel. For a moment he listened and watched, thinking how little humankind really changed from one age to the next. There would always be intrigues, romance and desire. It simply came in different packaging these days.

Solly grinned as he and Poliakowski stepped out into the night. There, as if to confirm his thoughts, a huddle of Goths stood around Royal Exchange Square swinging pumpkin lanterns. He laughed softly, causing his companion to follow his gaze. The conductor raised his eyebrows and gave an exaggerated shrug.

"They dress up to Trick or Treat?"

"You know about Hallowe'en, then?"

"Of course. Remember how well travelled I am, my friend. I see this often. Especially in the United States."

"Do they have Goths there too, then?"

Poliakowski frowned. "Goths?"

"They're not dressed up for Hallowe'en tonight. That's how they always look," Solly laughed softly, stopping to regard the group more closely.

It was true. The boys and girls were clad in their usual blacks and reds, some of the girls with banded stockings, hair dyed black or shades of purple, variously spiked.

The studded dog collars were almost a ubiquitous element of their dress, another feature that caused Solly to smile. The psychology of group dress fascinated him. Here were youths who sought some individuality away from what they saw, no doubt, as the strictures of school uniform. Yet they had created such uniformity without realising it: that was what was so amazing, their lack of self-perception. Several of the girls carried a pumpkin lantern, jagged teeth and eyes hacked from the orange skin. Old traditions died hard, though it had been smelly turnips singed by old bits of candle ends when he had been a boy. Their eyes shone with the same excitement, though. Some things never changed.

"Children dressing up," he murmured to himself.

Poliakowski shot him a puzzled look then walked away from the scene, leaving Solomon no option but to follow his dinner companion through the stone archways. It was only a short walk from Café Rogano to Lang's Hotel where Poliakowski was staying and so the two men set off along Buchanan Street. Glasgow Royal Concert Hall loomed large on the horizon, its video screen advertising events in neon pink and blue.

It was like a rock, solid and safe against the city's swirling currents; people were out in party mood tonight, groups of revellers laughing after the office night out, their faces shining in the myriad lights spangling the trees that lined the street.

Solly thought about Derek Quentin-Jones and Edith Millar. How much more difficult it was to cope with grief in such a carnival atmosphere. And who else within the Orchestra might still be grieving? That was something he might just try to find out.

Chapter Fifteen

Flynn sat up in bed slowly, the neck brace moving his head forward. He'd been asleep since lunchtime and the muscles across his shoulders still ached. Even to see out of the window Flynn had to negotiate his whole upper body sideways. He looked out at a grey November sky heavy with the threat of more snow. No change there, then. There was a television in one corner of his room angled just so that the patient could watch comfortably without straining to see. They'd been thoughtful about setting things like that up here, Flynn realised. Patients in the spinal injuries unit couldn't complain about the quality of service. No indeed. Flynn had been cheered to find the hospital telly had Sky TV and he could flick all the channels using the remote that nice wee nurse had left on his locker.

Between the nurses all fussing over him and the meals that appeared at regular intervals, he was almost glad he'd run in front of that van. The driver had even been in to see him. He'd been dead apologetic and all that but Flynn had told him it was no sweat. He'd been entirely to blame. The guy had looked pretty relieved and they'd ended up chatting about the football. He'd left Flynn a newspaper and a bag of jam doughnuts. When he'd gone, Flynn had picked up the paper, greedy for any news that might have been written by Jimmy Greer.

The headlines had made him sink back into his pillows. Another violinist murdered? What the hell was going on in there? Flynn tried to straighten up then winced as the pain shot through his head.Even yawning was fraught with difficulty. Since his accident he'd slept fitfully, the nights one long dreary darkness only relieved by the night staff coming in to check his temperature and blood pressure.

Still, it was nearly Visiting Time again. Flynn hadn't been surprised to see Raincoat coming in that first evening. He'd called in twice since then, bringing sweets and magazines. The police officer's concern made Flynn wonder just how badly injured he was. What were they telling Raincoat that they hadn't told their patient? Or was it just Detective Sergeant Wilson's conscience bothering him?

The door to Flynn's single room was ajar and he could hear several pairs of footsteps coming along the corridor with a chatter of voices that he'd learned to associate with Visiting Time.Half of him wanted to see a visitor sliding through the door and half wanted peace to watch the telly. He flicked a switch and Bart Simpson appeared resplendent in yellow and blue cartoon colours. Flynn settled back into the pillows, the neck brace propping his head upright.

He was giggling at some self-deprecating remark of Homer's when Lorimer walked into the room.

Flynn's eyes flicked across at his visitor then focused on the TV screen once more.

"Sorry if I'm interrupting anything."

"Naw, you're no'," Flynn shifted his gaze towards the tall man who had drawn a plastic chair over to his bedside. He met Lorimer's look, recognising the blue eyes that were regarding him with interest.

"How're you feeling?"

Lacking the ability to shrug a cool, indifferent shoulder, Flynn said, "A'right. S'pose."

"They looking after you okay?"

"Aye," Flynn grinned suddenly. "Cannae complain. Nice bed, food when I want it. A' the comforts of hame, right?"

"I was wanting to ask you about that, Flynn. About home. Where exactly is it you come from? Originally, I mean."

The smile died on the boy's face. "Ach. Did I no' tell yer other man? A Barnardo's boy, that's whit I wis. There's nae originally aboot it."

"Left on somebody's doorstep?" Lorimer suggested with the ghost of a smile.

"Aye, somethin' like that. Look, gonnae jist leave it, eh? Ah havenae got a hame. Never had. There's naebody waiting tae see me when I get oot o' here."

"Okay. Point taken. Anyway, I saw your surgeon on my way in. He says he's very pleased with you. Says he expects you to make a full recovery. He told me the temporary paralysis was caused by shock to the spine. Maybe they'll shift you into a different ward if they get short of beds."

"Oh, aye," Flynn replied, his eyes on the 'Simpsons' but his heart beating that wee bit faster. "Tell you when I'm for the heave, did he?" the boy asked, the question almost sticking in his throat.

"Oh, a couple of weeks, he thinks. The fractures are mending nicely." Lorimer hesitated. Despite the surgeon's positive report, Flynn still looked a mess, the bruises yellowing across his face. "Depends if you've anywhere to go."

The voices of Homer and Bart filled the room but Lorimer's words seemed louder than the TV programme. Flynn continued to look towards the screen, deliberately ignoring this bearer of bad tidings. Sure, it was nice to know he'd be fit and all, but fit for what? And in this weather?

The detective cleared his throat. "Do you have anywhere you could stay? A friend's place, maybe? Somewhere you'd be properly looked after?"

Flynn thought about Allan Seaton for a brief moment then dismissed the idea. Seaton's pad was always loupin' with druggies and nutters. He'd never get a minute's peace. Flynn suddenly realised how vulnerable he felt. This injury to his neck had damaged more than flesh and bone; he'd lost his nerve under that white van.

"Naw. There's nowhere," he muttered.

Lorimer had suspected as much from his discussions with the social work department connected to the hospital. He'd spent time thinking over how to say what he wanted to say to this boy, wondering how he would react.

"There's a spare room at my place," Lorimer told him.

Flynn's eyes swivelled round, trying to engage with Lorimer's. Their expression held more doubt than surprise.

"Ye serious?"

Lorimer nodded. "There's just me at home right now. My wife's working abroad for a while. We've got a spare room doing nothing. You could stay for a few weeks if you liked. How about it?"

Flynn turned back towards the television screen, obviously considering the detective's offer. When he grinned, Lorimer cocked his head to one side, curious to know what the boy's answer would be.

"Aye, why no. Hiv ye got Sky TV?"

"You've done what?" Alistair Wilson slammed down his half empty coffee cup on Lorimer's desk.

"I've asked him to stay at my place."

"And did you clear this with Maggie?"

As soon as the words were out, Wilson wished them back. It was none of his business what Maggie Lorimer thought, after all.

No," his boss replied shortly, "I didn't. Anyway, it's just until the boy has somewhere else to go. The officer at the Hamish Allan Centre says they might be able to sort out a furnished flat for him. I'm sure he'll be fixed up by Christmas. It's still over a month away."

Wilson shook his head. "You could be setting yourself up for a whole load of trouble."

"I don't think so. He's still pretty weak. He needs a bit of time and anyway..." Lorimer tailed off. How could he explain the unspoken feeling of trust that had sprung up between himself and this street kid? Flynn had told them about his relationship with George Millar. He'd made it clear that he'd only been the drug courier, nothing more. There would be no charges brought against the boy, though. Lorimer had assured him of that. He was simply helping the police with their enquiries. He wasn't willing to name sources, yet, and Lorimer hadn't expected him to grass up any of his mates.

But he had hinted that he could tell Lorimer something else about the late Leader of The City of Glasgow Orchestra. Maybe, just maybe, he knew something that could lead him to the missing violin.

"D'you expect him to sing for his supper, then? Is that your game?" Wilson's tone was cynical, breaking Lorimer's train of thought.

Lorimer ran a hand through his hair. "Look, I know this is unusual. And yes, perhaps he will tell me more, but that's not the real reason I offered him a place to stay."

Wilson looked troubled for a moment. Lorimer wasn't known for being soft hearted but he suspected there was a genuine sense of caring behind the man's decision to take the boy into his home.

"There but for the Grace of God…?"

"Something like that," Lorimer mumbled.

"I still think you're mad," Wilson told him. "But it takes all sorts," he shrugged, getting up and heading for the door.

"Oh," he added, turning back for a moment, "Betty's bound to tell me that you're a star. God knows if Maggie will agree, though." He was out of the door before Lorimer could reply.

The Chief Inspector swivelled his chair round towards the window. What Wilson had said was probably true. It was a bit mad to take in a stray like Flynn without even telling Maggie what he'd done. But was that part of the reason he'd invited the boy?

Was he trying to prove that the house was his home and his alone? Was it the action of a man who secretly believed his wife would never return? Was he trying to tell himself that he could do what the hell he liked? Lorimer shook his head as if trying to clear away all this introspection. Psychobabble was for the likes of Solomon Brightman.

"No he's no'," Sadie Dunlop protested. "He's as normal as you an' me!"

"Well, what's he doin' takin' a wee lad into his hame, then? Looks guy fishy tae me."

"Aye, well a lot of things look fishy tae you, Martha McKinlay. Ah'm telling ye, Lorimer's straight."

"Aye, well, it's jist whit they're all sayin', know what I mean? Mebbe that's why the wife up and left, eh?" The cleaner finished rubbing down the glass shelving and dropped the paper towel into the waste bucket. The snap as she removed her rubber gloves seemed to reinforce her opinion.

Sadie Dunlop seethed as she watched the other woman waddle through to the kitchen. What a thing to suggest about Lorimer! Okay he was on his own while that daft wife of his was off galli-

vanting in America but that was no reason to suggest that he had
turned into a shirt lifter. Heaven sakes, the very idea was ridicu-
lous! It was all the fault of the wee man who'd got himself killed
in the concert hall. Now he'd been a real poofter, Sadie told herself and not the only one in the band, from what she'd heard.
That was what all this was about, all this investigation into a
homosexual murder. Sadie gritted her teeth. Once an idea had
taken hold, though, it was hard to convince folk of its validity.
Despite the current trend to recruit gay officers into the force,
Lorimer would be in for a less than charitable time in the run up
to Christmas if gossips like Martha had their way.

Chapter Sixteen

Maggie Lorimer put down the phone, her hand trembling. What on earth had possessed him? The lad could be into anything. Hadn't he already admitted dealing in drugs, for heaven's sake? Yet the sensible half of her had kept quiet as Lorimer related his plans for Flynn's recuperation. Her husband was a policeman, after all; he knew the score better than any of them. Any error of judgement regarding this boy would be utterly out of character for him. So why did she feel so shaken?

It's your home, that's why, a little voice reminded her.

Suddenly the vision of her untidy lounge with its shelves of books on two walls came to mind. It would be dark there, now. Would the table lamp be switched on? She'd left it on a timer, but that was back in August when the nights had still been light. Maybe it was raining, the cold wind sweeping the rowan leaves over the grass at the front. Would any of the neighbours have lit their Christmas trees at the windows yet? Okay, it was still only November, but here the razzmatazz of the holiday as they called it had been in force since Hallowe'en. Fairy lights flickered all along the street where Maggie lived, her own apartment windows blank. It was something they always left until the last minute, usually when school broke up at the end of term.

Then Maggie would fling herself into a frenzy of shopping and decorating, usually ending up asleep on Christmas afternoon.

She wanted to be there, she realised, preparing things for this stray that Bill had found. "You're jealous!" she whispered aloud, the truth of her feeling shocking her. This boy, this vagabond, who had usurped her home; she wanted to be there to provide for him, to make up a Christmas stocking, to see that he was warm and loved. But it was Bill who would be responsible for these things, if he thought about them at all.

"Maggie Lorimer, stop all this at once!" she scolded herself, recognising the latent maternal instinct for what it was.

Christmas. Christmas had always been home with Mum and Dad then just Mum and the two of them. What had Christmas been like for this Flynn person? And what, since Mum and Bill were intending to come over by December 25th, would it be like for him this year? Had Bill even thought this through? In their conversation nothing had been mentioned about where the boy would go when her husband left for Florida. Surely he wouldn't leave him there alone? But then, where else would the lad go? Maggie asked herself fretfully.

Her hand hovered over the telephone once more then dropped. No. Bill would sort it out. She'd left him to get on with his life in Scotland. Somehow it robbed her of her rights to make decisions about their home. Maggie bit her lip. Not for the first time she wondered at the driving force that had taken her all the way across the Atlantic.

Lorimer pushed his foot against the cupboard, hearing a clatter as the vacuum's nozzle fell against the closed door.

Well, at least he'd made up for all those weeks of indolence, he thought with some satisfaction, then smiled wryly as he recalled Maggie's dictum that real housework only got done whenever they were expecting guests. It was true, he supposed. Flynn's imminent arrival had catapulted Lorimer into a frenzy of vacuuming and cleaning. Several black bin bags were stacked by the front door to be taken to the dump, some full of bottles for the bottle bank. When Maggie had been here, she'd religiously taken stuff every week, papers and all, for recycling.

The spare room was tidy now, at least; the single bed made up with an extra cover over the duvet in case the boy felt cold after the heat of his hospital room. The weather had been bitter all through November. Lorimer had spoken to the social worker attached to the hospital about Flynn's longer-term prospects. It was agreed that it "was not reasonable for the patient to continue to occupy temporary accommodation" (i.e. Lorimer's spare room) when the DCI was to be away in Florida. There would be a furnished flat made available to Flynn, well away from his old haunts and from anyone who might try to harm him.

The hostels were out of the question. All too often pushers from outside preyed on the vulnerable men and women who sought temporary refuge in the spaces provided by these bleak rooms. It was a moral dilemma for the case-workers attached to the Hamish Allan Centre. By law they had to find accommodation for these folk, but sometimes they knew only too well that there were pushers just waiting near the hostels to march some poor soul up to the benefit office for the handover.

And the movement of drugs within the hostels was rife; there were no locked doors, a double-edged sword that was meant to protect the men and women who tried to shelter from the streets but which could also make them a danger to one another.

In the end it had been fairly straightforward to arrange for the boy to stay for a short time. Flynn could at least apply for a benefit book now that he was to have some sort of an address, then it would be transferred to his new flat. That way the social services could recoup the housing benefit. There had been no mutterings about setting a precedent and disregard for correct procedure, as Lorimer had feared. In fact the senior emergency services officer had been more than helpful; a community nurse would be calling on a regular basis, he was told. Flynn's neck injury was healing and the broken ribs and fractured skull no longer required quite so much in the way of pain relief.

Lorimer experienced a sudden twinge of guilt. Would Flynn be better off in some country nursing home? Somehow he doubted whether he'd be able to keep tabs on the boy if he were to be hauled out to Mearnskirk Cottage Hospital or wherever they went these days. This was an ideal opportunity to let the boy open up to him, to reveal what he could of the life he'd been living in the streets of Glasgow. That hadn't been his underlying motive, though the thought had come pretty hard on the heels of his offer to stay, Lorimer admitted.

They'd reached an impasse in this case now, a state he'd never contemplated happening in the beginning. With a wealth of forensic material and hundreds of statements, he had been pretty sure that an arrest would have been made by now. Solly was busy drawing up a profile on what evidence there was, though there had been little feedback from the psychologist so far.

In some ways there was simply too much to handle. Much of the work done was now on computer and the IT boys had sorted things into a variety of patterns for Solly to see.

Several of the instruments in the City of Glasgow Orchestra had been bought from George Millar and their provenance was being investigated. It was clear that most of the musicians had been genuinely astonished by the First Violin's scam. Over and over their statements expressed a gratitude at having a decent instrument made available by instalments to a colleague whom they had trusted.

As Lorimer had foreseen, the overtime bill on this case was massive. Today was the first whole Saturday he'd spent in the house since that night at the Concert Hall. Working practices were quietly ignored at times like this, despite Mitchison's continual attempts to bring them into line with maximum shift times.

A ring on the front doorbell startled Lorimer from his thoughts.

Solomon Brightman stood on the doorstep, a tentative smile on his face.

"Solly, what on earth?" Lorimer began, then, "Has something happened?" he frowned, opening the door and ushering Solly inside.

"Yes and no," Solly smiled again, catching sight of the instant irritation his words produced.

Lorimer ran a hand through his hair. "Well, let's have it, then."

Solly unravelled his long knitted scarf and set it down on the edge of a settee before removing his heavy black overcoat.

"Come, on, sit yourself down."

Solly pulled aside a plastic basin full of cleaning materials before sitting down. His eyebrows were raised in a silent query that Lorimer deliberately ignored.

"It's the profile," Solly began. "Mitchison has been on at me to draw something up. Oh, I know," he said, gesturing with his hand in the air as if to ward off any verbal assault. "It's your case and he's interfering. But be that as it may, I do have a duty to provide some form of paperwork on this."

"And?"

"And I have," he replied, simply. "There's not such a mystery over all of this. It's not as if it's a stranger killing. You should have no fears that we are dealing with some damaged person who has an escalating hit list."

"I never thought we were."

"No," Solly looked thoughtful. "There wasn't a very strong reason for my presence in all of this, except your Superintendent wanting to be certain that there was no outside element involved. No loner attaching himself to the Glasgow music world."

"Himself. You've established that, then?" Lorimer's sarcasm was cutting.

"A large man," Solly went on, oblivious to Lorimer's tone. "Somebody with the strength to wield a percussion hammer effectively and to strangle a fit woman with a harp string and dispatch her body beneath the stage. Someone who is conversant with the music world from a professional point of view."

"Not necessarily another musician, then?"

Solly shook his head.

"But it could be?"

"Of course. Many of them had the opportunity. It remains to be seen if they might also have had a motive. There was forethought into George Millar's death, the evidence itself shows that. The crime passionel it was not, and yet…"

Lorimer drummed his fingers impatiently against the leg of the chair. Solly's ponderous silences maddened him.

"There could well be some high emotion behind this. There's a personal motive. George Millar was careless with his relationships."

"Was he also careless with his business affairs?" Lorimer asked. "Could it be that his colleagues in the dealing of stolen goods or those in the drug scene had a reason to put out a contract on the man?"

"But it is the instrument itself that causes me to question our killer," Solly murmured into his beard.

"Go on."

"There is a certain amount of irony, is there not, in a killer choosing a musical instrument as a means to kill a musician. We agree that this was a well-planned murder. So." Solly counted off on his fingers, "There is the time to think things through. Time to immobilise the CCTV cameras, to know about the technician's illness, perhaps? He even had inside knowledge of Maestro's habit of secluding himself in his dressing room, let's assume. So why not arrive prepared for killing with a more effective instrument than a hammer picked up from the percussion stand?"

"He enjoys the risk?" Lorimer suggested.

Solly shook his head. "Maybe that happens at the time, but he does not anticipate the thrill. No. We must try to think what goes on inside his head prior to the killing. What his intentions really were."

"Wait a minute," Lorimer stared hard at him. "Are you trying to say that this was not intended as a murder at all?"

Solly shrugged. "One blow to the skull might have felled him to the ground if it had been a massive weapon. In this case the killer was lucky. Or perhaps not."

"Why attack George Millar, then?"

"To stop him from playing at the concert? Or maybe as a lesson to him from an outside agency, though I don't really think so."

"No," Lorimer frowned. "If it had been a professional hit then he'd have been targeted somewhere far less public."

"My point exactly!" Solly beamed.

"But you haven't made any point yet," Lorimer protested.

"He wanted George Millar to be brought down in a public place. And not just any place. It had to be the concert hall and it had to be during a performance," Solly exclaimed, his eyes shining. "Don't you see? It was part of a performance itself, this drama. Whoever the killer is, he shows a certain penchant for creativity."

"Sounds a bit unhinged to me," Lorimer replied acidly.

Solly shook his head vehemently. "Not at all. He is quite lucid. Clear in his intent and maybe even anticipating the effect his actions will have. He's making a statement. And there's a reason for that."

"Do you think it's a member of the Orchestra?"

"Could be, could be. Someone fit and healthy, strong, young, too. Early thirties at the most and single."

"How do you work that out?"

Solly shrugged again. "He's willing to take such risks. It is as though there is some youthful bravado to his nature, foolhardiness, maybe. An older person is more inclined to worry about the consequences of their actions. And I feel he's unhampered by any ongoing relationship. A single person has more freedom. He's not worrying about what a partner might think of him if he's caught."

"Carl Bekaert, maybe?"

Solly frowned. "I don't think the Danish man has enough irony in his soul.But that's just my own feeling. He certainly fits any physical profile I'd draw up."

"And that's why you're here, isn't it?" Lorimer said. "You don't want him arrested, is that it?"

"What evidence have you against him?"

"He was the last musician out of the concert hall the night of Karen's death."

"There's no forensic evidence, though. No DNA at either scene of crime to match up to anything on Bekaert."

"We've arrested folk on less than that before," Lorimer reminded him.

"And what good would it do? If Bekaert's not your man the real killer will simply breathe a sigh of relief and continue with his life. Unless he feels threatened by anyone else."

"Yes, that's something I've been concerned about," Lorimer frowned.

"Flynn?"

Lorimer nodded silently. Joseph Alexander Flynn of no fixed address, who was to be his house-guest until Christmas, might easily be a target if he still had some knowledge about George Millar. And Lorimer was certain that he did.

Jimmy Greer had hinted as much and the journalist had sounded a tad put out that the boy hadn't opened up to him completely.

"Couldn't you put an officer to watch the house?"

"Nobody outside the investigating team will know he's here;

even the ancillary staff at the Division have been warned to keep quiet. No, he'll be safe enough. Anyway, I expect he'll be watching TV all day. He's not fit to go out. In fact there'll be a nurse coming in to see to that head wound. It'll still need dressing for a while."

"So," Solly smiled as he indicated the plastic basin. "You're preparing for his visit?"

"Aye. Och, the place was becoming a midden. I should've asked you for a loan of that cleaning woman you have in. Maybe I still will," he added thoughtfully. "D'you think she'd come in after Christmas?" he asked.

Solly laughed then his face became serious again. "To get back to Bekaert. What are you going to do?"

"We're not intending to arrest him. Yet. If you must know, we've had a tail on him since his interview, hoping that he could lead us to whoever supplied the cocaine. Probably the same source as George Millar used."

"And, anything?"

"No. Seems he's turned over a new leaf," Lorimer grinned wryly. "Maybe we frightened him off."

"But, what if my profile should be seen by your Superintendent? He'd jump to the conclusion that Bekaert was the killer."

"Maybe you need to work on it some more?" Lorimer suggested.

"Oh, I do. I do," Solly wagged his head then, catching sight of Lorimer's grin, continued, "but Mitchison wants a progress report."

"Ach, make him wait. Tell him you need more time."

Solly sighed loudly. "You know I talked to Poliakowski and asked him about the musicians. Remember I said he was quite forthcoming? Didn't really notice anything that would be incriminating? But since then I've had another thought."

"Yes?"

"What if George Millar's killer was a member of the Orchestra? Would he be on stage then or not? Weren't there others who were only needed for the second half?"

"True. Among them were the percussionists. We've already spoken to them."

Solly was silent for a moment, contemplating the carpet. "Hm," he said at last. "There's one other thing. Did Poliakowski see anyone playing in the first half who was suddenly inspired?"

"What?"

"The aftermath of a successful killing; it might produce an adrenaline rush of quite a different kind than you had anticipated."

"And how would the conductor know?"

Solly shrugged. "Perhaps he wouldn't. He doesn't know the Orchestra members well enough for such subtlety."

"Then who would?" Lorimer asked and before the question had even left his lips he thought of two men right away: Brendan Phillips and Maurice Drummond.

Chapter Seventeen

Simon Corrigan sprayed the last shelf then polished it in a rhythmic motion before scrunching the duster in a ball. There. It was as clean as he could make it. He looked at the pile of books laid neatly on the carpet. Each one had been carefully wiped clean of the offending dust that had gathered over the past few months. He'd put them back in alphabetical order, leaving a wee space at one end of the shelf for Chris's ioniser. Simon's eyes fell onto the rust coloured silk covering the bed. He'd even vacuumed the mattress and hauled out the bed so he could suck up all the dust balls from underneath.

Simon sat back on his heels, his imagination fast-forwarding to the evening ahead. There was no rehearsal tonight so they could have some of that Thai curry he'd defrosted before settling down for the evening. It would be just like old times again. He heaved a huge sigh that was somewhere between relief and tiredness. He should never have let Chris leave in the first place, he told himself. That had been so stupid. Well, he was coming back now, wasn't he? Poor old George was well and truly out of the way. There'd be nothing else to come between them, would there?

Brendan Phillips put down the phone with a shudder as if it were something alive in his hand. Just what were they asking him, now? He sat staring at the desk for a moment trying to conjure up a picture of the stage on the night of George's death. But he'd not been out front, he'd told Lorimer. The Director and Maurice had been, though. Why didn't he talk to them? Lorimer had said that he would.

There was something, though, that he hadn't thought of, wasn't there? CCTV footage would give a clear picture of that half concert. Didn't Lorimer have the tapes impounded still? If he could have them back and see the concert again, maybe he'd be able to answer the DCI's questions.

Brendan picked up the brown envelope and pulled the folded pages out. For a moment he thought about their contents then he let them slide back into the envelope. He'd read the letter over and over until he was certain it was perfect. If they took him, fine, if not, he'd want to know why. An Orchestra Manager of his calibre and experience was not to be sniffed at. After Christmas, he thought. They'll let me know after Christmas. Brendan breathed a sigh. What a relief to be out of Glasgow and all it had come to mean for him! If they took him, a little voice reminded him.

The telephone's ring made Brendan start from his reverie, reminding him that there was still work to do before he could make good his escape.

'Belshazzar's Feast' was sounding out the brass when the doorbell rang. With a curse, Maurice Drummond pressed the hold button of the video recorder, leaving his Chorus open mouthed across the frozen screen.

"Yes? Who is it?" he rasped into the intercom.

"DCI Lorimer, DS Wilson, Strathclyde CID. We'd like to see Mr Drummond."

"Hold on," Maurice grumbled. He picked up a discarded jacket and slipped it on, then straightened his tie before pressing the buzzer to let them in. Living on the first floor didn't give him too much time to prepare for unexpected visitors, he thought ruefully.

As he opened the door he remembered the DCI. It was the same man he'd seen at the Concert Hall, a man easily as tall as himself and with him a solid looking chap in a raincoat who looked every inch the plain clothes copper.

"Come in," Maurice stood aside to let the two men into the darkened hallway and closed the door behind them.

Stepping into the light, the first thing that Lorimer saw was a grand piano placed in the bay window of the huge lounge. It was one of those older flats with ornate cornicing around the high ceiling that gave an impression of a more graceful era. Apart from the piano, however, there was nothing graceful about Maurice Drummond's furnishings. A couple of ancient easy chairs covered in shabby cotton covers sat either side of a television and video. The screen was blurred, showing that they'd caught the Chorus Master in the middle of watching something. Piles of musical scores were stacked against the wall by the piano and other papers spilled across the carpet as if by design.

"Sorry to disturb you, sir. We wanted to ask you some questions in connection with the death of George Millar," Lorimer said.

"Sit down, won't you?" Maurice picked up the piano stool and hauled it towards the two chairs so that it was facing them then sat down on it, leaving Lorimer and Wilson no option but to sink into the easy chairs or perch on their edges. Lorimer chose to do the latter.

"Now, what can I tell you?" Maurice asked abruptly.

Lorimer nodded to himself. The man was trying to be helpful in his own way but it was clear he'd much rather get back to whatever he'd been doing.

"Did we disturb you, sir?" Wilson asked, his eyes travelling towards the television.

"Yes, actually. You did."

"Watching something interesting?" Wilson continued, feigning innocence.

"A recording by the City of Glasgow Chorus. 'Belshazzar's Feast', if you must know."

"Thou art weighed in the balance and found wanting," Lorimer quoted.

Maurice Drummond's raised eyebrows spoke volumes. He hadn't expected a mere policeman to know the scripture text, Lorimer thought to himself.

"The fall of a great king. The rejoicing of a persecuted people," Maurice said slowly, taking a closer look at the tall man whose eyes met his in a sardonic smile.

"You're performing it soon?" Wilson asked.

"Next May. But we begin rehearsals straight after Christmas."

"Could you cast your mind back to the performance the night of George Millar's death?" Lorimer asked smoothly.

"Hard to forget. Don't think any of us will ever get over that."

"The actual performance is what I'd like you to focus on, if you will, sir," Lorimer persisted. "The first half of the programme when Mrs Quentin-Jones took over as Leader of the Orchestra. What can you remember about the quality of the performance?"

Maurice Drummond sat up straight and frowned, hand to his

chin. "I'm not sure I can recall, Chief Inspector. There was nothing really memorable about the performance. Karen played the Albinoni beautifully and my singers were in top form. I do remember watching Poliakowski, though, because I'd never seen him conduct our Chorus before."

"He's not a man for Choral music, then?"

"On the contrary, he's renowned for his expertise with singers," Maurice replied dryly.

Lorimer cocked his head. Was there something underlying the man's words?

"And were you satisfied he treated your Chorus well?"

Maurice Drummond hesitated before answering. "They were all pleased with their performance. I think they enjoyed having him conduct them on the evening."

"But not at the rehearsal?"

"You heard, then?" Maurice looked up as Lorimer gave a nod. "He gave them an absolute bollocking in the afternoon. Some of my sopranos were in tears."

"Oh? What exactly was the cause of the Maestro's temper?"

"You mean you didn't know?" Drummond looked at Lorimer accusingly.

"Only that the rehearsal had been a bit fraught. Mr Phillips didn't go into any details," Lorimer replied.

Drummond gave a sigh and shook his head. "The man's a monster. All charm when it suits him, fawning over the ladies of the front row then screaming abuse at them if he thinks they're not giving of their best."

"And were they?"

Drummond scowled. "Of course. But it was a rehearsal. I always tell my singers to save something for the actual night. I won't have their voices wrecked just because some Russian Bear wants a sustained top c over and over again."

"But he was good with them on the night?"

"Had them eating out of his hand. You should have heard them afterwards, positively cooing."

"So the afternoon rehearsal was put behind them?"

Drummond nodded.

"You were in the audience before the concert began, that's correct?"

"Yes. Once the Chorus are on stage I make my way upstairs to the back of the Circle. Somewhere I can see all that's going on," he smiled wryly.

"There was nothing about the performance, perhaps by one of the musicians, that you found unusual, perhaps?"

"What sort of thing?"

"An extra nervousness. Maybe caused by the Maestro's earlier temper?"

"Not that I recall. The band was fine. No jitters from any of them. But they're all pros. Hysterical conductors are like water off a duck's back to that lot."

"And no outstanding performers among them?"

"Karen, of course. But I've already mentioned her. No. I can't think that there was anything else," Drummond looked towards the carpet and bit his fingernail as if trying to run the concert through again in his mind's eye.

As he closed the door on the two policemen, Maurice's heart was beating loudly. Had they seen his hesitation? Would they have figured out that he was lying to them? And what on earth did they think an individual player's performance had to do with George's murder?

Maurice sank into an armchair. Had his concern for the Chorus deflected attention from the other aspects of the performance? He hoped so.

There was no way C. Maurice Drummond wanted his name linked to a particular member of the City of Glasgow Orchestra, someone who had held his undivided attention for the whole performance; especially during a murder investigation.

Chapter Eighteen

Superintendent Mark Mitchison put his hand to his stomach. The pain was worse than ever today, a gnawing that began in his gut and travelled all the way upwards like broken glass. Stress, the doctor had said. He'd thought it was just acid reflux at first and had prescribed the usual pills but they hadn't worked.

Another spasm made him groan and lean over, clutching his stomach, just as he heard a knock on the door.

"Sir!" WPC Irvine crossed the room in double quick time. "What's the matter?" she asked as Mitchison tried to straighten up.

The policewoman saw the handsome face change colour from white to grey and watched, mesmerised as the man stumbled then fell forward, one hand clutched tightly to his middle.

"D'ye hear the latest? Mitchison's been signed off on the sick," Martha McKinlay wagged her head at Sadie as the two women finished drying the formica tabletops in the staff canteen.

"Aye, well, that'll please some of them. He's no' that well liked, is he?"

"Och, Sadie, that's terrible. An' him that ill."

"Why? Whit's wrang wi' him?"

"Collapsed in his office. Someone said it might be a heart attack," Martha's voice lowered in a conspiratorial whisper.

"Hmph. Well, we'll see. Who'll be taking over from him? Someone from outside again?"

"Well, rumour has it that Lorimer's been asked to be acting Super."

"That'll no please him. He's up to his neck in this concert hall case. He'll no' want tae gie' that up."

"There's no question of you being taken off this case," the Assistant Chief Constable told Lorimer. "You'll still be the investigating officer as far as we're concerned. But your time will be split between the two jobs, of course. Superintendent Mitchison has a pretty full diary," she frowned.

Lorimer watched the woman on the opposite side of the desk.

She was older than him by about ten years, her fair hair short and neat, her face made up discreetly. Yes, Joyce Rogers was still a feminine woman despite all her experience in the Force. Some of the women became hardened after a while, the dark underside of police work showing on their faces. Had she been instrumental in Mitchison's appointment in the first place, he wondered? If so, then this was the woman who'd rejected Lorimer himself for the job. He'd never know, and that was just as well.

"How long is the Superintendent expected to be off?" he asked mildly.

Joyce Rogers smiled thinly. "How long's a piece of string?"

She shook her head. "He's suffering from stress and will be off until at least the end of the year. His doctor has told him to take a complete break and our own medical man has endorsed that."

Lorimer nodded. That made sense. None of them would take time off willingly. So. The police doctor had had the last say. Mitchison must have gone off under protest, then. Lorimer wasn't sorry. The man had been acting strangely for weeks now, behaviour that could be explained by his present illness.

"He's not the first senior officer to have succumbed to stress and he won't be the last," Joyce Rogers looked Lorimer directly in the eye. "You've got your work cut out in the next few weeks, Chief Inspector, but that is no reason not to take the leave you'd planned." The Assistant Constable's eyes twinkled. "We can't have all our senior officers stretched to the limit. And I suppose Mrs Lorimer would be very put out if you didn't arrive for Christmas?"

"Indeed," Lorimer agreed, wondering just how much this lady knew about his domestic arrangements. Maggie would be more than disappointed. It would drive another huge wedge between them if her were to fail her this time. "Who'll cover since Superintendent Mitchison won't be back from sick leave before Christmas, Ma'am?"

"We've taken care of that, Lorimer." She grinned suddenly. "Just see if you can shed some of Superintendent Mitchison's workload in the meantime, eh? Spare a few trees."

Lorimer raised his eyebrows in surprise. Word about

Mitchison's paper trails had reached the highest levels, had it? "Certainly, Ma'am. I'll be glad to oblige."

"And one more thing, Chief Inspector. We would appreciate a result on the concert hall case. Not that I'm putting you under any pressure, you understand..."

"Bill, that's great!" Maggie enthused. "But will you still be able to come out?" Lorimer could hear the sudden quiver in her voice. The telephone had been serving him well these past weeks as a means of telling him just how Maggie was feeling. He was used to the nuances of the human voice. It was one of those skills that had grown with the job.

"Of course we will," he assured her. "The Assistant Chief Constable herself assured me of that."

"Joyce Rogers?"

"The same."

"Well, that's all right, then. I like her. This can only do your career some good. After all, acting Super is just a step away from being appointed somewhere else, isn't it?"

Lorimer shrugged. It wasn't something he'd considered until now. Leaving the Division and all his team behind wasn't a thought he particularly relished. And did he really want to be bothered with all these Superintendents' meetings that seemed to be par for the course?

"Maybe I'm happy just as I am," he told his wife at last. There was a silence that he took for her disapproval. "Catching criminals," he added at last. "Talking of which I must get some sleep. There are a hundred and one things I want to delete from Mitchison's diary tomorrow. The concert hall case has gone quiet on me for now."

"Just as well."

"Hm," Lorimer sounded at odds with Maggie's remark. He'd rather have a solution to these two murders any day than a promotion, no matter how temporary it was.

Chapter Nineteen

Karen Quentin-Jones was the headline in bold at the top of Lorimer's latest report. He'd continually been putting out feelers about the woman who had spoken to him on the night of George Millar's death.

She'd been born Karen Scott, the only daughter of a merchant banker and his wife. Both parents were deceased now so there were few to tell about her earlier years. He read the words on the first page, details about her musical background and early education: private school, year away, RSAMD then marriage to Derek Quentin-Jones. They'd had one child, a girl, who was now a student at the University of Glasgow.

The surgeon had tried to be helpful, but Lorimer guessed that he had been selective in what he told the police. It was all just too much a glowing account of a talented young musician. Karen had been more than that, Lorimer knew, even from his brief acquaintance with the woman. There was a hard core to her that he wanted to try and crack, if he could.

Some of the older members of the Orchestra had added snippets of information to the stuff Quentin-Jones had provided but it hadn't amounted to very much, really. What had she known about George Millar? Was she really unaware that her violin had been stolen and sold to her husband? Perhaps.

Maybe she was vain enough to take such things as her due. She hadn't liked the First Violin, though, had she? That had been patently clear from her attitude and Derek Quentin-Jones had corroborated that.

No. There would have to be more investigation into her background. Someone somewhere must know why she had lingered in the concert hall after that rehearsal.

Lorimer cast his mind back to his interviews with the technical staff. They had simply left the music stands where they had stood ready for the next day's rehearsal. And there had been no close circuit televisions trained on the stage. Lorimer thumped the report onto his desk. She'd been dressed for the street, probably just about to leave, so who had called her back? He imagined her standing somewhere in that labyrinth of corridors, violin case in hand. And why did they go onto the stage? Lorimer's glance fell onto the red folder. His report was based on several officers' work, their original typewritten sheets all crammed together.

Had they missed something? Mitchison had got them all into the habit of submitting neat copy to the investigating officer. Had something been left out of the hotchpotch of margin notes and post-it notes that covered their working drafts?

"Mrs Edith Millar," DC Cameron said. "She was questioned about the victim and gave some background information. I did have the impression she could have said more. She's quite a funny woman, that," he added, his lilting Lewis accent understating what his boss already knew.

Lorimer nodded. Edith Millar was an unusual person. Maybe it was time to pay another visit. If only he didn't have all of Mitchison's stuff to contend with. A sudden thought made him look at the Detective Constable narrowly.

"Fancy taking Doctor Brightman back there? Just to see if you can glean a bit more?"

Solly tramped by the side of the young detective, his feet having to make larger strides to keep up. The city was still in the grip of an early winter, bare trees thrusting their branches into a sky that promised more snow. The very air seemed to tremble on the brink of something momentous; not even a breath of wind blew the last fallen leaves from the frozen lawns.

Solly was between lectures and had only agreed to the visit because Huntly gardens was a ten-minute walk from his department. "Lorimer trusts my intuition, it seems," DC Cameron had told him with a self-deprecating grin. Well, it remained to be seen if this Hebridean officer had a glimmer of the second sight or if they were simply wasting their time going over old ground. Mrs Millar would be at home, Cameron told him. She'd be expecting them. Solly looked around him intently as they turned from the street, noting the polished brass bell pull and the freshly scrubbed steps. Somebody had had the energy to make an effort, he mused. Was it George Millar's widow?

Solly's first impression of Edith Millar was of a sensitive face framed with fine grey hair and eyes that looked directly into those of her visitors.

"Come in," she told them and Solly found himself ushered into a dark wood panelled hallway then into a bright sitting room where a grand piano dominated the large bay window.

"I'm Doctor Brightman," Solly told her, taking her hand in his. She was cold, he noticed, despite the warmth of this room. Perhaps she'd been outside?

"Please sit down," she said, her hand sweeping towards a flowered chintz armchair across from a matching settee. "Some tea? Coffee?"

"No thank you. We don't want to keep you too long," Solly answered, his mind half on the class that would expect him in less than an hour.

Perching on the edge of the settee, Solly began. "We would like to ask you a bit more about the violinist, Karen Quentin-Jones."

Edith Millar stared at him. "Yes?" she answered, just the faintest hint of curiosity in her reply.

"How long had you known her?"

Edith Millar nodded as if the question had been long expected. "Quite some time, Doctor." Solly saw her bite her lower lip as she hesitated. "You see, she was one of my husband's pupils."

"You didn't tell us that before!" Cameron began to protest but the woman's raised eyebrows stopped him in his tracks.

"Nobody asked me," she said. "It hasn't been an issue. Till now," she added, looking towards Solly once more.

Detective Constable Cameron looked outraged and on the point of protesting but a gesture from Solly stopped him.

"So, did Karen Quentin-Jones come here for her lessons?"

Edith Millar shook her head. "We lived in Great George Street in those days. And the young girl who came for her lessons then was known as Karen Scott."

"Did you know her well at that time?" Solly asked.

Edith Millar smiled at him. "I'm not sure if I did. I thought I knew her fairly well at one time, but then..." Her voice trailed off. The woman sat up and cocked her head to one side suddenly.

"How much do you want to know about Karen's teenage years?"

"Everything you can tell us," Solly replied. "The more we know the better we are able to understand the victim. And perhaps that will assist us in finding her killer."

And George's, he expected her to reply, but curiously the words remained unspoken.

"Very well," Edith Millar folded her hands on her lap and looked down at them as if bracing herself for something hard. "Karen came to George for lessons for about three years. She was a superb pupil, the best he ever had, but she had an attitude, you know. Karen was an only child and rather indulged. I haven't been blessed with children, Doctor Brightman, but I know enough about them to tell a spoiled child from one that is loving and giving. Karen, I'm afraid, fell into the former category. She was never a giver. Except," she broke off and glanced at Solomon. "She did give herself to a boy. But it didn't last."

"What happened?"

Edith Millar sighed heavily. "Oh, dear. I never thought I'd have to tell this story to anybody."

"Go on, please," Solly nodded his head encouragingly.

"Karen left to go to Bristol. She was away for a year during which time she had a baby. It was adopted and she came home again. I don't think anybody else knew outside the family."

"And the boy? The father of her child?"

Edith smiled serenely. "A lovely boy. He was far too good for her. Quiet and studious, but with real charm." She lifted her eyes to meet Solly's. "He was one of my piano pupils, a gifted lad with a place in the Royal Scottish Academy for Music and Drama all ready and waiting. But he didn't go. Karen's betrayal finished him."

"Her betrayal? What exactly do you mean?"

"Oh, he wanted to marry her, have the baby. He was that type of boy, Doctor. A giver. And besides, he was totally besotted. Not like Karen. She ended it all and left. The bitter irony was that she came back to Glasgow and waltzed straight into the Academy. Then of course she met Derek. And that was that."

"And the father? Is he still in the Glasgow area?" Cameron

asked.

"Oh, yes, Detective Constable, very much so."

Solly smiled at her. He'd expected that answer. There was more than a teacher's warmth in her description of her piano pupil. This was someone who might still be close.

"A name would be helpful," he nodded.

Solly watched as the woman's dark eyes filled with tears.

"Maurice Drummond," she whispered, then, covering her eyes with her hands, Edith Millar began to sob.

Chapter Twenty

Lorimer whistled as DC Cameron related Edith Millar's story.

"Okay. Let's see what Drummond's got to say about all that. Not mentioning his relationship with the murder victim is worth a bit more probing, don't you think?" Lorimer had already reached for his jacket when he remembered his new status. An acting Superintendent couldn't just waltz out of the building on a whim to interview somebody. He let the jacket slide onto the back of the chair.

"D'you want Drummond brought in?" Cameron asked, swiftly interpreting his boss's action. Lorimer chewed his lip. Did he? Maybe a quick visit after office hours might be better.

"No. Leave it with me. I want time to think about this first."

Cameron's face closed. He'd hoped for an immediate command to interview the Chorus Master himself, but evidently it was not to be. Catching sight of his officer's expression, Lorimer reminded himself of just how far this young policeman had progressed since being transferred to CID.

"Well done, by the way. We'd not have got this far if you hadn't thought of Edith Millar's reticence."

After Cameron had left, Lorimer sat, chin propped into his fingertips, pondering his next move. Would it profit the case to rake up Karen's past? Perhaps.

One question that certainly required an answer was what sort of relationship had existed between Maurice Drummond and Karen Quentin-Jones in their grown-up lives? Had that earlier animosity rankled between them? Casting his mind back, Lorimer could not recall anything adverse that Drummond had said about the dead woman. On the contrary, he'd been fulsome in his praise of her playing the night of George Millar's murder. Had their affair resumed, then? And what, if anything, did the surgeon know about his wife's teenage pregnancy?

Lorimer looked at the clock. There were hours to go before he could leave, with meetings that he couldn't duck out of. Blast Mitchison! For once the DCI heartily wished his senior colleague back in his own office building, his little empire. Then at least

Lorimer could pursue this new information to his heart's content. The telephone rang, intruding in his thoughts and signalling a resumption of his other, temporary duties.

Lorimer parked the car under the trees that lined the river Kelvin. Maurice Drummond had chosen a quiet area in which to live, yet it was only a short walk to the bustling activity of the West End.

"Well, his light's on anyway," he remarked to Solly, looking up at the bay windowed lounge. "Seems our Chorus Master is at home."

As the two men stood waiting for a reply to the security buzzer, a cyclist wobbled to a halt below them then heaved his bicycle up the short flight of steps to the doorway.

"Going in?" the young man asked them, inserting his key into the lock.

"Aye," Lorimer replied shortly. This was answered by a curious once up-and-down look from the cyclist.

Apparently deciding that the tall man and his bearded companion posed no threat, he pushed open the door and wheeled his cycle into the cavernous hallway.

"Thanks," Lorimer said as he headed for the main stair that led to Maurice Drummond's flat.

Solly's nod and smile appeared to disquiet the young man more than Lorimer's brusque manner for he stood staring after them as they turned the angle of the stone staircase until their footsteps had faded away.

"Mr Drummond. Good evening," Lorimer smiled as the Chorus Master opened his door.

Caught unawares, a flicker of something akin to fear crossed Maurice Drummond's face as he saw the two men standing on his doorstep. Interesting, thought Solly. Does he think we're here to arrest him? He watched carefully as Lorimer made the necessary introductions, smiling politely and extending his hand to the man whose evening they were about to interrupt so rudely. Drummond regained his composure quite quickly, but there was still that wariness that told Solly something: here was a man with secrets to hide.

"What can I do for you, Chief Inspector?" Drummond asked,

waving them into the big sitting room with its grand piano. "Please sit down," he added.

"Thanks," Lorimer replied, unbuttoning his coat and laying it across the piano stool. Solly followed the Chorus Master's eyes, sensing his inner dismay at Lorimer's small action. This was not merely a passing visit, then.

"We've recently received some new information regarding the murder of Karen Quentin-Jones," Lorimer began. "Information that directly concerns you, Mr Drummond."

Maurice Drummond's face was suddenly drawn as he sat down facing his two visitors, yet he continued to look straight at Lorimer, caught by the policeman's gaze almost like a rabbit trapped in the headlights of a car. He sat still and silent, moistening his lips with the edge of his tongue. Lorimer waited for a moment before continuing, increasing the man's discomfiture.

"We have been told that you and Mrs Quentin-Jones had an affair some time ago. Is that correct, sir?"

Maurice Drummond blinked as if he had been struck. "Yes. It's true," he whispered. "How did you find out?"

"Edith Millar told us."

An expression of relief instantly transformed the Chorus Master's face and he sank back into his chair. "Oh. That. But you can't seriously consider one youthful indiscretion has any consequences so many years down the line?" he scoffed.

Solly smiled. How much human behaviour revealed of itself, he thought.

"But perhaps that wasn't your only indiscretion, Mr Drummond?" he suggested quietly. He could sense Lorimer's eyes turning his way, and knew without looking that the policeman was frowning at him. But it was Maurice Drummond's eyes he wanted to see and they were once more full of anxiety. Then, dropping his gaze, he shook his head.

"No, it wasn't" he replied, his voice hoarse with emotion.

"Tell us how it all began again, would you, sir?" Solly asked politely.

Drummond's mouth tightened as he sought to regain his composure.

"I hadn't seen Karen for years," he began. "Not since, well you know about her trip down south. Oh, she had our child, right enough. He was given up for adoption. But you'll have had all the details from dear Edith," he said bitterly. "Anyhow, I met Karen again by chance. She was married to that prat, Quentin-Jones, and had just begun to play with the City of Glasgow. I was accompanying a soloist who was doing a one-off concert with them. We got talking afterwards and, well, one thing led to another," he finished lamely.

"So you resumed your relationship?" Lorimer asked.

"Yes. But it didn't last all that long. A year at the most, I'd say."

"Who broke it off?"

"She did. I expect the novelty of cheating on her husband had worn off. She became the dutiful little wife again and settled down to family life." Drummond passed a hand across his brow, "Look, that was nearly twenty years ago. We didn't remain lovers, in fact we didn't even remain friends. But I had no reason to kill her, you have to believe me!"

"Nobody has accused you of her murder, Mr Drummond, but any new information that comes to light has to be taken into consideration. Surely you realise that?" Lorimer said.

"Did Mr Quentin-Jones ever know of your relationship with his wife?" Solly asked.

Drummond frowned. "Not so far as I'm aware. I doubt very much if Karen ever admitted her infidelity. That wouldn't have been her style at all."

"And the earlier affair? When you were younger?" Lorimer continued.

"No. I'm certain she never told a soul. It was something she seemed to be thoroughly ashamed of. Karen was a person who liked to be in control, Chief Inspector. That youthful lapse was not something she'd have liked to acknowledge to anyone."

"Even her husband?"

"Especially her husband. The man thought the sun rose and set on his wife. There was no way Karen was going to spoil that illusion."

"But Edith Millar knew so presumably George Millar also

knew about it?"

Maurice Drummond gave a shrug. "If he did know he never referred to it. I don't like to speak ill of the dead, but George could be a nasty old queen when he wanted to. He'd have enjoyed tormenting Karen with a juicy titbit like that. So, no, I'm sure Edith never told him about us."

Lorimer's head was spinning with possibilities. Could Karen Quentin-Jones have murdered her lead violin to shut him up? Was this a case of blackmail rearing its ugly head? He could quite easily imagine the late Leader of the Orchestra adding that to his list of misdeeds. And what of Derek Quentin-Jones? Was the man really unaware of Karen's past? A doting husband had been known to strangle his cheating wife often enough.

"Where were you on the night of Karen's death, sir?" Solly asked quietly. He knew the answer already but needed to see the man's reaction.

"I've already told your colleague," Drummond said testily, "I was at the concert hall with the Chorus for their rehearsal. We have to fit them in around the Orchestra's schedule. I was out front the whole time then I went home."

"You weren't backstage at all, then?"

"No. I even had my coat and bag with me. I'd come straight from work, like most of my singers. You said that could be confirmed, didn't you?" he turned to Lorimer.

"Yes, the CCTV footage seems to corroborate what you say. As it does for most of the choir and members of the Orchestra," Lorimer replied slowly.

"Very well then." Drummond stared at each of them in turn. "I think that's about enough, gentlemen. If poking around in my dim and distant past has any bearing at all on Karen's murder, which I very much doubt, then I'll be only too pleased to have been of assistance, but now I'd like you both to leave."

Maurice Drummond had risen to his feet and was positively glaring at them both. Why this sudden volte face? Solly was curious. The man's irritation had no clear focus whatsoever. Lorimer had complied with the Chorus master's request, however, and was gathering up his coat.

"We'll keep you informed of any progress, sir," he remarked pleasantly as Drummond pulled open the door and held it wide. Solly thought about offering his hand in a polite gesture but one glance at the man's face changed his mind. His smile and nod were rewarded with a scowl as the door was shut firmly behind them.

Well," remarked Lorimer as they stepped into the night once more, "we certainly rattled his cage and no mistake."

"I think we did rather more than that," Solly replied.

"Aye. You fairly picked up on his vibes, didn't you? So he'd had another fling with the victim. Says it only lasted a year. Says they were never on great terms again. How are we to know he's speaking the truth?"

"Are you going to ask her husband?" Solly looked at Lorimer questioningly.

"Oh, God!" Lorimer groaned, running his fingers through his hair. "That's not a prospect I relish, believe me. Quentin-Jones is beside himself with grief. Am I supposed to add to that by telling him Maurice Drummond had his wife in the sack twenty years ago?"

They had stopped by the car and were standing under a street lamp. Weeks of sleepless nights had taken their toll on this man, too, thought Solly as he regarded the lines etched cruelly around Lorimer's eyes. Not for the first time he realised that Lorimer was a man on a crusade. He'd not rest until he'd found out who had committed these murders, and if they never came to light, then that would only add to his inner turmoil. He's lonely, too, Solomon thought, seeing the bleakness in the other man's face. And the pity of it was that the one person who could ease Lorimer's strain was Maggie.

Chapter Twenty-One

Rosie Fergusson knelt down in front of the living flame fire, her knees tickled by the white furry rug that Solly had placed there.

"Heavens!" she gasped, "Is there never any end to this cold! I can't remember when we've had such bitter weather so early in the year."

"Our just rewards for a terrific summer," Solly reminded her.

"Hmph! Maybe Maggie Lorimer had the right idea after all. Bet she's not freezing her socks off in Sarasota. What d'you think?" Rosie twisted round to catch sight of Solly's expression. "Would you up-sticks for a warmer climate?"

Solly regarded her thoughtfully through his horn-rimmed spectacles. Rosie's moans about the Scottish weather were nothing new, but he hesitated to share her feelings. Winter in Scotland had produced some of his best days out, the air clear and crisp giving views over the icy hills for miles and miles.

"That's a no then, I take it?" she grinned impishly up at him. "You wouldn't fancy trailing across the world with me to find some sunshine, eh?"

Solly tilted his head thoughtfully. She was teasing him, he knew, but there was an underlying question there. Would he go with Rosie if she were to leave Scotland?

"Would you stay here with me if I asked you to?" he replied gently, hunkering down by her side so that their two heads were inches apart.

Suddenly Rosie's face reddened and Solly watched with interest as she blinked rapidly. He put one finger against the bloom of her cheek and stroked gently, watching her eyes all the time.

"I didn't mean..."

"Oh, but I did," he interrupted her smoothly. "I really did."

Solly drew her chin towards him and kissed her lips then, as Rosie wriggled to be closer to him, his arm folded her into his embrace.

"Stay with me over Christmas. That could be a start. What do you think?" he said softly as they broke apart and was gratified to see Rosie's blonde head bob up and down in immediate agreement.

※　※　※

Flynn shivered as the frozen air hit his face. For ages now he'd imagined being outside, wished for it every day of this past week, but now, with DCI Lorimer by his side, he wasn't so sure. The naked trees swayed in the wind as they made their way from the hospital causing the boy to pull the parka hood over his head. It would hide the dressing as well, he thought, conscious of the pad still taped across his skull.

"Hope you've got central heating," he remarked.

"Aye," Lorimer grinned, "and an electric blanket for your bed. Don't worry, it's quite civilised even if the wife's away!"

"Good! Ah'm freezin' out here!"

"Come on, the car's just over there. I got the last space opposite the main door."

"Jeez!" Flynn's eyes were round with astonishment as they stopped next to Lorimer's car. "You got a second job, pal? What's with the wheels, then?" he asked, running his finger across the passenger door.

"No kids," Lorimer answered, his standard reply to the perennial question. The old Lexus still raised a few eyebrows among the younger members of the Division. Somehow, as he'd once overheard a new PC remark, a luxury car like that didn't sit comfortably with the other vehicles in the car park.

"Must cost a packet to run," Flynn went on, bending over to peer at the dashboard.

"In you go," Lorimer replied, opening the door for him. "It gets me from A to B, only quicker." He flashed a conspiratorial grin at the boy. For a fleeting moment Lorimer sensed that this was what it would feel like to have a son of his own, a lad he could share talk about cars and stuff.

Well, it hadn't happened for them and there was no more they wanted to do about it. Maggie and he had gone down the IVF road more than once before deciding it just wasn't to be.

"Hey, man, pretty smooth," Flynn grinned at Lorimer as the car purred out of the hospital gates. "I could get to like this!"

Lorimer smiled. If Flynn was as easily impressed as this then he'd be okay about the house. He had done his best to make the place homely, even remembering to switch on the heating to warm up the rooms.

It was a fifteen-minute drive from the Southern General Hospital during which time Flynn had asked Lorimer things about the job.

Why had he become a Busy in the first place? How had he come to work in CID? What was his wife doing abroad? The questions seemed to cover everything except the murders in Glasgow Royal Concert Hall, the very reason for Flynn being with him at all. Strangely, Lorimer was grateful for that. The case had caused him too many sleepless nights lately. As he turned into the driveway a few flakes of snow were beginning to smudge the windscreen. The security light beamed on revealing the red door of the garage and the white painted front door beyond the porch.

Flynn fell silent as he stepped out of the car and regarded his new home. It wasn't quite what he'd expected, a two-storey house on the corner of a street full of similar properties. Somehow he'd thought Lorimer would live in a bigger, grander place, a house in keeping with the smart old car.

There was a brass nameplate by the side of the door with the single word LORIMER engraved upon it and some evergreen plant growing up the wall, its tiny yellow flowers like wee stars shining in the overhead light.

"This is it," Lorimer told him, turning a key in the lock. "Home."

Joseph Alexander Flynn hesitated for a moment. It had been years since he'd stepped over any threshold that he could call home. What must it be like for Lorimer to come back here night after night, knowing a warm bed was waiting for him?

Interpreting his hesitation as reluctance, Lorimer put out a hand. "Come on in. It's freezing out there."

Flynn followed the tall policeman into a long hallway, pushing shut the door behind him. A waft of cold air crept up his back, making him step further into the house.

"This is the dining room and the kitchen's in here," Lorimer was saying, striding away ahead of him. Flynn looked around him. The room stretched from the front to the back of the house, divided by a pair of wooden doors that had been left wide open. Lorimer had disappeared into a kitchen beyond and he could hear the sound of a kettle being filled.

From where he was standing the dining room was at the far end, a round wooden table and four chairs placed in the centre. Here the two walls on either side were lined from floor to ceiling with books. Flynn's eyes roamed up and down the shelves. How could anyone find the time to read all that in one lifetime? Then he remembered what Lorimer had said about his wife being a teacher. Well. They always had their noses stuck into a book didn't they? There was desk under the window by the door where he'd come in. It held a lap top computer surrounded by heaps of paper and a framed photograph beside a green reading lamp. Flynn picked up the photo. It was of a woman, her head thrown back, dark curly hair blowing behind her. She was laughing into the lens, looking at the photographer as if they'd just shared a joke. Flynn replaced it on the desk exactly where it had been, wondering what it must be like to have a woman look at you like that.

"That's Maggie," Lorimer had come up unheard behind him, holding a tray with mugs of tea and chocolate biscuits. "My wife," he added. Flynn glanced at the man, catching sight of something softening in these hard blue eyes as he looked at the photograph.

"Come on upstairs. That's where the lounge is." Lorimer pushed open the door with his foot and re-entered the hallway. Flynn saw the light suddenly flooding the hallway and heard him pad upstairs. He turned his attention back to the laughing woman and gently touched the frame.

"D'you know ah'm here, missus?" he whispered.

Lorimer sat nursing a glass of whisky, listening to the rain pattering steadily against the upstairs windows. Flynn had been asleep for hours now. He'd wolfed down the meal that Sadie Dunlop had thrust upon Lorimer earlier in the day. ("Chicken broth and steak pie. Naethin' tae beat it!") Then the two of them had watched some television before the boy's eyelids had drooped shut, signalling an early night. He'd left Flynn to decide whether to close his own bedroom door or not and had been surprised when the boy left it ajar. The hospital room had been open at all times for security. Perhaps he'd simply become used to that, he mused. Tomorrow he'd be off duty and there would be plenty of time to see to Flynn's immediate needs.

For now, Lorimer realised, he needed a bit of quiet to himself to sort out his own thoughts. He'd been struck by how Flynn had reacted to Maggie's photograph. Okay, maybe he took her for granted, but seeing his wife through the eyes of another man made him realise just how lovely and desirable she was. Only three and a bit more weeks, he told himself. Then young Flynn would be happily ensconced in a wee flat of his own and he'd be off to sunny Florida.

But before that happened, would he be any further forward with solving this double murder? Perhaps that depended upon the boy sleeping across the landing. He took another gulp of whisky, remembering his recent interview with Derek Quentin-Jones. At least he still had a wife, he'd reminded himself, even if she was several thousand miles away. The surgeon had been so terribly bereft, crying once more as Lorimer had revealed his wife's infidelity as gently as he could. Had he known about it?

Lorimer pursed his mouth into a thin line as he recalled the man's words.

"I'm sterile, Chief Inspector. Now I know that man fathered not just one but both of Karen's children." Seeing Lorimer's scepticism, the surgeon had assured him it was true. A urinary infection had led to other, more discreet tests, confirming that the consultant surgeon could not have been the father of the child he had believed to be his daughter. He'd never asked Karen for the identity of her lover, choosing instead to engage a private detective to have her followed. With no further signs of her infidelity, he had eventually settled back into what he'd believed to be a secure marriage.

Having the identity of Tina's father made known to him was obviously a fresh blow and Lorimer had let him linger in his office until he could regain his composure.

Far from blaming the acting Superintendent for being the

bearer of bad news, Quentin-Jones seemed positively grateful to have another man to talk to. All the anguished emotion poured out. Behind his words of sympathy, Lorimer was taking a professional note of the man's behaviour: this wasn't the kind of man who committed a crime of passion. He might be brave enough with a scalpel when it came to saving lives, but Lorimer would lay money on it that Derek Quentin-Jones was incapable of any act of violence.

As he drained his whisky, his eyes fell on the telephone out in the hallway. Should he try to speak to Maggie? Best not, in case he woke the boy, he thought. His eyes closed and he let the glass slip from his fingers onto the carpet. Another minute and he would shift, just another minute.

Flynn saw the light on in the lounge and from the doorway of his bedroom he made out the sleeping form of the policeman curled into the sofa. Glancing back into the room he noticed the extra blanket that he'd tossed onto the floor.

As he draped the thick blanket over Lorimer, the policeman muttered something in his sleep and turned over. An unfamiliar feeling swelled up in the boy as he looked down at the figure under the blanket. He swallowed and blinked, staring at this man who had taken him into his own home. Then, with a sigh that seemed to come from his very soul, he switched off the table lamp and quietly tiptoed back to bed.

Chapter Twenty-Two

Jimmy Greer grinned with satisfaction as his fingers flew across the keyboard. There! That would fix the smarmy bastard! Weeks had gone by since his encounter with Lorimer but the event still rankled with the journalist. It had given him some little pleasure to see the lack of progress in the concert hall case although as time went on it was harder to find copy relating to the two murders. He pressed the print button as he reread his piece.

POLICE FAILURE TO MAKE CONCERT HALL ARREST

Despite the time and manpower spent on the recent murders of George Millar and his colleague Karen Quentin-Jones, Strathclyde Police have failed to make any significant progress in this case. Lack of concrete evidence seems to be the underlying problem, according to police sources, although extensive forensic testing has been under way since the first murder. Even the presence of Doctor Solomon Brightman, criminal profiler, has made no apparent impression on this case.

A senior Strathclyde officer insisted that reports that the Crown Office had insufficient evidence to arrest a prime suspect were not true.

"There is no prime suspect in this case," acting Superintendent William Lorimer claimed. "The case is ongoing and there are many aspects still under investigation."

What these aspects are Superintendent Lorimer refused to say but there is a feeling of disquiet within the force over the failure to make an arrest almost two months after the first murder. The two murder weapons, a percussion hammer and a harp string, are believed to be crucial to the investigation and sources close to the case believe that the perpetrator of the killings is still in the city. The victims were both killed in Glasgow Royal Concert Hall within days of one another and extensive police work was required in and around the area. George Millar, Leader of the City of Glasgow Orchestra, and Karen Quentin-Jones, his second in command, were well known figures to Glasgow concert goers and their loss to the city's musical life has been immense. Despite the tragedies, the Concert Hall's programme continues as normal and the Orchestra will be performing their usual Christmas Classics concert this Sunday.

Although several of the Orchestra members have been questioned by the police, it seems that Superintendent Lorimer, who continues to lead the case, is no nearer to finding the killer.

A source at the Crown Office claimed to be under pressure to release the bodies for burial with the result that the funeral service for Karen Quentin-Jones is scheduled to take place in Glasgow Cathedral this Friday.

Greer smirked as he picked up the newly printed page. That would be one in the eye for Lorimer!

Lorimer was perfectly aware that the Crown Office had deemed it possible to release the body of Karen Quentin-Jones for burial before Christmas.

Of course cremation would have been out of the question given the circumstances of her death. It was three days since Greer's piece in the Gazette and Lorimer was poring over the latest memo from Edinburgh. As he read the document in his hand, he wondered if there would ever be a need for an exhumation. He hoped not. Rosie and the forensic scientists had amassed a huge quantity of material that could be used as evidence if they were ever lucky enough to come up with the other half of its equation. Carl Bekaert had given swabs for testing but so far there was no matching DNA trace. If he could have his way, Lorimer would have the whole damn orchestra tested, the Chorus too, if need be. He knew fine, as Greer had so unsubtly hinted, that the trail had gone cold.

The only good thing about that, he thought to himself, was that he'd be able to take his holiday to Florida. Five more days and he'd be picking up Maggie's mum and heading for the airport.

Lorimer felt in his pocket for the black tie that he'd folded this morning. The service was at two o'clock in Glasgow Cathedral and there would be a considerable police presence there, not just representatives from the investigating team but with uniformed officers providing security measures.

He'd made his peace with the consultant surgeon, thankfully.

At first the man had been outraged at the Orchestra's decision to carry on with their Christmas programme, demanding that Lorimer make them stop. Quentin-Jones had shouted at him, his anger reaching a peak then he'd broken down again. Now, with the revelations about Karen's past and the seeming insensitivity of the Orchestra, he simply seemed exhausted by it all.

Lorimer was used to grown men weeping in his office, one of the more unpleasant aspects of this job. Sometimes emotional storms would result in a confession, just like the television, but that didn't happen often enough in real life. He wondered briefly whose tears would fall today for Karen Quentin-Jones.

The clouds that had threatened rain all morning seemed to have shifted to the east letting a pale shaft of sunlight filter through the stained glass windows of Glasgow Cathedral. Lorimer heard the sonorous notes of the organ and felt its vibration through the soles of his shoes as he made his way forward. Glancing towards the choir stalls, Lorimer saw the members of the City of Glasgow Chorus. Someone had pulled out the stops for Karen's funeral, he realised, wondering if Brendan Phillips's hand was in this. He looked around, recognising several members of the Orchestra before taking a seat near the back.

Whether or not Karen Quentin-Jones had been a popular member of the community, the turnout at her funeral was certainly respectable. Most of the congregation were middle aged or older but there was a row of youngsters near the front. Beside the consultant surgeon sat a girl with long dark hair falling down her back. As she turned her face towards Quentin-Jones, Lorimer saw the pale face with its firm jaw. Younger and perhaps even prettier, there was no question whose daughter this was. What else might Tina Quentin-Jones be feeling, apart from the obvious grief at losing her mother? Lorimer ground his teeth. There were so many victims never taken into account in a murder case; children, parents, friends, a whole gallery of suffering.

His eyes slid along the row to where an elderly lady sat, her face veiled from sight. She sat upright, hands crossed on top of a stick, staring straight ahead as if to blot out the murmur of conversation around her. Beside her a woman's grey head was bowed in prayer. For a moment Lorimer thought he recognised Edith Millar then his view of the front row was masked by the arrival of the undertaker and the request for the congregation to stand.

He watched as the coffin was brought forward, noting that it was being borne by professionals in their black livery, not by family members. Then, as the coffin was laid across the trestles, a sound like deep organ pipes came from the choir stalls as the Chorus began their vocal tribute to the dead violinist. Lorimer listened, moved in spite of himself as they intoned Taverner's "Song to Athene". As the women's voices reached the triumphant crescendo, he felt the hairs on the back of his neck prickle then the Basses resumed their sonorous notes, letting the sound fade into darkness. There was a long moment of silence as the notes reverberated into the vaults. After the obligatory coughing and shuffling, the minister began his address.

Lorimer hadn't intended to follow the funeral party to the hotel afterwards but professional curiosity managed to subdue any qualms about obeying protocol.

Quentin-Jones had booked a room at Lang's, the upmarket hotel directly across from Glasgow Royal Concert Hall, much to Lorimer's surprise. Okay, it was the nearest decent place to the Cathedral, but surely its proximity to the murder scene was in poor taste? Or was the bereaved husband so consumed with grief that such niceties had been lost on him?

Sipping the whisky he'd been offered by a solemn faced waiter, Lorimer glanced around the room.

Brendan Phillips was in conversation with the Chorus Master when he caught sight of Lorimer. His beckoning finger and tentative smile were all the invitation Lorimer required. That Maurice Drummond was there under the circumstances surprised Lorimer. How would Quentin-Jones feel about seeing his wife's former lover there? But, he reasoned to himself, as musical director for the funeral service he might be expected to put in an appearance afterwards.

"Chief Inspector. This is someone I want you to meet," Brendan began. His companion tilted his head towards Lorimer in a gesture of politeness. "Maurice, Chief Inspector Lorimer.

Maurice Drummond, Director of Music for the City of Glasgow Chorus."

"Actually Brendan, we've already met," Maurice Drummond replied dryly. He took Lorimer's hand in a firm grasp. "I didn't think I'd have the pleasure of meeting one of Strathclyde's finest today," Drummond said, dropping Lorimer's hand like a stone.

"No? Well we usually have a presence in such cases," Lorimer replied. "That Taverner was something pretty special," he said, swiftly changing the subject. Well done."

The Chorus Master shrugged. "He wrote it, I only hold the stick."

"Maurice, the Chief Inspector was asking me some time ago for your first name. I don't think that's something I've ever known," Brendan said teasingly.

A tiny frown crossed Drummond's brow. "No, Brendan. I don't think I've ever mentioned it to you, have I?" he said, his voice quiet, belying the obvious disapproval in his tone. "Excuse me, gentlemen, there's somebody over there I need to talk to. Nice to have met you again, Lorimer," he said politely.

"Oh, dear, looks like I've ruffled poor old Maurice's feathers," Brendan laughed, regarding the Chorus Master's retreating back. Lorimer eyed the man speculatively. Had Brendan Phillips deliberately riled the man? And if so, why? He'd never come across as a particularly malicious individual; in fact he'd appeared quite the opposite up until now, anxiously solicitous for his musicians. But perhaps that was the answer: the choristers weren't within his jurisdiction, were they? Was he beginning to sense some sort of rivalry between orchestra and Chorus?

"What does the "C" stand for, Chief Inspector?" Brendan asked.

"Well, if he doesn't want you to know I don't think I ought to say," Lorimer told him, his voice flat and even as though the conversation bored him, then drained the last of his whisky. "Better be going. I'll be in touch."

Lorimer made his way across the room to where the Quentin-Jones party stood, placing his empty glass on a convenient table without breaking stride.

The consultant surgeon saw him at once.

"My condolences, sir, once again," Lorimer said, taking the man's hand in a firm grasp.

"Thank you, Chief Inspector. It was good of you to come," Quentin-Jones replied, his words gracious enough, but his voice husky with emotion.

He looked suddenly older, the handsome face drained of colour. Lorimer guessed the man hadn't had a decent night's sleep in the weeks since Karen had first gone missing.

He recalled the surgeon's guilt as he'd agonised over his purchase of the stolen violin.

"If only I'd told her. If only I'd known!" he'd cried to Lorimer in his storm of remorse. Lorimer had kept silent. How could he placate the man when his own suspicions were that Quentin-Jones's dealings with George Millar might indeed have led to Karen's death? Suddenly Lorimer regretted his impulse to follow the funeral party. Surely the very sight of the policeman was heaping anguish on the bereaved man. Besides, he should really be getting back to work.

Lorimer was almost at the door of the hotel when a touch to his sleeve made him turn. It was the girl with the long dark hair, Karen's daughter.

"Chief Inspector?"

"Miss Quentin-Jones." Lorimer put out his hand but the girl seemed not to notice. She was looking at him in a distracted manner.

"I just wanted to ask you. Will you find him? Whoever killed my mother?"

"I hope so."

"Oh!" Suddenly the girl appeared more agitated than before. "But how would you be sure that you'd got the right person? I mean…what if you made a mistake?"

Lorimer frowned at her, unsure of how to reply, wondering what had prompted the strange question.

"Tina!" a voice called from within the room.

"I'd better go. Sorry."

Lorimer watched as she practically ran across the room to

where her father was standing then he looked up to meet the surgeon's gaze.

There was no disguising his expression of utter hostility. But to whom was it directed, to his daughter or Lorimer himself?

Pulling the door towards him Lorimer felt that Karen's funeral had raised more questions than ever, not least about the relationship between her husband and her daughter.

Chapter Twenty-Three

"Play something to me, will you?"

"Like, what?"

Simon rolled over onto his side, considering. "Something sad. Sad but not morbid," he added, qualifying his request with a grin that lit up his eyes.

Chris tucked the fiddle under his chin and paused for a moment, bow in the air, his eyes looking beyond the man on the bed and out towards the grey patch of sky framed in the window. Then he looked back fondly at the strings and began to play.

The strains of the music filled the room with their sense of unfulfilled longing as "The Dark Island" reminded the two men of a people who had been bereft of their homeland so long ago. As the music trembled and died, Chris lowered his bow and smiled.

"Will that do you?"

"Ah, such sweet music! You're a born romantic, so you are, Hunter!" Simon teased. "All that Scottish sentimentality, it's really got to you, hasn't it?"

"We learnt that at school," Chris told him. "Lots of the old pipe tunes were standard fare for violin lessons down in Bristol. That one's always stuck with me for some reason, though." He smiled a secret smile to himself.

"Thinking about when you were wee?" Simon asked, watching the other man's face.

Instead of replying to his question, Chris picked up the bow again and began a lively reel. He swayed from side to side in exaggerated sweeps, his foot tapping wildly on the bedroom carpet.

Simon leapt to his feet, clapping his hands and twirling around in time to the music, sending out the occasional "Heuch!" The music became louder and faster as the violinist changed the tempo, jigs and strathspeys following in rapid succession until Simon fell, exhausted and laughing, back onto the rumpled bed-clothes.

"Oh, man," he said, weak with laughter and the effort of prancing around the room, "That was just what we needed!"

Simon sank back onto the pillow, one hand behind his head, his cheeks flushed and the red-gold hair clinging damply to his forehead. "The perfect antidote to a funeral," he murmured.

Chris Hunter turned away to put the violin back into its case. "Blast!"

"What's wrong?"

"I need a new bow. This one's a wreck. Look at it!"

Simon yawned and waved a dismissive hand. "Forget it. Come to bed. Brendan'll get you something tomorrow if you ask him." He looked over at the man sitting on the edge of the bed, noting the sudden slump to his shoulders. "Wish you'd taken up George's offer, now?" he asked, a malicious glint in his eye.

"Hell, no! I couldn't afford it then and I can't now. A new fiddle? Any idea what a decent one would set me back?"

"Aye, poor old Georgie boy. Who'd have thought he was dealing in suss instruments, eh?"

Something in the other man's voice made Chris Hunter look up.

"Did you know what he was up to?"

"Me?" Simon feigned innocence, his eyes laughing behind their wide stare. "A clean-living country boy like me? Come off it!"

"Did you, though, seriously?"

Simon shook his head. "Never suspected a thing. Knew he did the odd line, well he hardly kept that a secret, did he?"

"No," Chris replied. "Liked to flaunt that, didn't he?"

"Aye, it fair annoyed the old women, didn't it? Remember how Karen used to go on about it?"

"Come on, Si, she's only just been buried, for goodness sake," Chris protested.

"With full honours," Simon replied. "Wonder how much Drummond charged for the Chorus's services today."

"Surely they'd be singing for free?"

"You don't know Maurice Drummond. I bet even now he's invoicing Quentin-Jones."

"I don't believe that," Chris replied shortly. "Nobody could be that cold-blooded."

Simon ran a hand through his hair. "Someone is, though," he

said darkly. "Someone's cold-blooded enough to do in two of our orchestra."

"You think it might be Drummond? Why?" Chris twisted around to look at Simon's expression.

"There was something between him and Karen."

"What sort of thing?" Chris asked, a frown creasing his brow.

"Och, I don't know really. I'd seen them arguing together. There was no love lost between that pair, I can tell you."

"Have you told this to the police?"

Simon made a face. "Tell them what? That Drummond didn't like our assistant principal fiddle? There were quite a few who would come in to that category. Come on, let's be honest, she wasn't everyone's favourite person, was she?"

Chris shook his head and sighed. "I suppose not, but it's wrong to speak ill of the dead. Especially today."

Simon laughed, "Nothing you or I can say will hurt her now, pal."

"I was just thinking of the family," Chris protested.

"Aye, I know. You're a soft-hearted lad, aren't you," Simon told him, reaching out and grasping Chris's wrist. "That's one of the reasons I love you," he whispered, drawing Chris's hand up to his mouth. He began sucking gently at their fingertips until Chris gave a groan and swung his body onto the bed beside him.

The light was beginning to fade when Chris finally fell asleep. Simon observed the faint shadow of his chest as it rose and fell in a steady rhythm. There was only that whisper of gentle breathing in the room now and the murmuring hum of the ioniser, mere shadows of sound. Even familiar shapes became blurred and indistinct; the fiddle in its open case was a dull gleam of polished wood. Simon stared at it for a long moment.

"I wonder what's happened to her violin," he asked himself dreamily, then a sudden shiver made him pull the covers over his naked feet.

Chapter Twenty-Four

"We've found the violin!" Jo Grant stood breathless opposite Lorimer, her hands on his desk, her face radiant.

"Well, well! Sit yourself down, Inspector, and tell all," Lorimer smiled at her enthusiasm but his own heart had jumped at Jo's words.

"It was in Vienna. In the back of a van that was transporting instruments for the Berlin Philharmonic. Can you believe that? I mean they're one of the best known…"

"Okay, just the main facts. How was it spotted?" Lorimer cut in.

Somewhat chastened, Jo continued, "The truck, van, whatever it was, had been stopped at customs for a spot check on the Austrian/Czech border. Seems they've had trouble with drugs coming over from Eastern Europe by way of Prague. The Orchestra had just done a series of concerts in Prague and had returned to Vienna for the next part of their tour."

"And the violin was found at the border?"

"No. The truck was stopped at the border for a check. Nothing was found. Squeaky clean lot the Berlin Phil," Jo remarked, "unlike some of ours," she grimaced.

"Anyway it prompted the driver and his second in command to take a look for themselves. And, bingo! Here was a violin surplus to their listed instruments."

"How did you find this out?"

"Well, we'd posted the violin as missing on a website that's dedicated to stolen instruments. Company called Smartaction operate it. The Berlin chap cottoned on to that and this fax came through," she glanced at her watch, "twenty minutes ago."

"What took you so long?" Lorimer asked dryly then smiled as Jo made a face at him. Here was one officer who didn't feel intimidated by her boss. The realisation came with something approaching delight. Suddenly all his misgivings about DI Grant and Superintendent Mark Mitchison vanished.

"Have the Germans any idea how the instrument came to be there at all or is that a daft question?"

"Yes," Jo grinned. "Not a single soul is putting up their hands for this one, but I will tell you that the First Violin in the Karlovy Vary Symphony Orchestra reported a Vincenzo Panormo missing a few years ago. They've collected the insurance now, right enough. There was a certain reluctance on the original owner's part to identify the violin, I believe."

"Aye, I can believe that right enough," Lorimer growled, remembering the fantastic price tag that the instrument had carried. With that kind of insurance money the owner would surely have bought some other violin by now. "So what's happening to our instrument?"

"We've got the full co-operation of the Austrian police. They've made sure nobody's touched the violin and just in case, they've kindly fingerprinted the whole orchestra and crew!"

"Good Lord! You have been busy while I was out enjoying myself, haven't you?"

"Was it grim?" she asked suddenly, remembering the funeral. Then, as Lorimer didn't respond, she made another face. "Well it's not been a typical Friday afternoon. Never is around here, though, is it? Anyway, they're bringing the violin over personally. One of their officers is apparently coming across to London for Christmas so she's arriving at Glasgow Airport some time tomorrow afternoon."

Lorimer sat back into his chair. If the Vincenzo Panormo hadn't been too messed about, could Rosie's team find anything on the violin that would link it to Karen's killer?

"Jo," he said slowly, "Get on to the Crown Office. Tell them we need a warrant to DNA test the City of Glasgow Orchestra and Chorus. Oh, and extend that to the backstage crew and the admin. staff, will you?"

Jo's eyebrows shot up in at his request but she rose immediately, giving Lorimer a mock salute as she left his office.

Less than a week to go, a little voice reminded Lorimer as he picked up the telephone. Just six days and he should be with Maggie once again. But would this new lead keep him in Scotland? The thought filled Lorimer with a feeling of foreboding. Would his career drive a total wedge between his wife and himself, destroying their marriage once and for all?

✳ ✳ ✳

Derek Quentin-Jones put down the telephone, noting the hand shaking as it replaced the receiver clumsily in its cradle. Would this nightmare never end? He pulled open the desk drawer and drew out the bottle of pills. At least they'd stop the shakes long enough to let him concentrate on what he should do next. He hadn't yet told Tina about the terms of her mother's will.

Her mother, he thought bitterly, who had betrayed them both for so many years. Or had she? Had Karen been aware that Maurice Drummond had fathered their daughter? Derek slammed his fist down hard on the leather surface.

It was time to stop deluding himself. Of course she had known! And she'd been laughing at him every time she'd looked at Tina and seen something of her lover in the girl's face.

Beyond the telephone was a portrait of Karen in evening dress, the Vincenzo Panormo clasped across her bosom. Her smile was confident as she looked at the photographer. Here is a woman who knows what success tastes like, she seemed to be saying with her eyes, her smile, the arch of her neck.

Suddenly Derek caught up the picture and threw it with all his force against the wall. It smashed with an unsatisfying tinkle of glass making him spring up and stride across the room to where it lay in fragments. Looking down at the shattered face he saw that her smile was still intact. With a cry of anguish he stamped his foot again and again over the splintered frame finally grinding it into the wooden floor below his heel.

His hands flew to his face, covering his eyes. She wouldn't make him weep. Not now and not ever again.

"I think someone's been following me," Tina said, putting down her coffee cup and looking across at Chris.

"Oh, Tina. You're just imagining things. It's the strain of everything, your term exams and your mum's funeral," Chris Hunter placed his hand over the girl's but she snatched it away angrily.

"No I'm not! I know there was somebody following me last night after I'd left Dad at home," she insisted.

"Where were you going?"

"Och, I know it was mean, but I just couldn't stand being on my own with him in the house any longer. He's been so odd lately, giving me strange looks all he time."

"Come on, Tina, think how he's feeling. Until they find someone for these murders he'll not be able to rest easy. I can't begin to imagine what the pair of you have been going through these past weeks."

Tina sighed, "Okay, I know he's under a massive strain. So'm I. But I'm not imagining things, Chris. That's the second time I've felt someone following me along the road. I was just going down to the underground. I wanted to be over here," she swept her hand from the coffee shop's glass fronted window towards Byres Road.

"Studentsville," the young violinist smiled at her. "Why don't you ask your dad if you can move into a flat after Christmas? Surely you can find some pals to share with?"

Tina shook her head. "I can't leave him on his own just yet; maybe next year when I start Junior Honours."

"Anyway, back to your secret admirer," Chris teased, in an attempt to lift the girl's spirits. "Did you get a look at him?"

"No. He was wearing one of these hooded tops. I couldn't see his face." She grinned suddenly. "Och, it was probably some ned wanting to nick my mobile phone."

"So you won't be going to tell the police?" he asked.

Tina looked up sharply. "Should I?"

Chris shrugged. "It's up to you, but they've got a lot on their plate right now, haven't they?"

"I suppose so," she said slowly, stirring the froth on her latte.

"Well, if you ask me, it's about time you passed your driving test then you wouldn't be wandering about Pollokshields at all hours."

"Aye, you're right," she sighed. "After failure number three I just couldn't be bothered. Mum had promised me a wee runabout for my birthday if I passed," Tina swallowed suddenly and reached out to grip her friend's hand.

Chris watched as she bit her lip and held back the tears. She'd been so brave, coping with all these weeks of horror. He'd have cracked up if it had been his mum, he thought, suddenly remembering the face of the woman who'd raised him and given him such unconditional love and affection. But Karen hadn't been like that, had she? The impression he'd had of Tina's mother was of a different character altogether, one for whom success and a wealthy lifestyle were paramount. Still, she'd been Tina's mum and the girl was obviously missing her. And it was extra hard at this time of year, Chris thought as strains of White Christmas floated over the crowded café as if to remind them of the retail countdown to 25th December.

"Anyway, how is life with Simon?" Tina asked, her lip curling in a way that startled Chris, it reminded him so much of Karen.

"Fine. Oh, I know you don't approve, my pet, but we get along just fine. He had the room all ready for me to move back in. Did I tell you? Even had an ioniser."

"You and your allergies!" Tina mocked. "Anyway, I'm just being selfish. Simon Corrigan doesn't like me so I know I'm not that welcome up at his place."

"Don't be daft. Anyway, it's my place too. I pay half the rent. Don't see why I can't have my friends over when I want."

"Maybe he thinks I'm trying to lure you away from him!" she teased.

Chris laughed, "I've told him you're my coffee-mate!"

"And what's that supposed to be? The gay equivalent of tea and sympathy?"

"Of course," Chris replied lightly. "Everyone knows a girl's best friend is her gay man. Right?"

"Mum thought you'd be a lovely friend for me. She told me that the night she introduced you. Did I ever tell you?"

Chris pulled a face. "Me? Your boyfriend? I can't see that happening, can you?"

Tina smiled up at him suddenly. "Well maybe you're right. I will try to get a flat over here next year. And pass my driving test. Then all the nice boys will come flocking!"

Chris Hunter smiled back at her. It was probably true. With her mane of glossy dark hair and these elfin features Tina

Quentin-Jones was a real babe. He was happy with Si, and surely he wanted her to have that same, settled feeling. So why did the idea of her having a host of male admirers fill him with a sense of dismay?

Chapter Twenty-Five

Sunday dawned clear and cold, the sky filled with the sort of pearly brightness that foretold the threat of a storm to come. Lorimer stretched under the duvet, remembering the previous day's events. That Austrian policewoman had been thoroughly efficient, bringing the old violin to them. It had been taken to Rosie Fergusson and the forensic pathologist had gone to work immediately. Weekend or no weekend, Rosie was ready and willing to drop whatever plans she might have made. Calling him late last night she'd told Lorimer that her first impression was that they might be in luck. There did appear to be traces on the violin case and the instrument itself that could provide fresh evidence.

Lorimer's thoughts turned to the Orchestra. Tonight the whole lot of them would be undergoing DNA testing, a procedure that might nail someone for the two murders at last. Today they'd all be up at Glasgow Royal Concert Hall for the Christmas performance. Harps and angels, Brendan Phillips had said. Well, if everything went according to plan, there could be one less angel in the firmament before Christmas.

Lorimer turned onto his side, dragging the cover tightly over his nose. There were so many threads to this case. George Millar's involvement in drugs might have been no more than a recreational sideline for the violinist.

Carl Bekaert had provided no leads there, unfortunately. Nor had Flynn. Despite the occasional hint, Lorimer had been unable to worm the names of the boy's drug dealing cronies out of him. It had disquieted the policeman to think the boy might be contacting them from this house and he'd been careful to monitor any outgoing telephone calls. But it appeared that Flynn really had dropped these low life friends of his for good. They'd got on well these past weeks, even Maggie's mum had called round to see the boy and fuss over him. As Flynn's injuries had healed so too had something within the boy, some chip on his shoulder that had formed over years of neglect and mistrust. But still he hadn't opened up to Lorimer about his links with George Millar's dealers.

At least Millar's stolen instrument scam seemed to be coming more to light now that the Panormo was back. The link with the Czech orchestra was being investigated and the Austrian police officer had hinted that there was sufficient evidence from loss adjustors in various parts of Europe to obtain some kind of pattern. Computers, he thought. Modern technology. It was a wonder anyone could sneeze without being noticed, these days, let alone get away with murder. But someone had, he reminded himself, and they were playing a dangerous game, if what Solly believed was correct.

The psychologist had insisted that the killer was still in the area, still working at a profession, still appearing to be a respectable member of society.

"Are you wanting your breakfast?" A voice interrupted Lorimer's thoughts and he squirmed around in the bed to see Flynn's grinning face at his doorway. In his hands the boy held a tray with cereal and toast and two large mugs of tea.

"A wee treat seeing as it's my last Sunday here," he went on.

Lorimer sat up suddenly, pulling the duvet around his naked form. Of course. The day after tomorrow Flynn would be going to his new flat.

"Shove over a bit," Flynn said, plonking himself down by Lorimer's side, tray still balanced in his hands. "Watch you don't spill the tea," he added, as Lorimer heaved himself up into sitting position.

"You sound just like my wife," Lorimer groaned.

"Miss her, don't you?" Flynn asked, giving Lorimer a shrewd stare.

"Aye," came the short reply as Lorimer bit into the slice of toast and marmalade.

"I wanted to say, well, thanks for everything. You know? It was dead nice of you to let me stay here," Flynn stuttered to a halt and picked up the mug of tea to hide his embarrassment.

"It's okay. It's been good for me to have you here. Meant I couldn't keep the place a tip the way it was after Maggie left."

"Doubt if I'd've noticed," Flynn grinned. "Don't suppose housework'll be a priority when I get the keys tomorrow. Still, you never know. It'll be nice to have my own pad, all the same.

Shame about the TV. I'll miss that," he added, giving Lorimer's arm a dunt with his elbow.

"Aye, well, you'll just have to save up for one of your own. And a licence," Lorimer told him. "That job with the parks department isn't bad at all. You can decide later on if you want to take a college course. I found out about the grants. You'd be eligible for the maximum allowance if you decided to go."

"That right? I might just do that, " Flynn said. "Know what, though? They're going tae keep me in the office for the first few weeks, just till they think ah'm fit for the heavy stuff. I get to do the odd jobs and find out all about how the parks are run."

"Anyway, how about finishing this lot through in the lounge and letting me get up?" Lorimer asked.

Flynn grinned at the policeman and scooped up the tray. It was funny how life worked out, he thought, as he wandered into the sunlit lounge. Here he was, living the life of Riley, a new flat and a new job awaiting him, things he'd only ever dreamed about. And all because he'd run into that van. If he hadn't, if he'd been caught by Raincoat that day, what might have happened? Would Lorimer have put the screws on him? Made him tell all about Seaton? So far he'd body swerved that line of questioning though he knew fine that the police still wanted him to name names. Well, Allan Seaton was far too tricky a customer to cross, safe flat or not. Glasgow was just too wee for comfort. He never knew when he'd run into Seaton and his cronies. And if he'd grassed them up he might as well have stayed under that van.

Lorimer knew it, he mused. He'd not pressed him too sore for information, guessing that Flynn was afraid of what repercussions could ensue. He'd made one mistake in telling that big ape, Greer, what he knew about George Millar. Life was suddenly a precious commodity to Flynn, something he wasn't about to endanger by any more loose talking.

"What are you up to today?" Lorimer asked, appearing at the door of the lounge, pulling his arms through his shirt sleeves.

"Dunno. Don't have a whole lot of packing to do, have I? How about you? Do you have to go into work?"

Lorimer nodded. "'Fraid so. We've got a hell of a lot to do

before I disappear on Wednesday."

"I'll miss it here," Flynn mumbled, turning away so that Lorimer couldn't see his face.

"No more of Sadie's soups, eh? You'll just have to frequent the station canteen," Lorimer chuckled. Sadie Dunlop might be the scourge of the Division but she had a heart of gold and had kept thrusting cartons of home made soup into Lorimer's hands every day since Flynn had come to live with him.

"Nae fear. You won't catch me doon there. Not for any reason."

Lorimer grinned. "I'll not tell Sadie that. She'd be raging at your ingratitude."

"Aw, man, don't do that! Och, you're joking. She's been dead nice giving us all that stuff. Tell you what. Ask her for the recipe for that chicken soup. I'll maybe try it in ma new place, eh?"

Lorimer whistled as he closed the front door behind him. It had been good leaving home knowing that Flynn was safe there. He'd drummed it into the boy to put the chain on any time he was alone. Sure enough most nights Lorimer had to wait for the front door to be opened to him on his return home.

They'd got into the habit of watching TV together, although Lorimer was careful not to fall asleep on the sofa as he'd done the night of Flynn's arrival. He'd been mortified to find himself wrapped in the boy's spare blanket early the following morning.

The tune in his head beat a rhythm, four more days, four more days, it told him. He glanced in the rear view mirror as he pulled into the street and headed back into town. It was early for churchgoers but there was one red estate car outside a neighbour's house with two men in the front; a taxi for Mrs Ellis, perhaps? He'd seen nothing of his nosey neighbour these past months and wasn't sorry.

As the Lexus turned the corner Lorimer was unable to see the red car creep slowly forward until it was level with his own gate.

When the front door clicked open Flynn assumed that Lorimer had come back for something he'd forgotten and so the footsteps on the stair didn't bother him. He was laughing out loud at Tom and Jerry's latest cartoon antics as the cat splatted against the garden gate but his laugh turned to a cry as the hands went around his throat.

"Havin' fun in the polisman's hoose, are ye, pal?" a familiar voice came from behind him. Flynn wrestled out of the grasp and shot out of the chair, standing panting as he watched Seaton grinning at him. The green eyes narrowed. Like cat's eyes, Flynn thought, suddenly seeing something flicker in their depths.

"Whit the hell are you doin' here?"

"Aw, that's no very nice, Flynn. Can a mate no' go and visit his old pals, eh?" Seaton stood laughing at him, arms folded across his chest.

He was a head smaller than Flynn but his stocky frame was all muscle from years in the boxing ring. He was quick, too and liked to hurt people for fun.

"How did ye know ah wis here?" Flynn rubbed the sore place on his neck where Seaton's hands had gripped him moments before.

Allan Seaton tapped the side of his nose. "Ways and means, man, ways and means. Anyway, now that I'm here how about making us a wee cup of tea, eh? That would be nice and friendly, now wouldn't it?"

Flynn hesitated for a moment. He didn't trust Seaton. How did he know he wouldn't nick something from the room while he was downstairs in the kitchen? But did he really have any alternative? The dealer was sitting down now, casually flicking channels with the remote control, legs crossed in front of him.

"Ah, this is mair like it!" he said, finding an old gangster movie where the action involved two men slugging it out on screen. He looked up and winked. Flynn got the message loud and clear. With an inward sigh the boy turned and headed for the stairs leaving the dealer absorbed in the movie.

The kettle was just coming to the boil and Flynn was trying to cut open a new packet of ginger nut biscuits when a noise behind him made him whirl around. In the moment that followed the scissors flew out of his hand scattering biscuits all over the kitchen floor then that searing white light that he'd known once before crashed into his brain.

* * *

Audrey Ellis watched in fascination as the two men came out of Chief Inspector Lorimer's front porch. What on earth were they doing carrying a carpet out? Did Maggie Lorimer know her husband was rearranging the furnishings on a Sunday morning?

Her eyes widened. The Lexus was nowhere to be seen! Then one hand flew involuntarily to her pearled bosom at the sight of two stockinged feet protruding from the end of the rolled up carpet.

For a moment she was rooted to the spot then common sense prevailed and she snatched up her well-used binoculars and hastily copied down the red estate car's registration. Even as the car sped away, Mrs Ellis was dialling DCI Lorimer's telephone number.

"He's what?" Lorimer paled as the woman recounted what she had seen.

"Removed your house guest by the looks of things," came the reply. Mrs Ellis actually sounded as though she were enjoying some drama this Sunday morning. Lorimer listened long enough to copy down the red car's registration and mutter a hasty word of thanks before grabbing the paper and jabbing out the extension number he needed.

"Get a check on this one would you?" He rattled off some more detailed instructions before adding, "And find Alistair Wilson. I need him. Now."

Lorimer pulled his coat off the stand in the corner and headed for the door. He was almost at the foot of the stairs when the Detective Sergeant appeared, clattering down behind him.

"What's up?"

"They've got Flynn," Lorimer answered shortly.

"Who?"

"That's what we're about to find out. Thank God for the Mrs Ellises of this world," he breathed. "She saw someone snatch him. We've put out a call for any available squad cars to track them. Meantime I want someone over at my place, see what's there. Here's the keys," he added, handing over the bundle.

"Doubt if I'll need them," came the answer and Lorimer nodded briefly. He was probably right. Whoever had taken the boy away wouldn't have bothered about niceties like locking up. He cursed himself. Why hadn't he told Flynn to put on the chain like he always did? It had become like a mantra every time he'd left the boy alone in the house.

The red car sped along the dual carriageway, oblivious to the notice that speed cameras lay just ahead. The driver took the roundabout at fifty screeching the tyres as the car wobbled between lanes. There was a straight stretch of road just ahead then he would turn along that country road just like Seaton had told him.

He put his foot on the accelerator and grinned as the rev counter flipped forward.

Then his face changed suddenly as a familiar sound drowned out the car's whine. For a moment he was tempted to hit the pedal again but the flashing blue light ahead and a glance at Seaton's angry expression told him he'd be wasting his time.

Flynn came to as the car thudded to a halt. For some reason he could hardly breathe and it was dark, wherever he was. Was this a nightmare? Was he going to wake up in his hospital bed? The blankets were stifling him and for some reason he couldn't pull them away. His legs were tucked under him but he wanted to stretch them out. Suddenly the memory of another man curled into a duvet invaded his jumbled thoughts. He remembered the feel of the tray handles in his hands as he'd carried in the breakfast.

Lorimer!

Flynn groaned aloud as memory came flooding back bringing with it an ache in his head. He heard car doors slam and voices rise in protest. Then suddenly the light came back as the boot was wrenched opened and unseen hands pulled his twisted body from its cocoon of carpet. Trembling, Flynn closed his eyes, waiting for another blow to fall.

"Flynn? You all right, son?"

Flynn opened his eyes and saw the familiar blue gaze of Lorimer staring anxiously down at him. The boy nodded then groaned as the policeman lifted him out of the car boot and tried to help him to stand upright.

"Aw, ma heid," Flynn moaned, his hands investigating the recent scar. He did not resist as Lorimer's fingers ran lightly across his scalp.

"It's okay. No apparent damage. But we'll get you checked out just the same."

"Ah feel sick," Flynn swayed suddenly and turned away, grasping the boot of the car for support. Lorimer flinched as the boy's breakfast exploded over the red paintwork.

"Come on, let's get you cleaned up and you can tell me all about it," he said gently, helping Flynn to straighten up.

"Where's…?" Flynn's question was answered as his gaze fell upon Allan Seaton and a fellow he knew only as Mick. They were being pushed into the back of a police car, their hands well and truly cuffed behind them.

Chapter Twenty-Six

"Just how did you know where he was?" Lorimer asked, his face grim.

Allan Seaton shrugged, "The big man, big Carl, he told us," he replied, avoiding Lorimer's angry stare.

The policeman sat back. How the hell had Carl Bekaert known his home address? Or that Flynn had been staying there?

"What're your dealings with Bekaert?" Lorimer asked, silently adding, as if I didn't know.

Seaton shrugged again. "Ach, he was a pal, y'know. We met up from time to time."

"Listen to classical music together, did you, Mr Seaton?" Lorimer's sarcasm even made his detective sergeant wince.

"Aye, well," Seaton's attempt at a grin failed as his eyes met Lorimer's.

"You were his supplier, son. We have this on good authority so don't give us any of your nonsense."

"Flynn tell you this, did he?" Seaton sneered suddenly.

"Not until you cracked him over the head in my kitchen," Lorimer thumped the desk between them. Seaton's expression changed, his sudden belligerence gone.

"Didnae mean tae hurt the boy, know what I mean?" he whined. "Should'a known he was a'right. A misjudgement of character on my part," he'd added, trying to retrieve the image of the big man he thought he was.

"Right then, let's just see what other misjudgements of character you've made, shall we? Let's start with the late George Millar."

"Aw, c'mon, man, that wis nothing tae do wi' me! Ah'm not intae killin' folk."

"Just whacking them over the head and driving them off in rolled up carpets?"

"We just wanted to scare Flynn, that was all," he muttered.

"Your pal, Michael O'Hagan, might have a different version of that story," Lorimer warned him.

"No he'll no'," Seaton said shortly. "I told him we were jist puttin' the frighteners on the boy. Wanted to know what he'd been sayin' tae youse."

"George Millar," Lorimer began again. "What was his involvement with you?"

Seaton sighed. "Okay. He wis after coke. I supplied it tae him through Flynn."

"How did Flynn come to know Millar in the first place?"

Seaton shrugged. "Met him in the street outside the concert Hall. Flynn was high and Old Georgie asked him where he could score. Put him onto me. Then the big Danish guy gets in touch, becomes a regular customer."

"And the stolen instruments?"

"Dunno," Seaton muttered.

For the second time the table between them shook as Lorimer's fist came crashing down upon it.

"Listen to me, Seaton. This is a murder investigation. Get it? Try to hide one little thing about George Millar and you might find yourself charged with perverting the course of justice!"

Allan Seaton flinched, his hands flying up as if to ward off imaginary blows.

"Okay, okay! Millar was just part of an organisation. He'd pick up an instrument here and there when the Orchestra were out of the country. Like on tour, see? There was someone he knew in Europe who supplied him with the stuff. He'd bring them back and sell them on here."

"How did you find this out?"

Seaton laughed. "Old George had a big mouth. Had a few sessions at my place, didn't he?" The dealer licked his lips nervously. "Told me all about his business. Wanted to know if I could do him a favour from time to time."

"What sort of favour?"

Seaton's eyes shifted from one policeman to the other. "Like puttin' pressure on a couple of guys when their payments were late, know whit ah mean?"

"George Millar used you and O'Hagan as his heavies?" Lorimer's eyes widened in disbelief.

"Aye, well no' very often. Word gets round fast when someone won't tolerate bein' messed around."

"And who exactly were the recipients of your persuasive techniques?" asked Lorimer.

"Eh?"

"Who did you duff up?" DS Wilson explained, seeing the blank look appear in the dealer's eyes.

Seaton nodded in sudden comprehension. "A wee nyaff called Ruskin and another yin called Karger. They're no' in the Orchestra onymair, by the way," he added. "Anyway, this wid be a coupla' years ago."

Lorimer saw in his mind's eye a younger Joseph Alexander Flynn. He couldn't have been much more than fifteen when he'd first met George Millar. The streets with their characters like Seaton had shaped the boy into becoming the dealer's go-between. Yet something had happened to the boy these past few weeks. It was a strange sort of Providence that had thrust him into the path of that van in Mitchell Street. Lorimer would swear that Flynn would never end up now like the man across the interview desk.

Seaton's statement had made interesting reading. Not only had Bekaert and Millar been supplied cocaine by the Glasgow dealer, George Millar had been one small part of an international ring, using the Orchestra's tour programmes as a cover. Lorimer hoped that the Austrian Police would benefit from another known link in what was undoubtedly a complex chain. The question now was, Lorimer told himself as he approached the Royal Concert Hall, whether he wanted to bring Carl Bekaert in for questioning just yet.

The Orchestra were at that moment rehearsing for the evening's performance. Lorimer had to remind himself that this was a murder investigation he was conducting. Taking him away to the station now might alert the killer. Solly was convinced that the Dane was not their man and somehow Lorimer's instinct told him to trust Solly's judgement. No irony in his soul, the psychologist had said.

Well, somebody's dark soul was full of irony and it was up to him to find out who that somebody was. The DNA testing would be undertaken straight after the concert, each member of the Orchestra and Chorus being given little warning of the impending tests. He didn't want anyone slipping through that particular net.

Lorimer nodded to Neville, the security man, as he entered the stage door and made his way through the now familiar corridors.

"Doctor Brightman here yet?" he asked one of the stage crew.

"Just arrived two minutes before you, sir. He's in with Mr Phillips, I believe."

Lorimer strode along the passageway that led to the Orchestra Manager's room. It was barely three o'clock and yet so much had already taken place on this, the last Sunday before Christmas. He glanced at the television monitor set at an angle inside Brendan's room. The rehearsal was already under way. He could hear the strains of Prokofiev's Troika from the Lieutenant Kije Suite as he pushed the door open to see Solly and Brendan seated at an overflowing coffee table. Several garment bags hung around the room, suspended from the window blind rails or the backs of cupboard doors, revealing the black evening suits that would be donned between rehearsal and performance.

Protocol demanded that even the administration staff were properly attired and men in full evening dress would drift in and out of Brendan's room several times before the Christmas concert began.

"Chief Inspector, or should I be addressing you as Superintendent?" Brendan smiled quizzically but the smile failed to reach his eyes. There was something bothering the man, Lorimer realised. Just what had the two men had been discussing before his arrival?

"Oh, that's only a temporary designation," Lorimer replied smoothly.

"I was explaining to Mr Phillips about what Dr Fergusson would require for her visit later on," Solomon glanced at Brendan as he spoke.

"I still can't believe that you are really going to test everyone for DNA. I mean, it's as if we are all suddenly under suspicion," Brendan protested.

"Look at it this way," Lorimer replied as he leaned casually against the door. "It'll help to eliminate an awful lot of people from our inquiries. That should give your players peace of mind, surely?" he smiled encouragingly.

"I suppose so," Brendan muttered. "It's gone on for so long now, we all just want things to go back to normal."

"They'll never be back to normal for Edith Millar or Derek Quentin-Jones," Lorimer reminded him quietly.

Brendan had the grace to look ashamed. "No, of course. And I'm sure the players will appreciate that more than anybody."

"We are grateful for your co-operation, sir. I know it's meant a lot of extra work for you, contacting so many people."

He pushed himself off the door and nodded towards the television monitor.

"We'll be starting with the musicians directly after the performance but perhaps the backroom staff would oblige Dr Fergusson by making themselves available from five o'clock onwards." Lorimer nodded at Brendan who instantly recognised his words as a command rather than a polite request. The whole procedure was going to take some time unless they got their proverbial skates on.

"I believe you've been asked to make rooms one and two available for Dr Fergusson and her staff," Lorimer continued.

"And you have given my officers a list of all the participants. You're quite sure the same people are here, including those who were augmenters on the previous occasions?"

The Concerts Manager looked up swiftly, but nodded.

"Yes. Rooms one and two are normally used as a place to relax and have their meals. You know I'll have a small mutiny on my hands when I tell them they'll have to restrict themselves to their own dressing rooms for the rest of the day? Chloe Redpath was a bit cross about having to come into the Concert Hall. Said she'd be rushing straight from a church recital," Brendan explained. A swift glance at the two men told Brendan that his attempt at pique seemed to be falling on deaf ears yet the Orchestra Manager struggled on, "It's not awfully convenient to cart a harp about all over the city, you know. And she's not going to be the only one who'll be put out."

"I'd appreciate it if you could make it clear that nobody is to leave the building from now until after tonight's performance. It just makes things a little easier," Lorimer told him, ignoring the vexation on the man's face. Any news that DNA testing was to take place could easily spook their killer; the unspoken words hung there as Lorimer watched the Concerts Manager flick his gaze from the Chief Inspector to the psychologist.

Brendan rose to his feet. "In that case, I'd better make a start, hadn't I?" He smoothed down his dress trousers as Lorimer opened the door for him.

The door closed behind him with a click.

"Our Mr Phillips isn't a happy bunny, is he?" Lorimer said wryly when he was certain the man would be out of earshot.

"Can't say I blame him," Solly said. "Did you know he had applied for a post with the Birmingham Symphony Orchestra?" he added.

Lorimer's eyebrows rose. "Trying to escape from it all, is he?"

"Put yourself in his position. Wouldn't you want a fresh start? It can't be easy going in there all the time," Solly jerked his thumb in the direction of the dressing room along the corridor where George Millar had been murdered. "He strikes me as a rather sensitive man, you know. And he did find the body."

"No irony in his soul, then?"

"If he has, then he's doing a remarkably good job of hiding it," Solly answered slowly.

Lorimer was suddenly reminded of Brendan's uncharacteristic, probing question to the Chorus Master after Karen's funeral. He had seemed almost a different man, then. Was that a mask slipping? Or did Maurice Drummond simply bring out a less savoury side to Brendan's nature?

"You're going to be attending every test?" he asked Solly.

"Most of them, hopefully. I still think that the behaviour displayed by each person could provide something tangible."

Lorimer nodded. "Especially if anyone tried to refuse being tested."

"Hence the warrant?"

Lorimer patted his jacket pocket. "Right here. Full authorisation. Signed and dated."

The possibility that DNA material could match the traces found on Karen's violin had given him new hope. Perhaps the events of the coming evening would prove extremely fruitful.

Chapter Twenty-Seven

Lorimer had been offered a seat at the back of the balcony. The show was a sell-out and even the Choir stalls were full but somehow they'd found an empty seat for the DCI. He suspected that it was the one Maurice Drummond usually occupied during concerts. The Chorus Master had been backstage with his singers all during the time between the rehearsal and the moment when they filed onto the stage. It was quite a sight, thought Lorimer, the entire platform covered with rows of singers above the ranks of the Orchestra.

As he settled down to watch the first half of the Christmas concert, Lorimer had the sudden realisation that he was seeing the whole orchestra and Chorus for the first time almost as it would have been on the night of George Millar's death. A stranger to the city would never suspect the aching void left by two of the Orchestra's leading violinists. As if to show that things were back to normal, the lights dimmed and Victor Poliakowsi strode towards the podium amidst thunderous applause. In the weeks he had been guest conductor, the Russian had evidently endeared himself to Glasgow audiences, Lorimer realised.

The first trumpet sounded a clarion call then the choir burst into a fanfare of 'Gloria in Excelsis Deo' that resounded around the concert hall. Lorimer watched the singers' faces.

Even from this distance he could see their clear enjoyment of the music and, as the conductor lowered his baton to more applause, various members of the City of Glasgow Chorus were smiling with pleasure. The programme continued with 'The Shepherds' Farewell', a quieter piece that showed off the sopranos' delicate upper register to advantage. Lorimer's gaze was drawn to the conductor. Poliakowski's hands were making graceful motions as he drew out the slightest of crescendos then brought a finger near to his lips to signal a pianissimo. Lorimer found his lips twitching into a smile. There was no doubt about who was in control on this platform, he thought.

It was easy to relax as the Orchestra rolled out its old

favourites in a medley that included 'Chestnuts roasting by an open fire' and 'Sleigh Bells'. For the first time that day Lorimer felt a pleasant tiredness wash over him. Christmas was coming and in three days' time he'd be on a plane winging his way to Maggie, her old mum by his side. Mrs Finlay had been marvellous, insisting on staying at Lorimer's house for the next two nights with Flynn.

"He needs someone to keep an eye on him," she'd told her son-in-law when she'd heard about his latest injury. He was okay, really, more shaken than anything else, and had not objected when Mrs Finlay had bundled him into a taxi at the Southern General Hospital's A&E Department. Lorimer had been gratified that Maggie's mum had taken such a shine to the lad. She might be an opinionated old so-and-so but her heart was in the right place. Trying to tell her as much had been met with the gruff reply, "Och, it's Christmas!" Nor would Flynn be alone over the festive season; there had been several offers of hospitality from folk within the Division that Lorimer intended to take up on the boy's behalf. Christmas seemed to be bringing out the best in even the busiest of people.

Suddenly a murmur from the audience made Lorimer look down towards the stage. A small boy in school uniform had appeared and was now standing on the conductor's left, his young face turned expectantly towards Maestro, waiting for a signal to begin. The lights deepened to twilight blue and, as the piano music began, snowflakes whirled magically around the walls of the concert hall.

"I'm walking in the air," the small, pure voice rang out clear as a bell sending a shiver of wonder through those whose eyes were fixed on that slight figure caught in the spotlight. Lorimer listened as the voice cast its spell over the audience, watched as the strings swept the music along on a tide of sound and heard his own voice cry aloud with delight as the clapping began. The string sections tapped their bows appreciatively against the music stands as the lad took his bow. For a few moments Lorimer let his eyes rove over certain of the other musicians to see if they, too, were responding to this highlight in the programme. Simon

Corrigan was looking towards the boy, his French Horn by his side, hands clapping in obvious delight. Now Poliakowski was shaking the soloist's hand to more tumultuous applause. Surely Maurice Drummond would be standing out of sight applauding this young singer? The conductor waved a hand towards the wings and a woman came forward, took the boy's hand in hers and bowed in recognition of the youngster's rendition. His singing teacher, then, thought Lorimer. She deserved to be included in the audience's adulation. It would be surprising if the boy were not asked to repeat his solo later on as an encore.

Finally the first half of the concert concluded with the resounding 'Hallelujah Chorus'.

As the lights went up, Lorimer made his way along the corridor towards the doors leading backstage. The rest of the audience would return to find a Christmas cracker laid on each of their seats, but the detective would not join in such niceties; there was too much work to be done on the DNA testing for him to remain out front. If he had hoped to see a sign of weakness from any of the musicians then he had been disappointed. There was nothing in their manner to suggest a guilty conscience. But was that what he should have been expecting? Lorimer could almost see Solly's dark head shake in disagreement. Wasn't he looking for someone with irony in his soul? Well, there had been no sign of that either.

He could never tire of gazing at the woman's face as she proceeded with her work, thought Solly. Rosie Fergusson had somehow become a feature of his life, as necessary to his continued existence as breathing. There had been no sudden explosion of fireworks, no moonlight serenade cascading through the inner reaches of his imagination, only a quiet but growing assurance that the woman before him was the person he wanted to see every day for the rest of his life.

Rosie had come to the last member of the Orchestra to be tested. She'd shown no fatigue whatever, dealing with each person as professionally as Solly had expected she would. His own remit, to note the reactions of those members of the Orchestra undertaking a DNA test, was far more tedious, Solly was sure. Nobody had caused a fuss nor had there been any refusal to comply with the request to volunteer, obviating the need for the warrant. Yet there had been some interesting behaviour from a few of the musicians, something he would discuss with Lorimer.

The Chief Inspector had been off and on his mobile phone all evening, checking up on Flynn and his minder. Solomon grinned. Maggie's mum might have been a traditional Jewish mother the way she'd fussed over Flynn. The boy didn't stand a chance of missing a meal or staying up later than he should. Mrs Finlay was staying over at Lorimer's home for the next couple of nights so Flynn would feel more secure. The lad was still determined to move into his flat, despite this morning's traumas.

Solly looked thoughtful as Rosie called "Goodnight" to the last musician on their list.

"Okay. That's it," she said, stretching her arms widely as she yawned. "But I promised you-know-who that I'd have the results back from the lab as soon as humanly possible." Her face held a mute appeal for Solomon's understanding.

"That means an all-nighter, doesn't it?" Solly asked. Rosie nodded ruefully, her face putting on that little-girl expression that didn't fool him for a moment.

"Fifteen hours from the time these babies hit the lab," she replied. "There's no way we can have them ready before tomorrow night at the earliest."

"Fine," he went on, "but you're going to have some company tomorrow, unless we can make a start on them tonight?" Solly's face creased in a beatific smile. He didn't feel at all sleepy, in fact the very thought of spending a whole night in bed alone seemed suddenly wasteful, especially when he was rewarded by a sudden hug.

"You're a sweetie, y'know that, Doctor Brightman?" Rosie murmured into his shoulder. "But I really think we'll need to leave it till the morning. Come on, let's get these down to the lab then I'll take you home."

Solly shrugged. DNA testing had come a long way in recent years but even Rosie couldn't perform miracles in the next twenty-four hours. And in that time there was the danger that their killer might well disappear from the city. Yet instinct told

the psychologist that turning tail and bolting did not fit the profile he had so painstakingly drawn up of the person who had
killed those two musicians.

Chapter Twenty-Eight

Chris Hunter felt the warmth of the arm around his neck as he came to drowsily. Slowly he shifted his position, leaving Simon's wrist free against the pillow. He propped himself up and gazed at his companion sleeping by his side. The red-gold hair had fallen back from his face. In sleep he looked like a child, his lips slightly parted, the pale blue veins of his eyelids so delicate, so very vulnerable that Chris wanted to reach out with his finger and trace each tiny line.

Simon had clung to him with such passion tonight, his moans interspersed with avowals of love that Chris, to his astonishment, had felt embarrassed to hear.

But why? a little voice asked him now as he saw the tiny rise and fall of Simon's chest. Surely this was just what he'd wanted, to be cherished like this?

Simon had felt soiled after the routine tests had been done, he'd told him. They'd been larking around in the shower when he'd suddenly become serious and started complaining about the police procedure. "It's a bit of me," he'd protested to Chris, "they've got something of mine and of yours. Something that's going to be on a file somewhere for the rest of our lives," he'd raged. It had taken Chris some time to calm him down, but afterwards they'd slipped between the silken sheets and that anger had been translated into quite a different passion.

Had he done it deliberately, wondered Chris? Had his lover's raging been quite intentional, working himself up into a frenzy that could spend itself against his own unresisting body?

Chris sighed. Love was so complicated. He'd never understand it and he wasn't at all sure that Simon Corrigan would, either. He'd flown into a fury when Chris had refused to stay in Glasgow over Christmas.

"I want to be with my mum because I love her," he'd explained with a simple innocence that had seemed to provoke Simon.

"What about our love?" had been the defiant rejoinder.

Chris had not answered him then and he was unsure if he could answer him now. Was what he felt for the man slumbering at his side truly love? Or was it an outpouring of some other emotion? Sometimes, as tonight, it felt like some selfish, primeval force that shuddered through his loins leaving him weak and dazed, its monstrous strength overcoming his very reason.

Loving George had been so different. There he had felt safe and secure, pampered almost by the older man. George had beguiled him, he knew, but he'd gone willingly down that road of charming seduction. They all had, he thought ruefully, remembering Carl's tense face earlier that night, Simon's outburst in the shower.

He was the only one of them who had maintained his usual easy control, Chris realised. Did that say something about him? Was he lacking in something? Tina certainly didn't seem to think so, he thought, fondly recalling his friend's flattering comments. A small frown creased his forehead.

Tina had not been there tonight though she'd promised she would be at the Christmas concert. Usually the girl came backstage and sought him out after a concert.

Maybe she'd known about the testing being done and decided it wasn't worth the hassle. Or had there been another reason? Chris had wanted to give her the gift he'd wrapped up that morning, a glass musical box with Mozartian figures that waltzed around together in a storm of fake snow. It was totally kitsch but he'd thought she'd have liked it nonetheless.

Now he probably wouldn't see Tina at all. He would have to get cracking if he were to catch that flight on Wednesday.

Chris looked back at Simon. He hoped they'd part amicably. His mind was quite made up now. There was no way he was going to stay here. After tonight his life might become increasingly complicated and it was time to bring certain things to an end.

Lorimer sat by the window gazing out at the pinpoints of stars that pierced the darkness. It would be night time in Florida too, he reckoned, almost eight o'clock on a Sunday evening.

Maggie had been invited to a colleague's home for a festive dinner, she'd told him. Lots of them would be there and carol singers were expected to show up early in the evening. It happened every year, she'd explained, her voice wistful for the kind

of Christmases they'd never known. Even the Salvation Army
had cut down its activities in Glasgow following an outbreak of
thuggish violence towards the bands' traditional Christmas offer-
ings. That didn't happen in America, Maggie had assured him
firmly. Over there folk could leave out a host of decorations and
Christmas lights and no one would dream of touching let alone
vandalising them.

Lorimer made a face to the reflection in the glass. What else
would be better over there? Would he be bombarded with comparisons the whole time or would his wife have any longings at all
for Scotland?

The Christmas concert at Glasgow Royal Concert Hall had
made him proud of the City of Glasgow Orchestra and Chorus.
Even Brendan Phillips had beamed his delight at the final encore.
He'd watched and listened to the second half of the programme
from the wings, standing by the Concert Manager as the
Orchestra and singers had filled the hall with familiar music.
Echoes of the traditional carols had flowed round the auditorium
like shadows from the past, shadows of sounds. Even in the
silence of this early hour, Lorimer could still hear their cadences
in his head. George Millar would have played these tunes year in,
year out, Karen by his side, he mused. As he stood there, Lorimer
had the feeling that their music was still going on somewhere out
of sight, behind a blanket of darkness.

Suddenly Lorimer drew the curtains across the window shut-
ting out the stars. It was up to him to silence these faint echoes,
if he only could.

Carl Bekaert twitched the window blind. They were still there,
then, those policemen in their unmarked car, watching and waiting. The Dane's lip trembled as he let the blind fall. Why could-
n't they leave him alone? Hadn't he suffered enough already?
There was no George to comfort him any more and even that
arrogant dealer, Seaton, had become unavailable to him.

Carl had not dared to seek out any sources of cocaine while he
knew he was being so closely watched. His mouth pursed in a
grim line as he realised the irony. He needed a line and he needed
it badly. But all the usual sources were closed to him because of

Karen's death. She had been a thorn in his flesh while she'd lived and now it was as if she was taunting him from beyond the grave. The whole night he'd tossed and turned, snatches of the Christmas programme coming and going in his fitful sleep.

Suddenly Carl heard the rumblings of an early morning dustcart from the next street. In a matter of minutes it would be outside his close, blocking the car across the road from view. The germ of an idea growing in his head, Carl grabbed his coat, stuffed some money into his wallet and headed for the front door.

The two detectives drew their gaze away from the flat as the dustcart rolled up to the close mouth, blocking the view from across the street. One of them stretched, clasping his fingers together and flexing them in front of him. The other yawned and blinked. It had been a long night but their relief would be here pretty soon. Then they could get some decent kip in their own beds.

The refuse collector nodded at the tall blond man as he hurried past but did not receive as much as an acknowledging glance.

"Aye, an' a Happy Christmas to you too, mate," he grumbled, pulling the wheelie bin towards the waiting vehicle.

"He's done a runner," Lorimer said, watching the pained expressions on the faces of his team. "Despite what Doctor Brightman's profile tells us, I want Bekaert arrested."

"Do you think he killed them?" Jo Grant ventured.

Lorimer scowled at her. What he thought and what he had to do were often at odds and she knew it.

"We have to act on the evidence, Detective Inspector," he said shortly, "And right now the evidence suggests that Bekaert's taken to his heels for some reason."

"But not because of the DNA testing being done today, surely?" she reasoned. "He had a sample taken ages ago and it hasn't shown any significant match."

Lorimer sighed deeply. "Look, just find him and bring him in, okay? He's going to be charged eventually with receiving stolen instruments and being involved in this European drug ring. But tread carefully. When he's found I'd like to know where he's been and whom he's been with. That's if you find him at all," he added darkly. Right now he'd give a lot to know the whereabouts of the missing viola player and even more to know the results from the lab.

"Look at this," Rosie lifted up two papers with bar coding shapes for Solly to see.

"What is it?"

Rosie screwed her eyes up and held the papers out at arm's length. "Evidence," she said in a tired voice.

"Evidence of what?" Solly asked, his head to one side, wondering at the lack of excitement in her manner.

"Paternity, I should think," she replied. "Look at the birth dates."

Solly pored over the details of names and dates of birth then he whistled softly.

"Well, that's one mystery solved," Rosie remarked tiredly.

"Or another one just beginning," Solly said, his eyes gazing somewhere in the middle distance. It had been a dreary Monday, the darkness barely leaving skies that had lowered over the city in what passed for daylight at this bleak time of year.

The artificial lights in the lab had hurt his eyes and more than once the psychologist wanted to lay his head down and drift off to sleep but Rosie and her team had just kept going, aware of the need to produce results for the investigating officer.

As the clock ticked towards midnight Solly felt his eyes drooping until at last Rosie gave him a nudge.

"Come on, better get these to our man. See what he makes of our find, if anything," she smiled wanly.

"Can we come in?"

Lorimer stared in surprise at the two figures on his doorstep. He held the door open wide, not speaking but looking intently at Rosie's face as if trying to read what she had to tell him. He hardly noticed Solly closing the door quietly and slipping past them into the lounge. Then Lorimer's eyes took in the bulky envelopes in Rosie's arms.

"You've got someone, then?"

As Rosie smiled a wintry smile and shook her head, Lorimer's mouth closed in a thin line of disappointment.

"There is something we want to show you, though."

Rosie Fergusson sat clutching a cup of coffee, her sheepskin jacket tucked around her shoulders. She had driven straight to Lorimer's home from the lab, Solly in the passenger seat at her side clutching the envelopes that contained the test results.

"Thanks for this," Rosie raised her cup, "we needed it."

"My pleasure. Least I can do after your efforts tonight. I just wish you'd brought me some good news," Lorimer sighed heavily.

"No. Sorry. There's no match for any DNA material taken from Karen's violin. It was a pretty long shot anyway after all this time and the handling that instrument must have had." She sipped her coffee, catching Solly's sympathetic glance.

"So, why come here at this hour in the morning?"

"Rosie made an interesting discovery tonight," Solly spoke quietly so that neither Flynn nor Maggie's mother, sleeping upstairs, would be disturbed.

"Maurice Drummond shares his DNA with another member of the Orchestra. Christopher Hunter."

Lorimer whistled softly. "Another violinist. What does that tell us?"

For a few moments there was silence in the room as three people concentrated on the implications of Rosie's discovery. Outside it was still pitch dark. No sounds came from the street, not even a sigh of wind at this dead hour of night.

"Maurice Drummond must have known he was Hunter's father," Lorimer said at last. "And Karen. She knew. I know she did," Lorimer punched his fist into his open palm. "I sensed the night of George's death that she was holding something back, something important."

"But does this man, this Christopher Hunter, know the identity of his real parents?" Solly mused. "Nobody else seems to have known. Edith Millar had no inkling of the fact that her husband was sitting only yards away in the Orchestra from Karen and Maurice Drummond's son."

"C. Maurice Drummond," Lorimer reminded him. "C for

Christopher."

Rosie looked up suddenly from the depths of her collar. "C also stands for Christina," she remarked.

"Of course," Lorimer sat up suddenly. "Tina Quentin-Jones. Christina! Derek Quentin-Jones told me that Drummond must have fathered his daughter. He'd found out some time back that he couldn't have kids himself. Karen deliberately named her children for their natural father."

"Grounds for murder?" Rosie murmured.

Lorimer shook his head. "I didn't think so at the time. Quentin-Jones had treated the girl as his own for years and Karen's affair with Drummond really did seem to have ended."

"Anyway," Solly pointed out reasonably, "why would he kill George Millar first? There doesn't seem to be any rhyme or reason to that, in my humble opinion."

Lorimer's eyebrows rose at the psychologist's words. Solly's opinion, as they very well knew, was anything but humble.

"Well why don't you ask him?" Rosie suggested.

"Which one? Derek Quentin-Jones or Maurice Drummond?" Lorimer asked.

"Oh, no, neither of them," she grinned, "I was thinking of Christopher Hunter, actually." She looked from one man to the other. "Isn't he a better fit for Solly's profile?"

"What was his reaction on being tested, Solly?" Lorimer wanted to know.

Solly flipped back the pages of his notebook. "There was nothing untoward in his manner. He was calm and relaxed. Like quite a few of the others he tried to crack a joke about it, but it wasn't to put himself at ease so much as to lighten the atmosphere for the medical staff, I believe." The psychologist looked up from his notes. "In fact he was so run-of-the-mill that I had to look this up, didn't I?" he smiled ruefully.

"What about the others? Were there any reactions worth noting?"

"Oh, yes, indeed. Nobody made a fuss about it, really. I mean there were no outright refusals, though that harpist chewed Rosie's ear off a bit. And some of the men were a bit stroppy."

"Oh?"

"Simon Corrigan laboured the point a bit about invasion of privacy and all that. Made a comment about Scotland turning into a police state."

"Did he, indeed?" Lorimer commented. "Wonder who's been rattling his cage? According to his statement he's been very co-operative up till now."

"And he's the right age," Rosie added.

Solly regarded her over the rims of his spectacles. "I hope I haven't been so dogmatic about the profile's age, you know. A single, fit male who has no fear of taking huge risks is more likely to be a younger man, that's all." He regarded Rosie fondly. "Thanks for being supportive, though," he smiled.

"It's like forensics, isn't it," she said sleepily. "Usually makes more sense after we've put the whole jigsaw together."

"Come on, you two," Lorimer stood up suddenly. "Go home while you're still fit to drive, Rosie. Get some sleep and I'll deal with this during the day. Give me a note of any of those reactions you think might be worth following up, Solly," he added, putting out his hand for the psychologist's notebook.

As Lorimer watched the tail-lights of Rosie's BMW disappear along the street he reflected on the day ahead. This would be the day when Flynn took possession of his new flat, when he'd have to arrange several visits to various persons connected with the case as well as clear the paperwork for the next acting Superintendent and try to find the time to throw some stuff into a suitcase. It was the shortest day, Lorimer thought as he gazed up at the stars still pricking the night sky. But with this early start it looked like being one of the longest in terms of sheer hard graft.

Chapter Twenty-Nine

Tina Quentin-Jones stared at her father in disbelief.

"But why? Why leave such a valuable instrument to someone she'd only known for a short time? It doesn't make sense."

"You mean your mother wasn't exactly known for her philanthropy," her father replied with a twist to his mouth.

Tina's eyes widened. She'd never before heard such bitterness in her father's voice.

"Perhaps there was a side to her that we didn't understand," she said slowly.

Derek Quentin-Jones ran an exasperated hand across his forehead. "There was quite a lot you didn't understand about your mother," he replied wearily. "And I think, my dear, that the time has come to enlighten you about what sort of person she really was."

Tina glanced down at the paper in her hand. The simple words Will of Karen Quentin-Jones made Tina realise that even beyond the grave there were things her mother continued to control.

The trouble was, the name that drew her eyes back to the document, the name she had uttered only minutes before with such astonishment belonged to the last person she had expected to see printed there in black and white.

"She did what?" Lorimer's voice rose in astonishment.

"My wife left her violin to Christopher Hunter, her natural son," the surgeon replied, his voice clipped with disapproval.

"And you knew nothing of this until her solicitors made contact with you?"

"Chief Inspector, I didn't even know my wife had made a will," he replied icily.

"But surely her solicitors...?"

"They contacted me when they'd heard about Karen's death. Of course they did. But I told them I wanted to leave things for a while," he looked up at Lorimer. "Well, you know what a state I was in," he added ruefully. "Then last week I instructed my own solicitors to ask for Karen's documents to be sent to their office."

"Well," Lorimer said slowly, "at least this proves one thing. She couldn't have known the instrument was stolen, could she? Not when she intended her violinist son to have it."

"No, I suppose not," Quentin-Jones agreed. "That's something anyway."

"Does he know yet?"

The surgeon shook his head. "That's the worst bit about it all. Karen introduced this lad to Tina. They've become quite good friends, as it happens. Ironic, isn't it?" he smiled grimly at Lorimer. "Tina was going to contact him today. She said she couldn't face him at the concert last night."

Lorimer's mind froze. What was it that Tina Quentin-Jones had asked him after her mother's funeral? How would they know if they'd got the right man? Had she harboured any suspicions about this young violinist? Or had the girl been thinking of someone else altogether?

"What were the other aspects of your wife's will, sir?" Lorimer asked suddenly.

Quentin-Jones shrugged. "Not much, really; a small insurance policy that comes to me. Her jewellery goes to Tina. Most of our assets are in joint names, Chief Inspector. Karen didn't really have any money of her own squirreled away, if that's what you're thinking." The surgeon looked closely at Lorimer as if trying to read his mind. "And, no, there was no little something left for Christopher Maurice Drummond if that's what you're wondering. He'd had quite enough already, don't you think?"

Lorimer sat back in his chair regarding the surgeon thoughtfully. There was a new edge to his voice. Something like a carefully restrained anger. But had it always been there? And was Derek Quentin-Jones really more sinned against than sinning?

"Oh, it's you?" Simon Corrigan stepped back from the door as he saw the girl standing there. "I suppose you'll want to come in," he added then called over his shoulder, "Chris! Your girlfriend's here!" There was a peculiar expression of malice in his face as he opened the door wider making Tina flinch. But the quick glance she threw his way confirmed something. If she was not mistaken, the horn player's red-rimmed eyes showed signs of recent weeping.

"Oh, hi," Chris Hunter emerged from the end of the hall, his face lighting up at the sight of the girl.

"Leave you to it, then," Simon muttered, sloping off into an adjacent bedroom.

"Come on through. Coffee?" Chris laid a hand on Tina's arm. His eyes registered surprise when she shook it off fiercely. "Hey, what's up? Have I done something to upset you?"

Tina looked at him angrily. "You tell me," she said.

Chris glanced at the closed door of the bedroom for a moment. "Come on through to the kitchen and tell me what's the matter, eh?"

The girl hesitated for a moment then with a shrug that was supposed to look nonchalant followed him down the darkened passageway into the kitchen at its end.

"Right, pal, what's all this about? First you stand me up at the concert and now you come up here with a face like thunder. Am I entitled to an explanation or not?" Chris folded his arms and smiled at her.

Suddenly Tina burst into uncontrollable sobs and threw herself into his arms. Her muffled words were lost as he patted her hair and held her close to his body.

"It's all right, wee one, come on, it's okay," he soothed.

Tina gulped back more tears and looked up at him. "Did you hear what I just said?"

"Not a word, sweetheart. Now how about starting again. It can't be that bad, can it?"

Tina took hold of both his arms and held them, still gazing intently into his eyes. "You never knew at all, did you? She never told you?"

"Told me what?" Chris gave a small puzzled laugh.

"You're my big brother."

For a moment the only sound in the room was the ticking of an ancient clock on the wall as Chris Hunter stared at the girl clutching his arms.

"God! I can't believe it!"

She nodded. "It's true. Mum left you her violin in her will. She's known about you for years, kept tabs on everything that happened to you, Dad reckons." She paused and smiled tremulously. "Only he's not my Dad. Nor yours."

"What? Then who…?" Chris Hunter's voiced came out in a whisper as he tried to resurrect some of the world that was crashing around him.

"A man called Maurice Drummond. He's the Chorus master of the City of Glasgow Chorus. He and Mum had a couple of affairs," Tina drew a deep breath, "and we're the result."

"Are you sure?" Chris asked, still staring at Tina as if she were the only credible thing in the room.

"Sure. Dad says these DNA tests were bound to prove it as well." She looked up at his face. "Did you know you were adopted?" she asked suddenly.

He nodded. "I've known for ages. Mum and Dad split up when I was little and she told me then. But I've never bothered about it. Mum was Mum to me. Still is," he broke off, the implication of his new identity hitting him suddenly.

"My real mother has been murdered," he said, an expression of horror coming over his face.

"Chris, I'm so sorry, I'm so very sorry." Tina began to weep again and buried her face into his jersey. But this time, as Chris Hunter stroked her hair, his attention was not on Tina but on something quite different that only he could see.

Simon turned away from the kitchen door, slipping into the shadows of the hallway. It all made sense now. Everything he'd just seen and heard made such perfect sense.

Chapter Thirty

The close mouth was in shadow when the man finally opened the street door. Four steps up and a long stone passageway ahead were illumined by the stained glass window high overhead on the first half landing. Flynn grinned as he turned his head, examining the old polished tiles along the walls. It was a "wally close", a mark of prestige in Glasgow tenements once upon a time, Flynn knew. His wally close. The grin grew wider as he followed the man up two flights of stairs. He'd be doing this every day, he thought suddenly. Up and down to his new job, in and out the close to the bus stop along the road. Flynn blinked, surprised by sudden tears. Such an ordinary thing to be doing, wasn't it? But it seemed like a whole new world to him.

"Right, pal, this is it," the man turned to Flynn and handed him the keys. "You've got all the stuff you need to start you off. It's not a lot, but it'll do you until you can afford to replace it, eh?"

Flynn nodded. The guy wasn't that much older than himself but he had the look of one who'd seen it all and more. Being assistant warden in a Glasgow hostel would have given him insight into the lives of loads of folk, he reckoned. Joseph Alexander Flynn was just another client being dropped off at his wee flat.

"Want me to come in with you?" The man smiled suddenly. "Show you how the oven works an' all that?"

"Naw, I'll manage fine. I'm no' goin' tae be cookin' a Christmas turkey, ah'm I?"

"Well, there's always Christmas dinner down at the Hamish Allan if you want to come?"

Flynn shook his head. He had other plans for Christmas Day. With a lift of his chin he looked at the warden. "Ah've already got an invitation, thanks anyway."

The man shrugged. He clearly didn't believe him. Who would offer hospitality to someone like Flynn?

"Okay, I'm off. But you can come down and see us any time. You know that. Right?"

"Aye. Right."

Flynn waited until the man had turned down the first flight of stairs then he inserted the key into the lock (his lock!) and pushed open the wooden door.

His hand immediately felt for a light switch as he entered the gloomy hall. Flynn dropped his two bags on the carpet and carefully closed the door behind him. The hall was a small rectangle with doors opening off on either side. He pushed open the first one on his immediate right revealing a small bathroom. A cursory glance showed him a strip of bare laminated floor with a bath on one side and a washbasin and loo at the far end. He pulled the light cord making the porcelain gleam suddenly under the naked bulb. Well, at least it was clean. He had a sudden vision of Lorimer's untidy bathroom with its rows of gels and jars that his Missus had left behind Och, it wouldn't take him too long to clutter up his own wee place.

Leaving both lights on, Flynn raced through to the other rooms. He barely took in the tiny kitchen with its basic appliances and formica topped table in the rush to find his bedroom.

"Jeez!" Flynn skidded to a halt as he opened the door. Once the front parlour of what had been known as a room-and-kitchen, the bedroom seemed bigger than any of the rooms back at Lorimer's own place. Flynn's eyes travelled up to the high ceiling with its remnant of plaster cornicing then to the huge bay window opposite the door. In a few strides he was across the room and gazing into the street (his street!).

Govanhill wasn't a bit of Glasgow he'd known too well up until now, he realised, watching the people in the street below scurrying past, their arms full of bulging carrier bags. Three days until Christmas Eve, Flynn thought, a shiver of long-forgotten boyish excitement making his arms all gooseflesh. Or was it the cold? He'd need to find out how to turn on the heating, he realised, his eyes falling on the gas fire. Maybe he should've let the guy show him how things worked. Well, he'd have Mrs Lorimer's old bossy-boots mum here by lunchtime. She'd be only too happy to show him what to do.

Flynn turned back to inspect the room with its single bed, old wardrobe and squashy chair. The bed had been made up already and Flynn ran his hand lightly over the brand new bedding. He smiled at the cartoon characters leaping across the duvet. This wasn't standard-issue-stuff-for-the-homeless, he thought, recognising Lorimer's hand in the choice of bedding. Well, he might be on his own but he'd have Bart Simpson for company at night. Throwing himself onto the bed, Flynn suddenly laughed out loud, the sound echoing around the bare walls of the room.

He was home!

Lorimer heaved a huge sigh as he closed the file. There was something very irksome about leaving this case unfinished with all its strands still hanging loose. They'd done an enormous amount of work compiling facts and figures since that October night in Glasgow Royal Concert hall. And what had they to show for it: a cocaine dealer with links to a vast European market and an expensive violin that could lead to the uncovering of an organised crime ring? Allan Seaton had offered names in the hope that he would have a reduced sentence when his case came to court. So far only Carl Bekaert and George Millar had figured as his customers within the Orchestra itself. There was no doubt in Lorimer's mind that the violinist's drug habit had been funded by the money he'd made from reselling the stolen instruments. Seaton and Bekaert had both mentioned George's sideline in their latest statements.

But was he any further along the road to finding the killers of the two musicians? Solomon Brightman's opinions and Rosie Fergusson's reports, for what they were worth, lay under the manilla folders piled in front of Lorimer. There had been eyebrows raised by the Assistant Chief Constable after the results of the DNA testing had proved so inconclusive but no criticism voiced. Yet, a little voice nagged in his ear. After the Christmas break would he have to return to face Superintendent Mark Mitchison and his sarcastic remarks? Or would a period of enforced sick leave have mellowed his superior? He doubted it.

Rosie had been such a wee star getting him these test results in double quick time, he thought guiltily. Just so he had the chance to wrap this case up before flying out to Maggie. And what had it achieved?

A young man named Christopher Hunter had suddenly appeared out of the woodwork as the illegitimate son of Karen Quentin-Jones and the Chorus Master. Lorimer clenched his teeth. It all seemed to come back to that damned violin. George Millar had received it from his source in Europe and sold it to Derek Quentin-Jones; Karen had played the instrument "like an angel" as Poliakowski had recalled on the night of the Leader's death and now, after its disappearance when she herself had been brutally murdered, it turned up again, only this time as the legacy to her estranged son. Lorimer glanced at his watch. Jo Grant would be at the hospital by now. Would she find anything else out from the consultant surgeon or was he simply wasting more time and manpower? Hunter was due in any time now. Just what would his version of events be, he wondered?

"This is quite outrageous, Inspector! After what I've experienced is it too much to expect some common decency from the police or does the season of goodwill pass you people by?" The surgeon thundered down the hospital corridor, Jo Grant matching his long-legged stride with her own. "In here," he snapped suddenly, coming to a stop outside his consulting room. Jo entered the room, aware of the man's instinctive courtesy as he held open the door for her. How many women had entered that room, trembling, with the handsome consultant smiling reassurance at them, she wondered? They'd certainly not been subjected to that look on his face. Right now Derek Quentin-Jones was not a happy man.

"I have already spoken to Chief Inspector Lorimer this morning!" he exclaimed, then seeing that Jo Grant was not prepared to budge, added, "I can give you ten minutes. I've a waiting room of patients to see," he snapped, waving a hand in the direction of the chair on the opposite side of his desk.

Jo sat down and began immediately. "You must have realised we'd want to ask you more about Christopher Hunter and Christina Quentin-Jones, sir," she said, watching the man's face flinch as she spoke their names. "We would like to know how long it has been since you were aware of their paternity."

The surgeon looked at her stupidly then leaned forward. "What are you really asking, Inspector? If I murdered my wife in a fit of jealous rage? Hardly possible given I was in the operating theatre at the time."

Jo Grant's face remained impassive. "When did you know about your wife's affairs, sir?" she repeated.

Quentin-Jones sank back into his seat and folded his hands, more to keep them in control, Jo guessed, seeing their reddened fingertips.

"I knew my wife had not been faithful to me. I discovered this fact about nine, no ten years ago," he began. "I'd had a minor medical problem that led me to discover my own infertility." He gave a mirthless laugh. "Karen had already given me details of her early pregnancy some years after we were married. Can't remember why she did, but it didn't seem to matter much until…"

"Until you knew Tina couldn't have been your own child?" Jo finished for him.

The surgeon nodded. "I put the matter behind us. We've been happy enough together since then." He paused then corrected himself slowly "We were happy enough together. There didn't seem any reason not to trust my wife."

Once you'd had her checked out by a private investigator, Jo told herself silently, wondering about the barely concealed anger in the man across the desk. Could he have simmered for years about her infidelity and suddenly snapped? Somehow she doubted it.

"When were you aware that Mr Hunter was your wife's son?"

"When I received the will from her solicitor," he replied simply. "Until that moment I had no inkling whatsoever that the young man was anything other than a musical colleague of my wife."

"Can you give me your honest opinion of Mr Hunter's character?" Jo asked suddenly.

Quentin-Jones smiled sadly. "That's just it," he said. "I thought he was a thoroughly nice young man." He looked shrewdly at Jo. "Am I to be proved wrong in my estimation, Inspector?"

* * *

"He said what?" Lorimer's jaw dropped in amazement as Alistair Wilson's words sank in. He listened for another few minutes then let the telephone fall back onto its cradle. "Don't shoot the messenger," Wilson had muttered, ringing off.

Lorimer whirled round in his chair until he faced the window. He'd deliberately cleared a space in his overcrowded diary to accommodate an interview with Christopher Hunter and now the violinist had had the cheek to postpone his appointment until tomorrow! Lorimer fumed. Okay, he would be here for a few hours in the morning.

His plane didn't take off until three o'clock from Glasgow Airport. But Hunter was taking a bit of a liberty!

Suddenly Lorimer's mind went back to the Christmas concert. He'd stood in the wings, listening to the festive music. What was the one he'd found particularly moving? Tchaikovsky's 'Swan Lake Waltz', that was it, he remembered. The string section's parts had been especially poignant. How hard had it been for these professionals to make sad, sweet music so soon after the tragic deaths of their colleagues?

But was Christopher Hunter even aware that one of these colleagues had been his birth mother? He'd a mind to send a squad car round to pick the guy up and have it out with him now.

Lorimer's shrugged. Och, he could wait. It would give him a wee while to nip round the shops at lunchtime today. Maggie deserved more for Christmas than a few hastily bought gifts from the duty free.

Lorimer grabbed the coat off its stand, putting his thoughts into action before he could change his mind.

The afternoon sped past in a whirl of activity, folk in and out of his office wanting signatures for this and recommendations about that. Annie Irvine had even ventured to ask for a donation to their Christmas night out. Lorimer would be well on his way to Florida, leaving his fellow officers to enjoy themselves, but he'd pulled a few notes out of his wallet anyway. Their acting Superintendent would be no loss to the Christmas revelry but his financial contribution would be appreciated, he reckoned.

It was after six when Lorimer finally dialled his mother-in-law's number.

"Yes, he's fine. Settled in no bother at all," she answered in reply to Lorimer's anxious questions about Flynn.

"Did he like my present?"

"The mobile phone? Aye. And he said to tell you he thought the Simpsons' bedcover was," she paused, "wicked, I think he said. Would that be right?"

Lorimer laughed. "Aye, that sounds like Flynn. Listen, could you ring him up, maybe? You've got his number. Ask him if he can take you to the airport tomorrow? Get a taxi and I'll pay you back."

"Och, I can manage fine on my own," Mrs Finlay protested.

"I'd rather Flynn went with you. Besides he wanted to see us off."

"I don't have to ask what's stopping you from picking me up, do I, William?" she asked, her voice heavy with disapproval. "Just don't miss that plane, whatever you do. I'm not going to be the one to explain to my daughter why her husband didn't make it in time for Christmas."

Lorimer put the phone down. He'd make a quick visit to the canteen for some of Sadie Dunlop's home cooking then come back here to deal with the rest of the paperwork that had mounted up on his desk during the day. Only then could he make it home to finish his packing. His glance fell on the red carrier bags leaning against his coat stand. He'd gone a bit over the top in Princes Square. Still, he thought, Maggie would love all that expensive lingerie. And how would she look?

A grin came over his face. Wicked, he told himself.

Chapter Thirty-One

Edith Millar bit her lip nervously. Should she have come here? It had been a moment of impulse, catching sight of her pale face in the hall mirror as she had been about to leave for the Mission, almost as if another person had suggested quite a different destination. Now all sorts of doubts assailed her as she stood uncertainly on the doorstep. A gust of wind rattled the few dry leaves left on the pavement and Edith glanced across at the railings that fenced off the swirling currents of the river Kelvin. She'd walked from Huntly Gardens across Byres Road and past the old BBC headquarters. Many a time she and George had played in studios there in the old days. But that was all in the past, she reminded herself. What she was doing here tonight was to make amends for that past, to try to salvage something for the future.

Glancing up at the light shining from the bay windows above, Edith saw that only one of them was without a twinkling Christmas tree, and she instinctively knew exactly whose window that was.

"Come on up," he said, then pressed the buzzer to release the locked door. Maurice Drummond moved across to the window and looked down into the street.

There was no sign of Edith so she must be on her way upstairs. Sure enough the doorbell rang out its shrill note just as Maurice was heading down the narrow hallway.

"Edith, how nice, come in," Maurice bent to kiss the cold cheeks of the woman who had been his piano teacher. She smiled up at him, drawing off her black gloves. "Hallo, Maurice," she said. "Have the police been here yet?"

"You'd better come in," he murmured, "through here, into the lounge."

Edith Millar's eyes widened as she caught sight of the Chopin Etudes displayed on the open piano. "You still play, then?"

"What made you think I'd ever stopped?"

"Oh, Maurice," she sighed. "What did we do to you?"

Maurice Drummond frowned. "Nothing that I know of, Edith. And what makes you think the police have been here?"

"But they have, haven't they?" She twisted the gloves in her hand. "I told them about Karen and you. About the baby," she added.

"Edith," Maurice Drummond took her by the elbow and steered her gently into one of his armchairs. "I know you did. They told me."

Edith looked up at him, a small frown creasing her forehead. "And you're not angry with me?"

Maurice Drummond shrugged and spread his hands in a gesture of defeat. "They were bound to find out sooner or later, weren't they?"

"What about Karen? Do you still hate her?"

"Oh, Edith, I never hated Karen. In fact," the Chorus master said lightly, "I probably never stopped caring for her." He sat down and took the woman's cold hands in his own. "There's something else, though, Edith." He paused then took a deep breath, "Karen and I had another child together."

"What?" Edith sat bolt upright, her hands pulling away form him. "Maurice, how could you do that!"

"The usual way," Maurice laughed shortly. "Oh, don't worry," he added, seeing the immediate look of disapproval in her face, "That affair didn't last long either. Karen was too damn fond of her marital status to take any risks with me."

"You mean her daughter is…"

"My daughter too. Yes, I know. I've known for years. She even called her Christina, can you believe that?"

"But the boy, Christopher. You must have known who he was, what he was doing?" she persisted.

"Edith, what's this all about? Just how much do you know about Christopher Hunter? You haven't just come to ask me about my illicit love affairs, have you?"

"No, Maurice," the woman said, her voice quiet yet controlled. "I've come to ask you about George's affairs." She looked straight into his eyes as she added, "You see, I think I understand now why he was killed. And it's all to do with Christopher."

From the front room of Edith Millar's home the phone rang out yet again into the darkness, its shrill insistence disturbing the silence. But no hand came to still the noise that jarred the dull air between the walls of the room.Eventually it stopped, the reverberation only a faint memory stirring the shapes of heavy furniture and the grand piano sitting sombrely in the bay window of Huntly Gardens.

It was after midnight when Maurice Drummond quietly closed the door behind him and slipped out into the street. The night mist had cleared from the river and now the moon was shining down, making tiny arcs of light along the swirling current. His heart began to thud as he jogged along the side of the railings in the direction of the taxi rank. Maybe he'd have a bit of a wait, after all it was Christmas week and all the bars and restaurants were filled with office parties whooping it up until the wee small hours.

But Maurice Drummond was in luck tonight. There was one single cab outside the Botanic Gardens, the driver lounging outside, his cigarette smoke rising in the cold night air. The cabbie looked up as Maurice slowed his pace to a walk then flicked the rest of his fag across the street as they made eye contact.

"Where to, pal?" he asked and Maurice told him.

Glasgow was alive with revellers as the cab made its way down Great Western Road towards the city centre. Term time might be over for a couple of weeks but the entire student population seemed to have taken to the streets. A group of lads in Santa hats with luminous bobbles flashing suddenly lurched off the pavement, causing the taxi driver to swerve and swear at them.

"Bloody neds!"

"Aye, Merry Christmas tae you an' all, Jimmy!" came the reply as they passed the laughing figures.

"They don't care, so they don't," the taxi driver grumbled. "Different story if they'd ended up under ma wheels," he added gloomily.

Maurice Drummond did not answer him, staring instead at the passing tenements, wondering if he would find what he was searching for at the end of this journey.

As he paid the taxi driver, giving him an extra tip because it was Christmas, Maurice noticed two figures leaving the mouth of the close across the road. He drew back into the shadows, pulling his coat collar up around his ears, watching the pair make their way towards the twenty-four hour shop on the corner. One of them suddenly threw back his head in a spontaneous burst of laughter, his face revealed by the street lamp above him. Maurice's heart thumped uncomfortably in his chest. The very sight of that smile caused a physical pain. And it was doubly cruel that the smile was not for him but for the younger man whose red-gold hair shone like a halo beneath the light. If only he had been alone, he thought, then everything would have been so much simpler.

Maurice watched as the two men linked arms and drew closer together. Then he shuddered. It was too much to bear, this love of his. He had to do something tonight. And he'd never have a better opportunity than this. He waited until they were out of sight then crossed the road. There were eight names against the security buzzers. Maurice pressed one after the other until a distant voice asked who he was.

"It's Chris from upstairs," he said, breathlessly. "I forgot my key."

There was a grunt from the unseen occupant on the first floor flat then a low thrumming sound that signalled the release of the lock. Maurice glanced along the street then pushed open the door, creeping quietly up the stone stairs until he reached the flat he wanted. He was in luck; the front door was unlocked, showing that his guess had been correct: they were only out for a quick errand.

Breathing a sigh of relief, Maurice Drummond slipped inside the flat and made his way along the corridor until he found the room he wanted.

He saw the violin first. Instinctively he lifted the instrument out of its case and cradled it in his arms. Chris had held this violin night after night as he'd watched and listened to his son making sweet music. More than anything he wanted to wait here and let the boy find him, tell him all the things he'd longed to say over the years.

The unmade bed stopped him in his tracks. This was where Christopher had been making love to another man. Was it also the place where he'd made love to George Millar? Edith's words came back to him suddenly like knives. The horrors of the past few weeks that he'd pushed into the deepest recesses of his mind resurfaced with startling clarity.

He couldn't do this, he simply couldn't.

With a groan of despair he put the violin back in its open case. Feeling in his pocket, he took out the gift-wrapped present he'd brought. Maybe he could just leave it here? He tried to picture his son's puzzled face as he opened the gift in the morning. Or would he keep it until Christmas Day? Whatever, it would be a surprise he wasn't expecting, that was certain.

Maurice's fingers were on the handle of the door when he heard voices from the close below. He was trapped! They'd find him here and he'd have to explain why he had come. Sweat broke out on Maurice's forehead as he envisaged the looks of incredulity and even pity on their faces. Hurriedly he pulled open the door of the bathroom next to the front door, praying that they would pass him by.

The voices grew louder and then the front door was opened and closed with a bang. Maurice stood stock still as footsteps passed him by only inches away. Surely they could hear the sound of his heart hammering?

At last the voices disappeared along the corridor and Maurice heard another door opening then music began to spill out from the far end of the flat. Holding his breath, Maurice slipped out from the bathroom and quietly turned the handle of the door. Mercifully there was no creak as he opened the door and crept outside, pulling it quietly behind him.

Saying a prayer to whatever spirit had been on his side, the Chorus Master felt his way down the steep stairs like an old man. Out in the street once more he sank back against the stone walls of the tenement, tears of shame pricking his eyelids.

Chapter Thirty-Two

"For you," Simon said softly, his eyes shining, "I made it specially."

Chris sat up in bed, pulling the duvet up around his waist. "That was nice of you," he remarked, his hands outstretched to receive the breakfast tray.

Simon shrugged. "It's nearly Christmas after all, isn't it? Goodwill to all men, even queers like us, eh?" he laughed and turned away, leaving the man in the bed looking after him, a puzzled expression on his face. Simon had taken it so well last night, he thought. They'd had a great night together, just like old times. He'd never even mentioned Tina and Chris had offered no explanation. That could wait. He'd hardly had time to adjust his own emotions let alone talk to Simon about the previous day's revelations. It was enough that they were still friends.

Chris spooned the porridge into his mouth. Great! Simon had made it just the way he liked it, big dollops of syrup sliding down the sides of the cereal bowl.

When the first spasm hit the back of his throat, Chris instinctively tried to balance the tray to stop it falling over the bed. His voice wheezed as the cry for help stuck in his gullet, the air refusing to flow through his trachea. With a crash the tray landed on the floor, the grey contents of the cereal bowl splattering in a sticky mess against the wall.

As Chris fought for breath he watched the lumps sliding downwards like slowly moving slugs leaving milky trails dripping on to the carpet.

The shock waves were making him dizzy now and he couldn't focus. Where was Simon? Why wasn't he here to help him?

Then from somewhere far away he heard a voice telling him terrible things. Things that weren't true. His hands clutched at the Christmas card beside his bed, its glossy picture crushing beneath his fingers as the darkness rolled over him.

When her front door bell rang, Tina was certain it would be Chris.

"Coming!" she called. So what if she wasn't even dressed yet?

It would be her brother. It had to be. "My big brother!" she said aloud, the very sound of the words like a caress.

"Oh, it's you," she said her voice registering sudden disappointment at the sight of the man standing on her doorstep. Then, seeing the expression on his face, her tone became anxious. "There's nothing wrong, is there? Nothing's happened to Chris?"

Tina stepped back as the man came into the house. He had not uttered a word but his eyes told her everything she needed to know. With a cry Tina stumbled against the edge of the banister as his hands caught her shoulders, pinning her against the staircase. Her scream was silenced as his fist slammed into her mouth then she heard herself moan, the taste of blood mingling with the sudden pain.

Before she could even try to scramble away, the blows began to rain down on her head then she felt his hands pulling at her dressing gown, releasing its cord.

"No," she whimpered. "Please. No!" Tina struggled against him as she felt her body being pulled this way and that, her hands fixed behind her and her ankles pinioned tightly with the cord.

"Stop it! Why are you doing this to me?" she cried, her breath coming out in great sobs.

Then the girl's eyes widened in alarm as he untied the kerchief from his neck and twirled it between his fingers. Her cry was muffled as the gag cut into her mouth, her final protests silenced.

"Why?" He broke the silence at last. "You have the nerve to ask me why? So that you and your bastard will never see the light of day, that's why," he sneered, panting slightly as he stood over her abject body.

Then Tina watched in horror as he pulled a familiar object from his pocket. It was a small cigarette lighter shaped like a harp. Her eyes stared wildly as the lighter snapped open, its flame rising higher as he turned the tiny cogwheel.

Then, laughing, he spun the flame around his head and let it catch hold of the curtains above her.

"Just for starters," he laughed, then dipped the flame against the carpet, watching as it licked a smouldering brown path along the floor.

❖ ❖ ❖

"Where the hell is he? I haven't the time for this today." Lorimer fumed. He'd only a few hours left before checking in at the airport and he was damned if Christopher Hunter was going to screw that up for him. "I'm going down there myself. Coming?"

Solly shrugged. With Lorimer in this mood, did he have a choice?

The door was lying open when they arrived at the top of the stairs. Solly glanced at Lorimer's face, recognising that grim look of foreboding. He shivered suddenly.

There was something not right about this. The two men made their way down the darkened hall towards a light that flared out from a side room.

"My God!" Solly breathed. "What has he done to himself?"

Chris Hunter lay unconscious, the sheets pulled away from his body as it slumped heavily over the edge of the bed. The smell of vomit made Solly take a step backwards, his hand across his mouth, but Lorimer was immediately at the bedside, seeing the swollen lips and the rash that was visible beneath pale, stubbly skin. As his hand felt for a pulse, his fingers met the touch of metal. Around the man's wrist was a bracelet. Lorimer peered at the inscription.

"He's still alive," Lorimer turned to the psychologist. "Look here. It says he's a severe allergy sufferer. This is a Medicalert bracelet. And there's a number on it." He pulled out his mobile, jabbing out the numbers. "Ambulance. This is an emergency."

The policeman explained the situation and relayed the membership number on the bracelet while Solly's eyes scanned the room, taking in the mess on the wall, the fallen tray and the ioniser on the shelf above the bed. He frowned suddenly, wishing that Rosie were here to tell them what might have happened to the man lying across the bed.

Solly's eyes returned to the black box above the bed. "See that?" he pointed it out to Lorimer. "My sister used one of these for her pet hair allergy. Could he have had some sort of asthma attack?"

"Check his things," Lorimer replied, still listening to the voice at the other end of the line.

"What do we want?" Solly spoke almost to himself as he moved across the room. "A medical card of some kind?" He bent down to retrieve a jacket that had fallen from the back of a chair. Lorimer's face darkened as he listened to the voice on the emergency line. "Okay. I'll try my best but for God's sake get a move on." He clicked shut the mobile.

"We've to look for an pre-loaded adrenaline kit. It's like the sort of pen that diabetics carry around. They say he should have one wherever he goes so it won't be far away. Looks like he's suffering an anaphylactic shock." Lorimer said. "Let's see if there's anything in here or that poor beggar hasn't a chance," he said, glancing down at the man on the bed as he rummaged in the bedside drawer.

"Bingo!" Lorimer breathed out in relief as he held up the sealed kit.

The psychologist looked away as Lorimer administered the drug. He focused instead on the arm drooping from the sheets, its clenched fist brushing the floor. Obscured at first by the corner of the duvet, Chris Hunter's motionless hand was closed around a Christmas card.

Solly bent down, his fingers prising the card from the unconscious man's grasp. His foot pushed against the bed linen revealing a torn envelope. Smoothing out the creases of the Christmas card Solly opened it. Inside was a photograph of a young girl smiling out from the crumpled gloss. He read the sloping handwriting, nodding to himself.

"What d'you make of this?" he began to say then both men turned their heads as the sound of feet came racing up the stairs.

"Thank God!" Lorimer breathed as the paramedic crew arrived at the bedroom door, stretcher and oxygen at the ready. "Here," Lorimer handed over the empty adrenaline pen. "I gave him this just before you arrived."

"Might help. How long has he been in a coma?" one of the paramedics asked.

Lorimer shook his head, his mouth a grim line. "We don't know. He was supposed to be meeting me an hour ago and didn't turn up. God knows how long he's been like this."

"Okay. We've got the rest of his details from the Medicalert database. Come on, fella, let's get you out of here."

The two men watched as Chris Hunter was gently lifted away from his bed. His body, wrapped in double cellular blankets and strapped onto the stretcher, looked ominously still as it was carried out of the flat by the paramedics.

"Think he'll make it?" Lorimer asked them.

"Maybe. Depends if he responds to that shot you gave him," one of the crew replied.

Lorimer turned back to see Solly by the window. The psychologist was examining a Christmas card that he'd picked up from the floor. Had it fallen from the window ledge? There were several others there in a row. Curious, Lorimer moved towards the window and looked over Solly's shoulder

"That's Tina Quentin-Jones," he said, seeing the photograph that had been stuck inside the card.

"See what she's written," Solly showed him. There, under Season's Greetings were the words, *From your new wee sister, with love, Tina. December 22nd. Happy Christmas.*

Lorimer's mind spun with sudden possibilities. He turned to face Solly. "What else could she have given him?"

Once more he recalled her desperate expression at Karen's funeral. Did Tina Quentin-Jones imagine that Chris Hunter had killed her mother?

"Could she have deliberately given him something to bring on this reaction?"

"Somebody did," Solly pointed to the porridge congealing on the skirting board.

"Who else lives here?"

"Simon Corrigan, but he…" Lorimer paused. "Wait a minute," he said slowly, letting his gaze fall to the window ledge. He picked up one card after another until he came to the one he was looking for.

"What does this tell you?" Lorimer held it up for the psychologist to see. "Not the sort of message you'd write to your mate, is it?" Solomon read the message on the card, his face serious as the implication sank in. Then he looked up.

"Where is he, then? Why's Corrigan not here if he's expressing his undying love to Christopher Hunter?" Solly asked.

Suddenly Carl Bekaert's words came back to Lorimer.

"*Love. It's not a dirty word?*"

"Love. You just said it. That's what it's all about," Lorimer stared at Solly.

"That's what it's been about from the beginning, only we couldn't see it." For a moment there was a triumphant spark in his eye then his expression changed.

"No. Oh, dear God, no." Lorimer's eyes flicked from one Christmas card to the other. "He's gone after the girl. Quick, let's get out of here."

As the flames began their ascent of the heavily embossed wallpaper, Tina struggled to free her hands from their bonds. She could still hear Simon in the lounge, the sound of a clinking glass against a bottle. Suddenly it reminded her of her father and his nightly tipples.

Dad. Where was he supposed to be this morning? She couldn't remember. Was it a theatre day? Or was he doing rounds? Tina couldn't remember. They'd had an awful row the other night, and she'd said some cutting things. If only she could take them all back now, unsay them.

She whimpered as the fire whooshed upwards, the wallpaper dissolving into its yellow tongues. He'd never get to hear her say that she really loved him; that he was her dad and that was all that really mattered. The girl struggled harder, a sudden urge to live, to fight against this terror forcing the adrenalin through her veins.

From her twisted position at the foot of the stairs Tina could hear the musician as he moved about her home. She heard the door of the stereo cabinet opening and the clunk of Simon's glass as he laid it down. What on earth was he doing now?

Her answer came moments later as the final movement of Tchaikovsky's 1812 Overture crashed at top volume through the rooms. He was mad. The man was totally insane, listening to Tchaikovsky and drinking whisky as he burned down her house.

If only she could reach the front door again! The panic button was at waist height, next to the chain that was hardly ever used, she thought, crazy tears filling her eyes.

Tina crawled towards the foot of the stairs. The fire had got a hold of the carpet between where she was now and the door. She'd have to roll her body through the lines of flames if she were to make it.

The pain shot through her legs as she inched down, elbows taking her weight.

The thump as her body landed on the floor made her stop, head craned to see if her attacker had heard, but the music had evidently drowned out the noise. She could see his back to her as he drank down her father's whisky, one arm conducting the unseen orchestra. Heart thudding, Tina grasped at hope. At least the cigarette lighter was laid aside for the moment.

With a jerk Tina rolled over the line of flame, her head bursting with the effort. Would her dressing gown catch fire? Or would she smother the flames? She could smell the burning carpet beneath her even as her body felt the heat.

Hardly daring to look, Tina forced herself against the corner of the wall beside the door, her spine protesting as she wrenched her body upright. The strain on her wrists and ankles made her wobble dangerously.

With a sigh she let her head fall forward towards the small steel box, forcing her face sideways so that her nose dipped under its rim.

For a moment nothing happened then she saw the man turn towards her, his eyes narrowing in disbelief.

"What the hell?"

No. She would never do it now.

As he lunged towards her Tina pushed her face against the space beneath the box with the last remnant of her strength then the whole world exploded in a shrieking wail as the alarm went off.

The sound of exploding canon fire roared from the house when Lorimer pushed open the door. He caught the girl's body as it fell towards him. Smoke billowed out in grey clouds from the house.

"Quick! Get her out of here!" Lorimer dragged the girl over

the doorstep as Solly hurried to take her in his arms.

Fanned by the sudden draught from the open door, the flames leapt higher. Through the layers of smoke Lorimer could just make out a figure moving inside.

"Lorimer! No!" Solly's cry went unheeded as the policeman thrust his way back into the burning house.

Coughing, Lorimer pulled a handkerchief from his pocket and held it over his nose and mouth. The flames were shooting up into the stairwell now, shrivelling the walls like a rising brown tide. Still the music thundered, the crackle of fire a deadly counterpoint. Still he struggled into the lounge, the smoke coming at him in waves.

Simon Corrigan turned to face him, his arms raised as he beat time to the music, one hand holding a half empty bottle of whisky. Through the smoke he could see the musician laughing aloud, his face shining with a delirium of pleasure. With each sweep of his arms the whisky splashed to the ground, flames shooting out around his feet.

Lorimer coughed, waving his free hand to clear the air between them.

"Get out!" he called hoarsely. "Now. Before it's too late!"

With a final crash the music rose to its climax and the musician gave a grandiose bow.

His screams as the flames caught his red-gold hair urged Lorimer forward. He grabbed the man's arms and hauled him backwards in the direction of the open door, Corrigan's heels dragging on the burning carpet, hampering them both.

The smoke was so thick now that Lorimer could barely make out the outline of the front door. There was a shower of sparks above him, making him look up as the walls seemed to move.

Choking, Lorimer pulled the musician out of the hall just as the banister above them gave way with a sickening wrench of timber.

"Over here!"

Blindly, Lorimer stumbled forwards, other hands taking Corrigan out of his grasp. He was dimly aware of the flashing blue lights and the uniformed officers crowding around him.

"Here," Solly was saying, "Over here!"

Lorimer allowed himself to be led away from the roaring behind him, his eyes smarting from the smoke. His legs felt weak as he was helped into the back of the police car.

"The girl?" he coughed as the words stuck in his throat. "Is she okay?" he croaked.

Solly nodded, his hands on Lorimer's shoulders. He was looking at Lorimer with an expression he had never seen in the psychologist's face before.

"You could have been killed!" Solly was shaking Lorimer by the lapels of his coat, tears brimming in his large, dark eyes. For a moment neither man spoke then Lorimer gently drew Solly's hands from his collar.

"What about Corrigan?"

Solly turned to watch as the ambulance drew away from the kerb. "Who knows? He was still alive when you brought him out."

"Sir! Chief Inspector Lorimer?" A uniformed officer was suddenly standing by the squad car. "We've just heard that Carl Bekaert's been picked up at a warehouse outside the city. They found him with a number of stolen musical instruments. He's been charged," the constable added.

"Great. Remember to wish Jo Grant and the team a Merry Christmas from me," Lorimer nodded.

"You all right, sir?" the constable asked, suddenly noticing his superior's dishevelled appearance.

"Never better, pal, never better," Lorimer started a laugh that rapidly turned into a cough.

"We should have you checked out at the hospital," Solly began. He turned towards Lorimer and sighed, shaking his head in mock despair. "That was one hell of a risk you took. Your wife will have kittens when she finds out."

Lorimer's mouth opened in horror as he looked at his watch. "Oh great! I'm supposed to be at Glasgow airport as of ten minutes ago! Forget the hospital."

"What about Mrs Finlay?"

"Flynn was picking her up by taxi." He slumped helplessly

against the seat. "Just in case I didn't make it in time," he added, his voice heavy with irony.

"Phone him. Tell him we're on our way." Solly signalled to the constable who was still regarding Lorimer with interest. "We need a driver. Now!"

Flynn put down the phone. The flight had been called five minutes ago and Mrs Finlay was fretting by his side, calling her son-in-law all manner of unseasonal names.

"Well?" she demanded.

"An emergency," Flynn told her briefly. "He's on his way now."

"That's not much good," Maggie's mother bristled. "If I don't make a move soon we'll both miss that plane."

Flynn looked around the departure lounge wildly. Surely there was something he could do? Over by the door he spotted two transport policemen, their jackets vivid yellow against the dreich December afternoon.

"Wait here a minute. I'll be straight back. Don't move. Right?" Flynn grasped his new mobile phone and leapt out of his seat, grinning slightly at the elderly woman's astonished face.

A few minutes later Flynn clicked off the mobile phone that Lorimer had given him. It was a wee cracker, but it just couldn't be helped. With a sigh he dropped it into the water bucket and turned away.

He had just time to return to Maggie's mum before the alarm went off, heralding the calm voice that resounded through the airport asking everyone to evacuate the building.

Coda

Christmas day in Glasgow dawned bright and clear with just a hint of frosting to transform the park below Solly's windows into a winter wonderland. The psychologist had risen early, moving away from Rosie's warm body as quietly as he could. Now he stood wrapped in his dressing gown gazing down at the scene below him. It was early but there were two little boys playing in the park, their heads bare but their hands brightly mittened. His gaze travelled to where a couple walked slowly behind them, hand in hand.

Smiling at them, Solly felt in his dressing gown pocket. His hands closed round the tiny box that had been so carefully wrapped by the jeweller. As he turned it over in his palm he gave a sigh, savouring the moment. He'd waken her soon, but not just yet. Solly watched until the family was out of sight before he turned back towards the bedroom.

Rosie lay sleeping, her hair spread out upon his pillow, the expression on her face so peaceful it almost seemed a pity to disturb its repose.

Solly's lips brushed against Rosie's cheek and he grinned as she wrinkled her nose, as his beard tickled her into wakefulness.

"Merry Christmas, darling," he whispered, his fingers drawing the box from his pocket. "Merry Christmas."

Derek Quentin-Jones knocked on the door of the room before quietly turning the handle. Tina lay asleep. In the half-light from the window the bruises on her face were like dark shadows, but her split lip was still dark and swollen. He opened the door, fingers to his mouth as he glanced at the others in the corridor behind him.

"Still asleep," he whispered down at the man in the wheelchair. "Let's leave her for a while longer." He looked up at the person grasping the handles of the wheelchair and at the woman standing by his side. "How about it, Maurice? Mrs Millar?"

Maurice Drummond bit his lip and smiled. "I've waited this long for my family," he said at last. "I think I can wait a wee bit longer," he added, his gaze travelling down onto his son's head.

Maybe he would tell Chris one day about Edith's visit. She had been quite adamant that Chris's homosexuality had been at the root of the whole business, spurring him on that night to confront his son. In a way she had been right.

Chris Hunter nodded. "I can't imagine why it took you so long," he grinned up at his father.

The surgeon watched them. Something new and good was growing there between these two. There were things that Derek Quentin-Jones had come to understand in these past few days that he'd never dreamed of knowing. Like the kind of love that turns to violent hatred or the way that people could share their love for the same person. Looking at Maurice Drummond he wondered if they would both come to love this young man who was Karen's son, Tina's brother. And Karen, he thought, remembering the way her loveliness had twisted his heart. Had that too been love? He supposed it had.

What he felt now was a sense of gratitude towards these people around him.

Edith had opened her home to him after the fire that had devastated his house in Pollokshields. Her Christian duty, she'd called it in tones that brooked no refusal. Now, on this Christmas morning, Derek had the sense of having found far, far more than those things he had lost.

Before he followed the others down the hospital corridor towards the day room with its bright paper garlands, Derek turned back to the room. Despite everything that had happened she was still his daughter, his darling girl. He stood there for a moment looking down on Tina as she slept, then blew her a silent kiss.

"Happy Christmas, son!" Alistair Wilson pulled the cracker with Flynn, the crack of the paper exploding as they both fell back, laughing. Flynn stuck his tongue out at the detective sergeant. He hated being called "son". It was dead naff.

"You're a couple of big weans, so ye's are," Sadie told them. "Just as well Betty an' me are here tae keep ye's in order, eh?" she winked as Betty Wilson placed the soup tureen carefully onto the red tablecloth.

Flynn pulled out the rolled up paper hat, letting the motto fall to one side. He laughed again out of a sense of sheer delight as he placed the yellow crown onto his head. Who would've thought it? Having Christmas dinner here with Raincoat and his missus, not to mention the wee woman who had been supplying his meals from the police canteen for all these weeks!

"Wonder what they're up to in Florida," Sadie went on. "Bet they don't have as good a turkey as us," she said, grinning up at her hostess.

"Ach, it's only about eight o'clock there. They won't have had their breakfast yet," Alistair told her. "Besides, the boss is probably still recovering from jet lag. Or the panic he had when he thought he was going to miss his flight," he added, giving Flynn a meaningful look. Nobody had asked him outright but everyone seemed to guess that Flynn had been behind the bomb hoax at Glasgow Airport.

"Aye, well," Flynn giggled, "At least he'll have a merry Christmas, won't he?"

Maggie sat up suddenly, hearing Lorimer roll over and groan. Gratefully she sank back against the pillows. The last two days had passed in a dream. After Bill and Mum had arrived (late!) Maggie had taken them back to the apartment to sleep off their journey. Her husband had spent most of the next day ostensibly recovering while she and Mum had busied themselves with preparations for Christmas dinner. She knew fine that Lorimer had been off and on the telephone to Scotland, anxious to tie up all the facts. He had not told them everything about the case until last night, and even then, he'd been considerate enough to leave out the nastier aspects to spare Mum's feelings.

Later, they'd sat side by side, his arms holding her close, while he had related the whole story. Simon Corrigan had been a man obsessed by his lover, his outward carefree personality hiding a deeply passionate, jealous nature. When George Millar took Chris as his latest conquest, that passion had been transformed into murder.

"But why kill Karen?" Maggie had asked.

"He thought she knew what he'd done," Lorimer told her.

He'd paused, making Maggie sense that he was unwilling to speak ill of the dead.

"Karen was the sort of woman who made insinuations. She liked people to think she knew more than they did," he had told his wife. "She had secrets of her own so perhaps she assumed that everybody kept things hidden. Anyway, Corrigan saw her talking to me and immediately thought that she was on to him. She was stupid enough to telephone him on the night that George was killed, let him know that she was aware of his affair with her son."

"How did she feel about Chris being gay?"

"I doubt she was thrilled about it, she seemed to have had an antipathy for the Leader of the Orchestra that I guessed was homophobic. Perhaps she simply didn't want Chris being involved with George Millar. Maybe Simon Corrigan seemed a safer bet?"

Maggie had shuddered, the thought of the man's double murder and his subsequent attempt to kill those two young people suddenly very real indeed. "He thought Tina and Chris were an item?"

"Worse than that. He saw them together the day Tina told Chris she was his sister. Somehow he jumped to the conclusion that she was pregnant with Chris's child."

"So he tried to kill them both?"

Lorimer had nodded. "If he couldn't have Chris for himself, then no one could. He gave the lad some ground almonds in his porridge, knowing full well the effect that would have then he went to the Quentin-Jones house."

"To murder Tina," Maggie finished for him. "Thank God you got there in time," she'd whispered.

Lorimer had nodded, his silence telling Maggie that there were things about the fire that he wanted to keep to himself. He'd tell her once he was ready to talk about it.

"Yes," he'd replied. "She was a bit of a mess but she'll be all right. More than I can say for Corrigan."

"Oh?"

"He's in a special burns unit. Most of his face has gone," Lorimer had turned away for a moment and Maggie wondered just what the clinician had reported. "But he was able to communicate with Jo Grant yesterday. Told her everything," he'd broken off suddenly, squeezing Maggie's hand.

"And the others? The families? What's happening to them now?"

She recalled her husband's smile as he'd related how Edith Millar was playing hostess to the surgeon. "Funny old world, isn't it?" he'd remarked.How long it would take before the surgeon could return to his burned out home was anyone's guess.

Maggie rolled onto her side with a sigh of contentment. Whatever had been going on these past few months was over, now. Oh, there would be other cases, some of them just as disturbing, but DCI William Lorimer would handle them. Maggie stared at the man lying asleep on the bed beside her. He'd rushed all the way here with no luggage, full of apologies for all the lovely Christmas presents he'd left behind. It was fine, she'd assured him. They'd keep till she came home.

Maggie Lorimer's face split into a radiant smile. It was Christmas Day and she had everything she wanted in the world.

Acknowledgements

I would like to thank the following people for their help in researching this novel: Anne Smith, Concerts Manager, the Royal Scottish National Orchestra; Superintendent Ronnie Beattie, former Deputy Divisional Commander "U" Division, Strathclyde Police; the late Margaret Paton, Procurator Fiscal Depute of the Crown Office and Fiscal Service; Dr Marjorie Black, Department of Forensic Medicine, University of Glasgow; Stringers of Edinburgh; the staff of Glasgow Royal Concert Hall especially Cliff Brown, Donald Ball, Keith Marshall and Jane Donald; Pat Leonard of the Hamish Allan Centre, Glasgow and last, but by no means least, Graham Taylor and all my friends past and present members of the City of Glasgow Chorus.